FRACTURED SOULS

FINDING SANCTUARY

BOOK FOUR

Copyright © 2024 by Natasha Madden

All rights reserved.

Cover Art Design by Bookcovertrove

This is a work of fiction. All characters are fictional and any resemblance to individuals is unintentional. Any references to people, places or events are only to provided authenticity and are used fictitiously.

ALSO BY NATASHA MADDEN

Finding Sanctuary Series
Chosen by Destiny
Marked by the Gods
Night of Shadows and Death (Novella)
Wicked Cravings
Fractured Souls

Crescent Moon Series
His Light in the Dark
A Spark of Madness (TBA)

The Fae Court Series
The Last Druid

Dedication

It is time, my fellow warriors, to reclaim our power and shine our light so brightly that it illuminates the darkness for others to find their way.

Triggers

To the women who have been through unimaginable struggles, who have faced adversity head-on, and who have fought tooth and nail to rise above the depths of darkness, I want you to know that your strength and resilience are awe-inspiring.

Sexual Harassment
Implied SA
Abuse
Violence
Sex Scenes

Chapter One

GABE

I tug at the collar of my jacket, trying to keep the frigid wind from seeping down my neck. My smile grows as I look over at my luna, my friend. We've been handing out coffees and muffins from Little Bites, a fellow pack members' café, all morning, and now Nesrin sits at the mouth of the alley with three homeless people, her long, auburn hair flying in the wind as she tells an animated story that has them all captivated. Our luna has a heart of gold and a streak of stubbornness a mile long. It shows in the way she stands up for the little guy, and always does what's right, despite the challenges.

The Shadow Lake Coven has made life difficult for our pack over the last few years, constantly vying for control. Lukas stood firm, unyielding to their demands. Then Nesrin showed up, and everything changed. The more her powers developed, the more she grew into a formidable and unstoppable force.

Then everything that happened with Hera last year set about new changes. Nesrin even managed to get the council to lift their laws on mixed species relationships. She seems to cause a stir with everyone, especially since she's the first hybrid luna. The change has had a ripple effect throughout the entire magical community.

Now, with Marcus as the new high priest, the coven and pack run Portland together. Still, convincing me and others that he has changed won't be an easy task, as he has a lot of ground to cover. But for now, Nesrin trusts him, and I trust her. That is good enough for me.

I bury my hands in the pockets of my leather jacket, trying to shield them from the cold as I scan the street. There's a young boy standing outside the florist shop a little way down. Looks to be around eight or nine, it's hard to tell from here. I don't know what it is about the boy that's caught my attention, but my eyes stay glued to him. I watch his eyes dart around the street as he shifts his weight from foot to foot, clearly nervous. My gut tells me that something isn't right, and my senses confirm it. I can smell his fear from here.

With a quick movement, I turn to Nesrin. *'Will you be okay for a minute?'* using the same telepathic bond she shares with each member of the pack. Despite her witch upbringing, she has fully embraced her shifter identity, and all that comes with being the luna.

Nesrin's amber eyes fly to mine, concern lighting her face at my tone.

'Is everything okay?'

'Yeah, I just wanted to check something out.'

'Okay, call if you need me.'

'You took my line.' I wink in her direction, before casually making my way down the street toward the young boy.

He stands in front of the shop, fiddling with his backpack and glancing in through the big bay window. Carefully, he plucks a small bunch of purple and blue flowers, before quickly trying to tuck them into his bag. He barely has time to react before the owner storms out of the shop, red-faced and yelling.

"I hope you aren't trying to steal those!" he yells, stepping up to the young boy, his round face red and flustered.

The boy's fear leaves a sharp taste in my mouth. It rolls off his small body in waves as he stands paralyzed, scared to death of this asshole. The distress the man is causing the boy pulses in the air between us, and in this moment, I want nothing more than to knock him down a notch. With a renewed sense of purpose, I step up to the boy, softly placing my hand on his shoulder. I give it a light squeeze, using my body to block him from the shop owner.

"Hey, bud. Are these the flowers you picked? I like them. Good choice."

Without waiting for the boy to reply, I ruffle his shaggy brown hair, then I pull out my wallet. I flash a reassuring grin and wink at him before turning to the fuming, diminutive man hoovering behind me.

"How much for these?" I motion toward the flowers.

The boy's hands tremble, fingers twitching with nervousness, a clear sign of his anxiety. I glance briefly at the shop owner, fixing him with a sharp look—daring him to slip up, to make one wrong move.

"Ten dollars," the man replies gruffly, his tone as rough as the lines etched into his face.

I hand over the money with a practiced, casual smile, silently dismissing him as if he's of no concern. He grumbles something under his breath, disappearing back into the shadows of his shop, but I'm already focused on the boy in front of me.

I squat down to his level, careful not to startle him, the distance between us closing as I study him more closely. "Hey." I keep my voice soft, hoping to put him at ease. "You okay?"

Now that I'm closer, I notice the tiny flecks of gold scattered in his deep brown eyes. But as my question hangs in the air, his pupils dilate in panic. His mouth falls open slightly, the words caught in his throat, and his eyes dart wildly around, looking for an escape.

"It's okay," I reassure him.

"Aren't you going to yell at me?" he questions.

"Nah, I figured you know what you did, but I am curious as to why you'd want to steal some flowers. Especially from grumpy Gary."

The boy's eyes widen at the mention of Gary, and I have to work at holding back my smile.

After a moment he hangs his head in shame. "It's my mom's birthday today, and I wanted to give her something pretty."

The words tug at my heart, making my chest constrict. Standing, I shift my eyes back toward Nesrin, who's been watching the entire exchange with curiosity. She raises her coffee cup to hide her smile.

I shake my head at her attempt to be discreet. *Mind if I walk this boy home?*

'Not at all. I'll head over to Blue's. I need new material to tease Zee about.'

I can't help the grin that takes over my face. Those two are impossible with their constant teasing and bickering. Turning back to the boy, I see him look around me to see what I was looking at.

"Want me to walk you home?" My offer must catch him off guard, because surprise flickers in his eyes as they meet mine.

"Thank you for paying for the flowers, but I'm not supposed to talk to strangers, let alone walk with them." He picks up his backpack.

"I understand that, but it's getting late, and I won't feel comfortable letting you walk alone."

His eyes are so expressive. The distrust and uncertainty he feels are clear. I'm proud of him for being cautious, and I can see he wants to say no, but he doesn't want to be alone either.

"I promise, I will just take you to your front door. That's it." My hands lift in a non-threatening manner.

"I'm not going home. I have to go to the diner where my mom is working."

I have a strong feeling he doesn't want me to know where he lives, so for whatever reason, I play along.

"Okay, I can take you there. Which diner?"

Shuffling his shoes on the ground, he mutters under his breath, "Greta's."

With my enhanced hearing, I pick it up, and I'm momentarily stunned into silence. I know Greta's. It's a nice little diner. The owner is as old as dirt and tough as nails. But what has me taken aback is the fact that it's an hour walk away, and the area is notoriously unsafe. What is a young boy like this doing walking the dimly lit streets of Portland by himself, especially in that part of town? What kind of mother would let her kid walk around the streets at his age? It doesn't sit well with me.

"How old are you?"

"I'll be nine in two months." His tiny chest puffs out, and I can't hold back my smile.

"Does your mom know you're walking around the streets, and that you're so far from where you're supposed to be?"

His face pales, and he shakes his head. "I'm supposed to go straight from school on the bus home, or to the diner. I messaged Mom saying I was home, but I came here instead to get her some flowers. The ones where we live are horrible and cheap, and I couldn't risk taking some from where we live."

That makes me feel a little better that this isn't a regular thing for him. Scratching my head, I peer down at the boy.

"Okay, fair enough, though I hope you don't try stealing again. That you learned your lesson today?"

Dropping his gaze, he nods his head.

"My car is over there." I point. "I can drive you to the diner, so I know you're safe."

The boy looks at my car then back to me. "My mom will be so mad if I get in the car with you. I don't know you," he whispers.

I feel a surge of pride as I watch the boy take a moment to assess the situation before making a decision. I sense Nesrin approach and feel her light touch on my back as she stops beside me. Her eyes radiate warmth as she looks down at the young boy.

"Hello, I see you've met my bodyguard, Gabe." She gestures up to me. Her sudden and friendly appearance causes his body to lock up, before glancing back at me with a questioning look.

"Bodyguard?" he inquires as he takes in my stance.

I roll my eyes and push her hand down. "It's rude to point."

Ignoring me, Nesrin continues, "Yes . . . well, no. He is my friend, but he walks around like my bodyguard." She laughs.

The boy eases slightly, beginning to relax, just like everyone else when she is present. Heart filled with a comforting warmth, I send her a grateful smile.

"What's your name?" she asks, softly.

I'm such an idiot. I didn't even ask the kid his name.

Shifting on the spot, he replies quietly, "Tyler."

"Hi, Tyler. I'm Nesrin"

"Hi." He blushes shyly.

"Tyler needs a ride to Greta's Diner. Feel like coming for a ride?"

Nesrin looks at me out of the corner of her eye. *'Greta's?'*

'Yes.'

I can tell from the look on her face what's going through her mind.

'That's miles away.'

'I know.'

Smiling brightly, she looks down at Tyler. "I'd love to. If that's okay with you, Tyler?"

His eyes dart around with uncertainty before he slowly nods in agreement. "Okay."

Exhaling a deep breath, my shoulders drop. I didn't realize how tense I was. We need to make sure he gets home. No kid should be alone on the streets of Portland, no matter what time of the day it is.

We make our way across the road, and Nesrin wastes no time in hopping into the passenger seat of my car, calling out to Tyler as she does.

"Tyler, jump in the back, it's super spacious back there."

He hesitates for a second, but he can't contain his excitement as he jumps in the car, flashing a wide smile and buckling up. The flowers lie across his lap as he looks around the interior.

"This is a nice car." His expression is full of awe, and a flash of satisfaction runs through me at his approval.

"Thanks. I like it, too. Took me a long time to save up for her." I pat the dash of my black Escalade. Nesrin chuckles beside me, and my eyebrow raises as I glance sideways at her. "Don't you start, woman."

With a wide grin, she slowly lifts both hands up in surrender. "Didn't say a word."

"Uh huh, I know what you're thinking." I smirk, pulling out onto the street.

Settling back in his seat, Tyler laughs, content to look out the window. We make our way across town, Nesrin rattling off details about conversations she overheard from the homeless people ear-lier—snippets of gossip, random observations, bits of information that might actually be useful later.

Traffic isn't too bad today—a rare blessing in this city. We weave through the streets with ease, and in about twenty minutes, we're almost there. Tyler's still silent, his gaze fixed on something far in the distance, while Nesrin keeps talking, her voice a steady hum of background noise.

As I indicate to turn into the parking lot, I immediately pick up on Tyler's worry. I can't quite explain why I'm so drawn to this boy, but the instinct to shield him from any harm or alleviate his worries is overwhelming.

The broken concrete crunches beneath my tires as I pull into the small parking lot next to the diner. Bringing the car to a stop, I glance over at Tyler, finding his gaze locked on the diner, lost in his own thoughts. His dark, shaggy hair hangs over his face, partially shielding his eyes, but the heaviness in his expression is clear, as if he's carrying the weight of the world on his young shoulders.

"You alright, bud?" I ask, turning off the engine and slipping the keys from the ignition.

He shakes his head slightly, as if trying to clear his thoughts, then nods. "Yeah, I just wish Mom didn't have to work so hard all the time."

His words hit me harder than I expect. There's a lot of emotion packed into that simple statement.

"Where's your dad?" the question slips out before I can stop it.

Instantly, Nesrin reaches over and zaps me with her magic, making me jolt. I glance over, meeting her eyes. They're sharp, warning me off, but it's too late.

"He's dead."

The words shock me out of my stare off with Nesrin. The way he says it sets off alarm bells in my head. It wasn't said in sadness or grief; it was said with venom and conviction. He's glad his father is gone. No kid should ever be made to feel that way.

Tyler opens the door and gets out, grabbing his backpack and the flowers.

"Thanks for helping me, and giving me a ride." He shuts the door and walks toward the diner, like he didn't just drop that information in my lap. No way am I letting him leave without my phone number.

Quickly, I jot my number down on a piece of paper, the ink smudging slightly, but it'll do. With the paper in hand, I push open the door, the crunch of broken glass under my boots sounds as I leap out of the car.

Nesrin immediately follows me, her door closing quietly behind her.

Tyler's eyes dart between me and Nesrin, panic flickering across his face. "What are you doing?" His voice is tight, edged with panic.

"Easy, Tyler," I murmur, trying to keep my voice calm and steady, hoping to soothe his frayed nerves.

The waves of anxious energy coming from him tug at something deep inside me, and I let out a heavy sigh. I step closer, moving slowly so as not to spook him further, and hold out the small piece of paper.

"We won't intrude, but here's my number. If you ever need help, don't hesitate to call."

Tyler hesitates for a moment before reaching out and taking the paper from my hand. Just as his fingers close around it, the front door of the diner flies open.

"Tyler!"

Tyler's eyes flare, and he quickly shoves the piece of paper in his pocket before turning. I glance up, and my breath catches in my throat. Rushing toward us is the most beautiful woman I've ever seen, her dark brown eyes lit with protective fury. Dark chestnut brown hair is in disarray, falling from her messy bun, tendrils framing her delicate face. When she reaches us, she pulls Tyler behind her, holding him there with one hand as if she needs the contact to make sure he is here and safe. Her cheeks are flushed a deep red, standing out sharply against her bronze skin, and there's a rawness in her eyes that makes me study her a little more closely. This is a woman who's been through hell and back, and she's ready to go through it again if she has to.

"Who are you?" she demands, her voice low and hard, laced with suspicion.

I raise my hands in a defensive gesture, trying to show her I mean no harm. "I was just talking to Tyler. Nothing more."

Her eyes narrow, and she takes a step closer, the scent of fear and anger rolling off her in waves. "I saw him get out of your car. Who are you?" she growls, the words coming out almost like a snarl.

"My name is Gabe, and this is Nesrin." I keep my voice calm and level.

My eyes connect with Tyler's, who is peeking around his mother, and she shifts, blocking him from my sight again.

"Don't look at him!" she snaps.

Nesrin moves forward a step. "We don't mean any harm, so please don't talk to my friend like that. We were helping Tyler out, making sure he got back to you safely."

Nesrin's calm demeanor is giving way to her instinctual need to protect her pack. The last thing we need is for her eyes to start glowing and ruin everything.

Tyler's mother looks between the two of us, distrust clear in her eyes. "Leave. Now"

I shake my head, my hair falling in my face. This beautiful woman is just being a protective mother. My own mother was the same, so I understand it completely.

"We didn't mean to upset you, we are just looking out for Tyler." I peer around her at Tyler again. "Bye, buddy. Look after yourself and your mom."

My hand instinctively reaches for Nesrin's arm, and I steer her toward the car. Nesrin looks like she has more to say, but I need to get her into the car, for Tyler's sake.

Just as I round the car, I hear Tyler's voice. "Thanks, Gabe."

I turn and see him being led toward the diner, his mother turning back to look at me over her shoulder. Her beautiful brown eyes narrow with caution as she looks back and forth between her son and me before ushering him inside.

Nesrin and I sit in the car, a heavy silence settling between us as we watch the scene unfold. The mother and son stand just inside the diner. The woman's distress is evident in her posture. Her body language speaks of inner turmoil and struggle, with every movement tense and guarded, as if she's constantly on edge. It's obvious she's carrying a heavy burden, and the weight of it shows in the way she holds herself. I get it, though. I really do. If I were in her shoes and saw my kid stepping out of a stranger's car, I'd be losing my mind, too. But it seems like more than that.

More than just unknown faces and potential threats.

Tyler holds out the small bouquet of flowers, offering them to his mother with a soft, almost tentative gesture. Even from where we're sitting, I can see the way her expression crumples, tears welling up in her eyes. She bends down, pulling him into a tight embrace, clinging to him like she's afraid to let go. It's a raw, vulnerable moment, and I find myself feeling like an intruder, witnessing something so private and profound. Tyler says something else, and whatever it is, it shifts her focus. Those fierce eyes lock on mine again, and I swear, even at this distance, her piercing gaze feels like a tangible force connecting with mine.

Chapter Two

SARA

My hands are trembling as they grip Tyler's shoulders, bringing him to a stop before me.

"What were you thinking, Tyler? Getting in a car with people you don't know?" I demand.

Fear and anxiety pound through me like a drumbeat, causing my chest to tighten. I thought I taught him better than that.

Standing up straight, I place my hands on my hips as I let out a breath, trying to relieve the tightness in my chest. The adrenaline that's been pumping through my veins is finally starting to ebb, leaving behind a dull ache that refuses to go away.

I eye my son closely. His dark brown eyes look up at me filled with regret. Tyler is on the smaller side for an eight-year-old, and he is my baby. If anything happened to him, I'd die.

I hate this place. I hate the peeling paint on our apartment walls, the cracked sidewalks, the sound of sirens that never seem to stop. I hate the dangers lurking around every corner, the feeling of always having to look over my shoulder. But this was the only place I could afford to hide, the only place where we could disappear.

My eyes flicker to the flowers Tyler is holding, a simple bouquet of bright blooms that seem so out of place here. My chest squeezes again, this time with a mixture of confusion and a strange, bitter-sweet tenderness. Where did he get those? How did he get them? We don't have money to spare for extras, let alone something as frivolous as flowers.

"I'm sorry, Mom. I didn't mean to upset you. I lied. I didn't go home after school. I went across town to get you some flowers. Gabe saw me looking at them. He bought them for me so I could get them for you. Happy Birthday," he says quietly, almost like he's afraid of how I'll react.

I can feel the weight of his emotions, and I can't hold back the tears as my heart breaks into a million pieces. I'm so mad he lied and put himself in danger for me, but he did it to make me happy. I can't fault him for that. But he needs to know that wasn't right. His safety comes before anything else.

"Tyler, they are beautiful. Thank you so much. But I'm not happy you lied to me and put yourself in danger."

"I know, but Gabe helped me, Mom. He isn't a bad guy. He just got me back to you safe," Tyler whispers.

I know he is still out there. My skin prickles with the sensation of being watched. I turn and look out the window at the car. The windows are tinted, but I can just make out his shape in the front seat. I was horrified when I saw Tyler get out of the car, my motherly instincts going into overdrive. I raced outside guns blazing, but as soon as I made eye contact with the handsome Asian man, I felt a sense of calm rush over me.

I have never felt that before. It made all my defenses come up.

It's hard to deny Gabe's attractiveness with his striking looks and magnetic presence. The way his hair is pulled back in a man bun, with some black strands framing his face, only adding to the charm. With a strong jawline, prominent cheekbones, and a mouth that is irresistibly kissable, his features are truly striking. *Shit . . . I shouldn't be thinking of his lips.*

Unlike the leering looks of most men, his brown eyes are warm and inviting, making me feel at ease. He looks like a strong warrior, and as much as I used to dream of a knight in shining armor rescuing me, I am a big girl now. I know that's all bullshit. I can take care of myself.

"I know, Tyler. We will talk about it when we get home, okay? Thank you for my flowers. I love them." I run a hand through his shaggy hair. I really need to get him a haircut soon. The one time I tried to do it myself was a miserable failure. Tyler has been wearing a hat for three weeks, to keep it at bay, though today he seems to have gone without. "Why don't you sit down and start your homework, and I'll get you something for dinner?"

"Okay, Mom." He turns to make his way to his usual seat. Stopping, he looks over to me. "I love you. Happy Birthday."

My heart swells and I smile. "I love you more."

Tyler's face lights up, and he flashes me a smile before he takes his seat in the far booth.

"Sweet boy you got there, Sara."

I spin to see Greta watching us, a look of longing on her face. I have heard from other waitresses that Greta's daughter passed away as a child and her husband left. She never remarried, just bought this place and spent her whole life here. It makes me sad to think about that kind of loss. To lose a child, no matter the age, would be absolutely heartbreaking.

"Thanks, Greta." Smiling at her, I walk past, reaching out to gently squeeze her hand. "And thanks for letting him sit here while I work. Means the world to me."

Greta clears her throat with a low noise before turning toward the office out back. I watch her walk away, the weight of her pain visible in the slump of her shoulders. Not for the first time do I wish I could ease her pain, even just a little. But Greta is the most private and closed off person I know, apart from myself, and when you've built those walls, it is hard to take them down.

The rest of my shift goes by quickly, and I don't see the black escalade anymore. Gabe sat in the parking lot for a few minutes before leaving, and it made me extremely nervous. There was something about the way he looked at me, the warmth in his brown eyes that didn't seem diminished by my anger. If anything, it was as if he understood it, like he'd been expecting it all along.

I can't shake the image of the woman who was with him either. She was beautiful in a delicate, almost ethereal way. But what really stuck with me was the way her eyes seemed to glow when I confronted them. It gave me pause, a flash of something strange and eerie that I couldn't quite explain. In the heat of the moment, my anger pushed the unease aside, but now that I'm alone with my thoughts, it creeps back in, making me second guess what I saw.

I must have imagined it, caught up as I was in the whirlwind of emotions. After all, I've been living on the edge for so long that paranoia has become second nature. I've learned the hard way not to trust anyone, not to let my guard down, and to always assume the worst. That's how I've survived this long.

I only have one friend, and I haven't seen Mallory in two years, not since I went into hiding. It isn't safe to do so. I'm sure my father still has eyes on her, even after all this time. He's not the type to give up or tuck tail, and I know better than to underestimate him. He's relentless, and he'll do whatever it takes to find us.

That's why I use a burner phone, changing it regularly to stay a step ahead. Once a week, I call Mallory just to let her know that I'm alive, and that Tyler is safe. It's the only contact I allow myself with the outside world, and the only tether to my old life. Everything else about me, about us, is buried deep. I've worked too hard to keep us anonymous, and I'm determined it will stay that way.

Making friends, forming connections—it's all too risky. Tyler struggles with it more than I do. He's a kid, after all, and he craves the kind of normal life that I can't give him. He wants friends, people to talk to, play with, to just be a kid around. But I can't let him get too close to anyone. Not when it could put us both in danger.

I hate it for him. I hate that I've had to strip away the simplicity and joy of childhood from him, forcing him to grow up too fast, to be wary of everyone and everything. But I don't have a choice. Keeping us safe is the only thing that matters.

Gathering my stuff, I walk over to where Tyler is packing up his school work. Glancing up, he spots me and beams, his smile brightening my world, and I feel my chest warm at the sight.

"Hey, are you ready to head off?" I ask, handing him one of his books.

Frowning, Tyler looks over my shoulder. "Yes, but I think we missed the last bus."

I shake my head. The last bus leaves from across the street at 9 p.m. "We still have a few minutes."

Tyler points frantically to the window, and I curse under my breath as I see the bus pass by the diner. Shit.

They came ahead of schedule. A heavy feeling settles in the pit of my stomach. I hate the walk home at night. It really isn't safe. Tyler's presence only makes me more cautious, and I don't want to take any chances.

I absently bite my thumbnail and contemplate who I can ask for a lift. The chef, Tony, is out of the question; he has asked me out multiple times since I started working here ten months ago, and I have always declined. I don't want him to get the wrong idea if I ask for a ride, or to know where we live, but he is the only one leaving work at the same time as me. A small hand reaches up, pulling my hand away from my mouth.

"It's okay, Mom. It's not that far, we can walk."

Shaking my head, I look down at Tyler. "I can ask Greta if she minds taking us." I hold up one finger. "I'll be right back."

My footsteps quicken as I approach the office at the back of the diner. When I reach the office door, I poke my head inside, half-expecting to see her sitting at the cluttered desk, finishing up paperwork or counting the day's earnings.

But it's empty.

The sight of the vacant room makes my heart sink like a stone in my chest. A heavy sense of disappointment settles over me. I hoped she hadn't left yet, but the empty chair and dark computer screen tell me all I need to know. She's gone.

This is the only downside to not having a car. If I miss that last bus, I have to walk the streets at night. Growing up where I did, I know there are things out there that can hurt me other than scumbag humans.

I move down the hall to the back door that leads to the alley. Maybe she's out there. It's worth checking. Pushing the door open, I spot Tony, cringing when he notices me standing there.

"Hey, Tony. Have you seen Greta?"

"She left about ten minutes ago. Why? Did you need a lift?" He flicks his cigarette to the ground as he makes his way to where I'm standing.

I take a nervous step back. "Uh, no. I just wanted to talk to her before I left."

The door groans as I tug it open and quickly scurry back to the front of the diner. I take a deep breath, trying to steady the nerves that are beginning to bubble up inside me.

As I round the corner, I feel a jolt of fear shoot through my body. Tyler is sitting in the booth where I left him, but my attention is drawn to the person seated across from him. I quickly make my way over to the booth, my stomach twisting in knots. Tyler sees me and stands quickly, with a look of guilt on his face. This kid can never keep a secret. He wears all his emotions on his face for the world to see.

"Mom, Gabe is going to give us a lift home," he blurts out.

Without hesitation, I put my arm around Tyler's shoulders, bringing him closer to me as I carefully eye the man sitting in the booth.

"What are you doing here?" I hiss, anger riding my words.

I don't even care how harsh I sound right now. Why is he back here?

Before he can answer, I sense someone at my back, and stiffen.

"Sara, it looks like you missed the last bus. Why don't I take you home." Tony's deep voice creeps up from behind me.

I freeze in shock as I become aware that he silently followed me back inside.

Suddenly, I feel boxed in. Trying to keep my panic at bay and my breathing normal, I turn slightly toward Tony. "I said I was fine, Tony."

"You don't want to be walking these streets at night, Sara. Anything could happen."

The way he speaks sends chills down my spine, making my skin feel tight and uncomfortable. Tony may have started out nice enough, but over the last month, his persistence with me is growing like a weed in a garden that I can't get rid of. Gabe rises out of the booth next to me, and I can see the muscles in his arms flex as he takes a step forward.

"She won't be walking the streets. I will take her and Tyler home," he growls.

Heart pounding, I quickly shift my gaze toward him.

Gabe's response doesn't seem to bother Tony, who merely shrugs back.

"Okay, then."

Without a backward glance, he spins on his heel and leaves. I exhale slowly, releasing the breath I have been holding, and turn to face Gabe completely. "Thank you for that. Now we have to go. Tyler, grab your stuff. We are walking."

Gabe's voice cuts through my fretting. "I'm driving you both home."

His warm brown eyes hold such kindness, a kindness I haven't seen since my mother passed away. I look to Tyler as he watches our exchange, waiting for my reaction. Once again, his emotions are clear to read: *hope*.

I can't let him take us home, can I? I don't know the man, and I'm not thrilled for him to know where we live. "Come on, Mom. I don't want to walk, and it's your birthday," Tyler begs. The hope in his voice and his pleading eyes will be the death of me.

"Okay, fine," I relent, shifting my eyes to Gabe and finding a slight smirk pulling at his lips. Pointing my finger at him, I threaten. "If you try anything, I will gut you."

Holding his palms up, his smile is full and blinding. "Noted."

My eyes narrow on him, internally shaking my head at my thoughts. "That was a threat!" I snap, annoyed that he's not taking me seriously.

"Oh, I know." Grabbing Tyler's bag, Gabe walks for the door.

Chapter Three

GABE

I don't wait to see if they follow as I stride purposefully to my car, and unlock it. My focus sharpens, and with a single thought, I send out a wave of magic, letting it ripple through the area like an invisible net. It's a quick, discreet sweep to ensure the creep who was eyeing Sara in the diner is gone. The way he looked at her set my teeth on edge, and I am not about to let my guard down.

Satisfied that the area is clear, I reach the car and open the front passenger door for Sara. Her initial reaction is one of bewilderment—her eyes widening as if she's not used to such gestures. But just as quickly, suspicion clouds her gaze, her brows drawing together in a wary frown. I can't blame her for being cautious; after all, she doesn't know me. I have a feeling that in her world, trust doesn't come easily.

Tyler, on the other hand, doesn't hesitate. He darts past her and jumps into the back seat, settling in with the ease of someone who's used to moving quickly, adapting on the fly. Sara still stands there and studies me, as if weighing her options.

"Is there a problem?" I ask innocently, raising an eyebrow at her.

She lets out a tiny huff and mumbles something under her breath, too low for even my ears to catch, before moving past me and getting in the car. With a grin, I softly close the door behind her and make my way around the front of the car and get in. Sara sits stiffly in the front, glaring out the windshield.

"You know I'm not here to hurt you or your son, right?" My words are soft.

Upon seeing her slight nod, I extend my hand towards her. "Let's try introductions again. I'm Gabe."

After a moment of hesitation, her eyes flicker to my hand, and then she takes a deep breath before reaching out and firmly grasping my hand in hers. She glances up, meeting my eyes once again.

"I'm Sara." Her hand slowly withdraws from mine.

I start the car and turn to look at her, a smile spreading across my face. "Nice to meet you, Sara."

With a slight dip of her head, she turns to gaze out the windshield again. It's clear that this woman won't open up to me until she feels a sense of trust.

"Where are we going?" I pull the car out onto the quiet street.

Sara is silent for a moment, and I turn my head toward her. She seems to be lost in whatever thought is going through her mind. Absently, she lifts her hand and starts biting her nail.

"Hey." I reach across and pulling her hand away from her mouth.

Startled, she looks at me and frowns. "Oh, yes, sorry. I'm over at the Parks apartment complex," she mutters, pulling herself together, and sits up straight.

I know the place, a low-income area for those who can basically only afford the roof over their head. It's full of dangerous people, and I hate the idea of them living there. I bite my tongue, though. It isn't my place to say anything. I'm sure she knows the dangers of where she's living and doesn't need the reminder.

During the almost ten-minute drive, Tyler talks incessantly in the back seat, while silence blankets the front. With a smile on my face, I answer all of his questions, doing my best not to look over and admire Sara. As soon as I stop the car in the dimly lit parking lot, Tyler jumps out. Sara quickly follows, but before she can close the door, I'm out of the car and waiting for her.

"Go up, Tyler, I just want to have a word with Gabe quickly." Sara shoos him toward the outside stairs that lead up to the second level apartments.

Tyler hesitates, looking between us, worry clear as day on his face. "Please don't scare him off, Mom," he whispers before running for the stairs.

Sara looks stricken by her son's words, and I can't help but reach out and lay my hand on her arm. Sara jumps, shrinking away from me.

I raise my hands in a placating gesture. "Sorry, I didn't mean to startle you."

"It's fine," she snaps, and then lets out a huff.

Reaching up, she slips her fingers into her hair, carefully pulling out the pins that have held it in place all day. With a gentle tug, she frees her hair from its bun, and I watch transfixed as it cascades down around her shoulders in messy, tangled waves. The strands, dark brown with hints of lighter shades caught in the dim light, tumble over her shoulders and down her back.

"Look, it's not that I'm not grateful, but why did you come back? I told you to leave."

I don't want to tell her that Tyler called me to ask if I was close enough to give them a ride home. She might make him delete my number. So instead, I lie.

"I was passing by and wanted to check on Tyler. He mentioned you missed the last bus, and I wanted to help."

Sara doesn't look convinced, but I have to give her credit—she is a good mom, doing everything she can to keep her son safe in a world that offers little security. There's something about them though that I can't shake. I find myself drawn to them both, an inexplicable need rising within me to make sure they are okay, to protect them in any way I can.

"Can I walk you up?" I offer.

Anger flares in her pretty brown eyes. "No."

With a furious glare aimed my way, she turns and storms up the stairs. I keep my eyes on her until she disappears onto the second floor. With a final glance in my direction, she enters the apartment and closes the door behind her. Dropping my gaze, I look around the parking lot, hating how easy it was to get to her apartment from here. Even worse, it's accessible from the street.

Chapter Four

GABE

My gaze wanders as I make my way through a quiet garden filled with vibrant flowers and lush greenery, the temples with their red beams standing out in the distance. I feel at peace here, my feet crunching on the pebbled path. The temple ahead seems to call to me, a tug pulling me forward with a sense of urgency. I summon my magic, swirls of gold wrapping around me, and in a blink of an eye I'm standing at the majestic torii gate, marking the transition from the mundane world to the sacred realm of the temple. The gate stands tall and imposing, its crimson paint gleaming in the sunlight, with intricate carvings and symbols adorning its wooden frame.

I take the winding path up to the stone steps, my footsteps silent as I approach the main hall of the temple. The air is thick with a sense of reverence, the kind that only centuries of worship can instill into a place. As I step inside, I'm immediately stricken by the beauty of the traditional wooden architecture—a masterpiece of craftsmanship that has withstood the test of time. Modern structures, with all their sleek lines and innovations, pale in comparison to the rich, timeless elegance before me.

The roof, a marvel in itself, features intricate eaves that curve upward with a graceful sweep, as if reaching for the heavens. The wood, weathered by time yet still strong, holds a warmth that feels almost alive, each beam and plank telling a story of devotion and artistry. The walls are adorned with stunning carvings, each one meticulously detailed to depict mythical creatures and divine beings. These carvings add a layer of enchantment to the already sacred space, their presence a reminder of the spiritual realm that seems so much closer here.

I move through the hall as if I'm floating, the serenity of the temple making me feel completely weightless. A pair of imposing guardian statues stand sentinel at the entrance. Their stern expressions, etched in stone, command respect and instill a sense of safety. Each statue, with its fierce eyes and powerful stance, symbolizes protection, their presence a silent promise to ward off evil spirits and keep the temple's sanctity intact.

Stepping inside the temple, the air is thick with the sweet aroma of incense, and my eyes are drawn to an elderly woman kneeling before the altar, lost in deep prayer to the deity before her.

Though I stand in silence, it seems as though she can somehow sense I'm here. Raising her head, she stands up slowly. My frown deepens as I take in the intricate patterns and vibrant colors of the traditional kimono and silk wrap she wears. They are very familiar. When she faces me, my stomach drops.

"Obasan?" I whisper.

My grandmother's loving smile warms my heart as she closes the gap between us. I'm so taken aback that I can't bring myself to move. I simply stand there, captivated, as she draws nearer.

Stopping in front of me, she gently cradles my face in her hands, drawing my head toward her, and plants a tender kiss on my forehead.

"My dear Makoto."

I haven't heard that name since my parents' deaths twenty years ago, it brings a sharp pang to my heart.

"I have something important to tell you." Her voice is gentle yet urgent.

"What is it, Obasan?" My words are barely above a whisper.

My grandmother takes a deep breath, her hands trembling slightly. "I want you to know that no matter what happens, I will always be with you. My love will surround you like a warm embrace on cold days. I'm sorry I couldn't be there for you, after you lost your parents. I felt their deaths." Her admission is filled with emotion.

"How . . . How are you here?"

Tears well up in her eyes. "We are kitsune, my dear. Our powers are limited only by our imagination."

"Is this real?"

Despite being aware that I'm in a dream, every detail seems impeccably real, fooling my senses.

When my grandmother looks at me, her kind eyes crinkle at the edges, radiating warmth and love. "This is real. I need to tell you that my soul will pass through to Yomi, the land of the dead, tonight. At which point, my magic will transfer to you, granting you my affinity for dream walking. You already have three tails, and when you receive my magic, you will gain a fourth."

Her words hit me like a brick to the face, the implication sinking in. "My parents . . . They are the reason I have two additional tails?"

She nods, a solemn expression on her face. "Their magic transferred to you, Makoto, when they passed. The magic of water manipulation runs in your blood, gifted to you by your mother, while the power of teleportation was bestowed upon you at the moment of your father's untimely death."

I stand there, speechless, as a wave of realization washes over me. The air grows heavy, suffocating me with the weight of all the missed moments and untold stories. I have been blind to my roots, my heritage, and now, I can't help but feel the strain of all that I have missed.

"Why didn't you find me earlier?" I whisper.

"To visit you like this takes a lot of magic. It will be my last act before I die."

A lump forms in my throat, and I have to look away, as the weight of unspoken emotions bears down on me. "If I had known you were alive," I choke out, my voice thick with regret, "I would have come home."

She shakes her head gently, dismissing my words with a quiet certainty. "Nonsense, boy. You are exactly where you need to be." Her voice is firm, but there's a tenderness in it that I haven't heard in so long, a tone that used to comfort me when I was younger, when the world felt smaller and safer.

I watch as her form flickers, a reminder that this moment is fleeting. The lump in my throat tightens. "I miss you," I manage to say, the words catching in my chest.

Her expression softens, her eyes filling with a warmth that makes my heart ache.

"I miss you, too," she replies, a whisper that seems to echo through the space between us, as if carried on the wind.

There's a pause, a beat of silence where everything seems to hang in the air, and then she speaks again, her words laced with a gentle command. "Take care, Makoto. The water spirits are with you. And should you need guidance, you know where to find us." Her voice is soft yet powerful, a blessing and a farewell all in one.

Before I can respond, she pulls me into her arms. It's a sensation long forgotten—the warmth of her arms around me, the feeling of being safe and loved. I close my eyes, trying to hold onto the moment, but I can already feel the temple beginning to fade away. The vibrant colors that surround us start to blur, melting into the darkness that encroaches from the edges of my vision.

I cling to her, trying to anchor myself in the fading light, but it's no use. The temple, the gardens, the warmth, even her touch—all of it dissolves into the void, leaving me standing alone once more. But as the darkness closes in, the memory of her lingers.

I awaken abruptly and scan the room, seeing my magic restlessly swirling about. The walls are adorned with a mesmerizing dance of golden hues. A heavy weight settles in my heart as I ponder the words my grandmother spoke.

Suddenly, a surge of unfamiliar magic permeates my being, seeping through my skin and finding a place beside the magic inherited from my parents, nestled within my chest. I close my eyes, trying to steady myself as the weight of the moment bears down on me. But as the warmth of the magic intertwines with my own, a profound sorrow washes over me.

She is gone, and I never knew she was still alive. The truth stings, a sharp pain that cuts deeper than any blade. All these years, I thought I had no one left, that my family was lost to me forever.

Now, I am truly alone.

The thought settles like a heavy stone in my chest, a cold truth that no amount of magic can warm. The power within me, both old and new, pulses faintly, a reminder of the connection I never had the chance to explore. The grief is overwhelming, a sorrow that digs deep into my soul and refuses to let go. I had family out there, someone who might have understood me in a way no one else could—and now, that chance is gone forever.

Chapter Five

GABE

Great, Gabe. You're sitting outside the diner in your car like a damn stalker, waiting to see if Sara is working. I drag a hand down my face, feeling ridiculous, but the thought of seeing her – even just a glimpse through the glass – keeps me rooted here, fingers. All night, thoughts of her raced through my mind, making my heart jump with anticipation at the thought of seeing her again this morning. But after my dream, my mood has been dampened dramatically. A heavy cloud of sadness lingers, though I know I hold fragments of my family, my chest brimming with their magic essence.

A knock on my passenger window has me jumping in my seat. I look over and my eyes clash with a furious set of brown eyes. Today, her hair is elegantly braided, accentuating the contours of her face. The light blue uniform perfectly complements her tanned complexion, and I can't help but notice how the dress hugs all her curves. She points to the window and signals for me to put it down. I do so, knowing fair well the chance of this firecracker letting me have it is extremely high. Despite her evasiveness, Sara's fiery temper is impossible to miss, and it only makes me more intrigued.

Though I am a bit annoyed that my heightened senses didn't alert me to movement outside the car. I'm not usually this distracted.

"What are you doing here?" Sara demands as soon as the window is fully down.

I reach up, rubbing the back of my neck, keeping my gaze fixed out the windshield. I don't have a good reason for sitting here. I just wanted to see her. But how do I tell her that without her building a wall?

"I'm talking to you, Gabe. Why are you here?" she snaps harshly, fire lighting up her beautiful brown eyes.

The distrust I see lurking there sours my mood even further, and I have no idea why I hate it so much.

"I don't know why I'm here, okay? I got in my car this morning and ended up here," I shoot back, immediately regretting it. I open my mouth to apologize, but she stops me short with a sharp look.

"Well, it's creepy, okay? At least come inside."

My eyebrows raise in surprise, and I tilt my head inquisitively, eager to unravel the mystery behind this stunning creature.

"I'll get you a coffee. It's the least I can do," she grumbles before turning on her heel, and heading toward the diner.

She walks with a clipped pace, not bothering to look back to see if I'm following. I sit there, stunned for a moment, before my brain catches up. Getting out of my car, I swiftly move toward the diner, my feet eating up the space between us. I reach the door just before she does and open it for her. Sara just stares at me for a long moment. I don't know her well enough to understand her facial expressions, but I know she is questioning why I'm here.

"After you." I bow slightly.

She rolls her eyes, which remind me of Nesrin for a second. I can see the slight twitch of her mouth though. She wants to be mad at me, but can't quite follow through. Stepping inside the diner, I am greeted by a comforting blast of warmth, along with the enticing scent of sizzling bacon, eggs, and steaming coffee. I see the man from last night staring at Sara as she approaches the counter. His gaze slowly moves to mine, and I glare at him, his smirk only infuriating me more. There is something about him that sets me on edge. My instincts are telling me he is bad news.

Taking a seat at the counter, I pick up the menu just as my stomach rumbles. I was in such a rush this morning that I didn't take the time to eat. Nesrin offered me a steaming cup of Blue's coffee, but I declined in my eagerness to get here.

"What would you like?" Sara leans on the counter in front of me. Her smile is friendly, but there is a hint of tension in her expression.

"I'm forgiven already?" I ask, not able to help myself.

"Oh, no. Not even close. But you know you catch more bees with honey." Pushing off the counter, she turns for the coffee pot.

"Right," I drawl.

She grins as she turns back to face me and fills my cup. "It's not the best coffee, but it's not the worst either."

"Anything is fine."

"Well, what will it be? I heard your stomach rumble." There's a thread of humor in her voice, but I don't know if that's just wishful thinking on my behalf.

I look to the kitchen where Tony is watching us and decide against ordering a meal. "I'll take a muffin. Whatever you think is good."

"A muffin?" She wrinkles her nose, scrunching her eyebrows, and I want nothing more than to reach over and smooth out her frown. She's so cute.

Instead, I cross my arms in front of me and lean on them, stopping them from doing anything crazy. "Yes, I don't think I will order food when, uhh … Tony, was it? Is glaring at me."

Sara stiffens before she glances over her shoulder. Looking back at me, she sighs, her shoulders dropping. "I'm going to have to talk to Greta about him, aren't I?"

"Probably a good idea."

Chapter Six

SARA

When I first spotted Gabe's truck in the diner's parking lot, I was furious. All sorts of scenarios ran through my head. Mainly, *did my father send him*?

I was so close to turning around and going home to pack up everything and leave. Despite my fear, I couldn't ignore the intense urge to confront him. My fiery temper always does interfere with the rational side of my brain. My feet took me across the parking lot straight to his truck, before I realized I had even made that decision. His response left me bewildered enough to regret my outburst. There is also something in his eyes, a sadness that pulls at me. Although I am going to be cautious, my intuition tells me that Gabe has no ill intentions toward me or Tyler. He definitely isn't working for my father. My father wouldn't send someone as patient and kind as Gabe.

"So, how did your birthday night go with Tyler?"

A smile spreads across my face as I recall the previous night spent with Tyler. Birthdays are a special occasion, so staying up later than usual was a given for us both.

"It was good. We stayed up, watched a movie, and ate a lot of ice cream. Thank you for the ride last night, and for getting Tyler back here. He told me what happened. You didn't have to purchase those flowers." Heat rises to my cheeks.

Even though it's brought so many mixed emotions, I am thankful he stepped in and helped us not once, not twice, but three times yesterday.

"That's okay. I'm glad I was around when I was. What time do you get off work today?"

Frowning, I look at Gabe. Despite his open posture and sincere voice, his interest in Tyler and me makes me anxious. The reason I've made it this far is that I've avoided forming attachments. Makes it a lot easier to up and leave when I have to, and leaves no one asking questions or putting out missing person alerts. Although Gabe wants to get to know me, I have a simple rule that I have followed for two years. A rule I am not willing to break. One that has kept me and the people around me alive.

No friends, no boyfriends, no connections or attachments of any kind. No one my father could track down and hurt to get to me.

"I'm only asking because I can wait for Tyler to get off the bus and take him to my friend's bookshop. You remember the woman who was with me the other day? Nesrin? She is my lu– friend," he quickly finishes.

Holding his gaze, I study the handsome man before me, trying to read his intentions. I can tell he wants me to trust him, but I just don't know if I can. Trust comes hard to me, having learned that nothing in life is ever easy.

"I'm not comfortable with you spending time alone with my son. I'm sorry, Gabe," I say finally.

I can see that he is trying his best not to let the disappointment show. Instead, he nods his head and stands up, throwing a bunch of notes on the counter.

"It's okay, Sara. I'll prove to you I'm someone you can trust," he promises.

With a smile on his face, he strolls out the door, leaving me to watch his back. I sigh and pick up the bills he left, noticing there is way too much money here.

"He seems like a good man." Greta comes to stand next to me.

I wipe the counter and pocket the money until I head over to the register. "Looks can be deceiving, Greta," I murmur.

Shaking her head, she nods toward the parking lot where I see Gabe's car leaving. "That man there isn't deceiving anyone."

"How can you tell what his intentions are?" I inquire, genuinely curious.

Crossing her arms, she gazes at me until I begin to squirm under her intense stare.

"I just know he isn't hiding or running from anything. Which can't be said for some, now, can it?"

A sinking feeling consumes me as my heart drops. Greta knows I'm hiding from someone, but she doesn't know who or why. Which is why she pays me in cash, and my apartment is under her name. Greta has been an absolute lifesaver, but she has never brought up my situation so openly before.

"Greta," I warn, my pulse picking up.

"I know, Sara. Just don't close yourself off from everyone. Especially a man who is decent and caring. Trust me, you don't want my life."

With that, Greta turns and walks down to her office. I lean forward, my hands gripping the edge of the counter in front of me. Deep down, I know that she is right. Tyler needs a male figure in his life, and I can't let my fear hold me back. Hell, the kid needs anyone around. It is a hard truth to face, but the reality is that we are both yearning for connection. Taking that leap seems daunting, and I'm not sure if I'm ready for it yet. If I were though, it would definitely be with someone like Gabe.

I shake my head at the thoughts swirling in my mind. It isn't going to happen, so I need to forget about it.

Unwillingly, my eyes travel back to the window, searching for him. His car is gone now, and for the first time, I wish someone would break through the walls I've built around myself. That he makes good on his promise.

I'll prove to you I'm someone you can trust.

For three long hours, I work tirelessly, hoping for better tips from unappreciative customers. Everyone seems to be in a bad mood today. Obviously, the stars are not aligned in my favor. By the time my twenty-minute break comes around, I'm exhausted. A cup of black coffee in hand, I head to the alley for some fresh air. Sipping coffee, I take a seat on some crates. The bitterness in my mouth is hard to ignore, but I force myself to swallow it down. I need caffeine to get me through the rest of my shift. The thought of going three more hours without caffeine is unbearable.

I sigh deeply as the image of warm, comforting almond eyes flicker in my mind, bringing a sense of calm. A sense of yearning washes over me, making my chest ache. Thoughts of Gabe keep invading my mind. My eyes darted to the parking lot this morning more times than I care to admit. I've been taken aback by how different he is from other men I've met. He has a generous heart and is strikingly good-looking, but never expects anything in exchange for his kindness. I have never imagined thinking of a man in that way before. The men around me during my upbringing were handsome at first glance, but their personalities were ugly.

With a resigned breath and aching feet, I make my way back inside. The clinking of silverware and chatter of people greets me as I step into the full diner. Right. Time to get back to it.

The hours pass by quickly, filled with the constant sound of clinking plates and the high energy of busy customers. I glance up at the clock and sigh in relief when I see it's time to go. My energy is completely depleted, and even the most basic tasks feel overwhelming at this point. I finish clearing the final table in my section and take the plates to the kitchen.

With a weary sigh, I untie my apron. "Bye, guys," I call out over my shoulder to the kitchen staff, who have just come in for the afternoon shift.

A chorus of goodbyes ring out, and I make my way to the back to grab my stuff. I am more than ready to leave. Today, an overwhelming number of customers tried to get my number, and the rest were just plain rude. I am completely fed up.

I pop my head into the office and smile at Greta. "I'm out. Have a good night."

Greta's eyes meet mine, and her face softens. "Okay, Sara. Thanks for today. I'm amazed you were able to bite your tongue with some of those customers. Not sure I could have."

A blush creeps up my cheeks as I release a nervous chuckle. "Yeah, well, they were pushing it. One guy even snapped his fingers at me. I'm not his dog," I grumble.

Greta grins. "Go home to your boy and rest up. Hopefully everyone is in a better mood tomorrow."

"One can hope," I mutter. "Bye, Greta."

"Bye, honey."

Chapter Seven

GABE

I don't know how I'm going to prove myself to be someone Sara can trust, but they've been on my mind all day. Surely it won't hurt to check in on them. Maybe swing by and see if she's working tonight. Perhaps keep Tyler company until she's finished.

That's the plan as I step into the diner. Then I immediately sense the chaos. The place is packed with people. Still, my gaze is drawn to Sara like a magnet. Her long, wavy brown hair is haphazardly tied up in a bun, loose strands softly framing her face. A light sheen covers her brown skin, giving her an enchanting glow, and her eyes are constantly in motion, never lingering in one spot for too long. Tucking my hands into my pockets, I make my way over to the booth at the back. Tyler's sitting there again, his head bent low, tongue peeking out between his teeth as he focuses on his homework.

"Hey, Tyler." I flash a smile as his big brown eyes look up at me.

"Gabe!" he exclaims loudly.

"Can I sit?"

"Yes."

"What are you working on there?" I point to the book in front of him, sliding into the booth across from him.

"Math," he replies, his face dropping at the mere mention of the word.

Chuckling, I lean forward and grab his workbook, pulling it across the table. A frown forms on my face, and I carefully scan the work before turning my attention to him. "Want some help?"

Tyler's eyes light up in surprise. "Do you have time?"

"Of course." I motion for him to pass me a pencil.

Tyler hands over his pencil, a slightly chewed-up number two, with a grin. Giving him a playful wink, I begin to explain how to do the formula, breaking it down into sections for him. As I speak, his eyes light up with focus and determination, and he leans in to listen intently to everything I say. So I take my time, ensuring each step is clear and concise, making sure he understands the logic behind each equation. Tyler nods in understanding, his brow slightly furrowed in concentration. Which is better than the glazed-over look some kids get when math is mentioned. Sensing someone's gaze, I raise my head, finding Sara's eyes flickering from me and locking on her son. When her gaze comes back to mine, I give her a reassuring smile. Biting her bottom lip, she motions me over. Her look of distress confuses me, but I want to ease her mind.

"I'll be back in a second, Tyler. Work on these while I'm gone." Ruffling his hair, I stand and begin making my way over to the other side of the diner.

As I approach, Sara's gaze shifts past me, her eyes fill with concern as she steals a glance at her son. I stop in front of her, and she meets my eyes, her lips parting slightly as if she were going to speak, but stops herself. Curiosity fills me as I tilt my head, wondering what could be going on inside her pretty little head.

"I'm not here to cause trouble. I just wanted to check in and see if Tyler wanted company."

Sara continues to just stare at me, a soft blush covering her cheeks. A playful smile forms on my lips as I wave my hand in front of her.

"Sara?"

Blinking rapidly, she shakes her head, curls flying everywhere. "Sorry. Um, that's okay. Is he okay?"

"Yeah, why wouldn't he be?"

Sara bites her thumbnail, drawing my eyes to her mouth. "He's falling behind in his schoolwork. I try to help him, but I'm left with little time and energy at the end of the day."

Seeing her distress, I take a step closer. "Hey. He is doing fine, and he seems keen to learn, which is always good. I will help him with his homework until you finish."

Sara sighs, her shoulders slumping with exhaustion. "I don't want to ask that of you."

"You're not. I'm offering my time to help him."

"But–"

"No, buts. I want to help."

Sara's eyes fill with fire, and she steps closer, her voice dropping low. "If you dare to mess with me or my son, I will unleash a wrath upon you that will make you regret ever laying eyes on me."

I hold my hands up and back away, a smirk on my face. "I have no doubt in my mind you will make good on the promise."

Sara blinks and then her cheeks turn a rosy hue. The playful nature of my kitsune side feels mischievous, and longs to continue the interaction with her. However, I don't want her to chase me away, so I give her a nod and gracefully turn, making my way back over to Tyler.

Chapter Eight

SARA

Making my way out the front door of the diner, I untie my braid and quickly weave my fingers through the strands. My thoughts drift to Gabe, and how he helped Tyler with his homework yesterday afternoon. I was honestly so surprised to see him at the diner after I told him I wasn't comfortable with him taking Tyler after school. I really didn't think I'd see him again, even with his parting words.

And even though yesterday was a whirlwind of chaos, I saw him the moment he walked through the door. It was like time slowed for just a second, and my eyes locked on him, following his every move. Gabe has this way of commanding my attention without even trying. And when he sat down to help Tyler with his math, leaning over the table with that calm patience of his, I couldn't stop the thought that flashed through my mind—I wanted to kiss him.

I shake the thought away, tipping my head to the side as I run my fingers through my curls, letting them fall into place. Standing up straight, I hear a low whistle coming from my left. Glancing over, I see Tony lounging against the side of the building, casually drawing on a cigarette. His eyes linger as he exhales, smoke curling into the air, and he flashes me a crooked smile.

Irritated, I ignore him completely, and walk down the pavement to the bus stop, hoping to make it home at the same time as Tyler. Just the thought of seeing my boy adds a bounce to my step, a bit of my fatigue vanishing. With the extra I made in tips today, I can take him out for pizza.

Suddenly, a rough hand lands on my arm, spinning me around. I yelp in pain as the hand squeezes my arm, hard. My heart slams hard in my chest, and I come face to face with Tony, his disgusting breath wafting over my face as he leans closer to me.

"You think your shit doesn't stink, you whore," he growls.

Despite years of self-defense training, my mind goes blank as I try to recall any of it. *Shit*.

"You're no better than me," he sneers, pulling me against his body. "Ought to teach you a lesson."

A cold shiver of revulsion runs down my spine. The feel of his body against mine snaps me out of my shocked state. With more aggression than is needed, I stomp down as hard as I can on his foot, bringing my knee up in straight succession. Tony bends forward in pain as my strike lands directly on his groin, yet he stubbornly refuses to let go of me. Nonetheless, I am able to twist free from his grip. Swiftly pivoting behind him, I deliver a forceful kick to the back of his knees, causing him to stumble and fall to the ground. The impact of the pavement is harsh, prompting a groan of pain to escape from him.

"Never touch me again," I seethe.

I'm furious at myself for not acting quicker. As the bus comes into view, I quickly start running to catch it. My determination to leave Tony behind intensifies with each step. That jerk will *not* ruin my evening.

Chapter Nine

GABE

Mist swirls around my paws as I make my way through the ancient forest surrounding Yomi. There is no doubt in my mind that I am either in a dream state or engaging in some sort of spiritual journey. Whispers from the towering cedar trees catch my attention, their branches reaching up to the heavens like silent sentinels guarding the path ahead.

I know that I'm treading upon sacred ground, guided by the spirits of my ancestors toward a hidden destination. The further I walk, the sparser the forest becomes, and soon I can see a vast, open plain of green grass ahead. With a leap over a massive tree root, I arrive at the edge of the forest, feeling a rush of energy coursing through my veins. Shifting into my human form, I come to stand before a shimmering veil of mist, the boundary between the mortal realm and the world of spirits. With a deep breath, I prepare to step forward and cross the threshold into the unknown.

Suddenly, three figures appear opposite me, halting my steps. The mist clears and fields of golden rice sway in the gentle breeze, while majestic mountains rise in the distance, their peaks shrouded in wisps of cloud.

Yet, it is seeing my family standing there, so close, that brings tears to my eyes. They stand beneath a canopy of cherry blossoms, their faces radiant with joy and love.

"Makoto, my dear boy," my mother whispers in a gentle voice, her words floating in the air.

My father wraps an arm around her, drawing her to his side.

"What are you doing here, boy?" my father asks.

"What do you mean?"

"You walk the road to Yomi, but you are neither injured nor dying."

Frowning, I suddenly realize that I have been aware of my whereabouts all along, but I never considered the reason behind it. My gaze travels from my father, his tall figure exuding strength and pride, his eyes mirroring the lighter shade of brown like mine. I then shift my attention to my mother, tears glistening in her onyx eyes, yet she still radiates youth and beauty, just as she did on the day I last saw her.

Finally, my eyes meet my grandmother's, and I notice a knowing twinkle in her eye, as if she holds a secret that only time will reveal. "He seeks guidance."

The desire to step over the threshold and reunite with my family makes me feel as if I've reverted back to my childhood.

"You can dream walk?" my mother gasps, her long black hair swaying over her shoulders as she jerks forward out of my father's embrace.

"Yes, I think so."

My mother walks toward the veil and raises her hand. The place she touches shimmers a soft gray, rippling outward.

My father's stern voice sounds from behind her. "You must be careful. Dream walking is dangerous."

"You've grown so handsome. So strong. I'm so proud of you, Makoto. I can see the kindness in your eyes."

With a gentle motion, I lift my hand and press it against the veil, meeting hers. Looking at our hands, I am aware of the subtle vibration of magic coursing through my body. I look back at my mother with her soft gentle smile, making my heart ache something fierce.

"I miss you," I whisper, tears choking my words.

"I miss you, too, Makoto." Tears begin to line her eyes.

As my father and grandmother approach, I drop my hand, lowering my head in respect.

"What do you seek, Makoto?" my father questions.

"I don't know."

"Something is troubling you?" He tilts his head, studying me.

I sigh, my hand running through my hair. Thoughts of Sara and Tyler rise to the surface.

"It's about a girl." My grandmother grins.

"How could you possibly know that?" my father grumbles at his mother.

"The boy has the look of someone completely smitten."

With a sigh, I drop my gaze and run my fingers along the tense muscles on the back of my neck.

"Is this true, Makoto?" my mother inquires.

"There is a girl," I concede.

"Knew it!" My grandmother whoops.

A wide grin spreads across my face as I gaze at her. "I feel drawn to her and her son. There is an unexplained connection there. I felt it the moment I first saw them."

"She has a son?" Concern lines my mother's eyes.

"Yes. He is eight." At their shocked looks I go on. "Her husband died."

My parents exchange a look, and a sinking feeling forms in the pit of my stomach. But it is my grandmother who speaks. "Makoto, you have always had a big heart. If you are drawn to this woman and her son, it is for a reason. Trust your instincts. Follow the pull of your heart, for it will guide you to your destined path."

"The moon goddess's actions are deliberate and meaningful, for she never does anything without a reason. Trust her," my mother urges softly, barely above a whisper.

I stand completely still and absorb her words. A warmth spreads through my chest at the realization that I am being guided to Sara and Tyler for a reason.

"She's right. Trust in the whispers of your soul, Makoto, for they will guide you," my father adds, his arms once again finding my mother. They were always like that, constantly touching, their bodies gravitating to each other.

Before I can even get another word out, the veil comes alive, shimmering and quivering, as if it were fortifying its barrier. The forest surrounding me slowly fades away, replaced by a comforting white void, lulling me back into slumber.

Waking up the next morning, I feel invigorated. Seeing my family after such a long time has filled a void in my chest, one that I have ignored for far too long. Deciding to go for a run, I transform into my fox form and cast an illusion over myself, just in case I come across any hikers. Although it's unlikely for anyone to venture this far, especially close to Lukas's land. Closing my eyes, I let my golden magic shimmer in the air. When I open them again, I find myself on the front porch.

I sit down on my haunches and marvel at the new addition to my garden.

Two towering nanten berry trees form a magnificent arch over the steps of my porch. The vibrant red berries adorn every inch of their branches, resembling a carpet of heavenly bamboo, renowned for its protective powers against malevolent spirits. The sheer size of these trees, seemingly grown overnight, is unprecedented. Intrigued, I approach, standing on my hind legs, and inhale deeply. A gentle breeze encircles me, carrying with it the familiar fragrance of my mother, evoking a sense of warmth and nostalgia.

Chapter Ten

GABE

"What are you doing hiding back here?" Nesrin's voice brings me from my thoughts.

It has been two days since I last saw Sara and Tyler. And it's taken all my willpower to resist the allure of the diner. Every time I get in my car, I start heading that direction like an invisible force is pulling me to her. But I don't want to scare Sara away, and I have a feeling that's what would happen if I push things with her.

Her beautiful brown doe eyes are imprinted in my memory. They are even more beautiful when they are full of fire, which they seem to be often around me. She has so much spirit, and I hate the way she hides herself from everybody.

"Nothing. I just thought I'd try one of these books you're always raving about," I lie, waving the book at her.

Nesrin's eyes light up with mischief, and she lets out a hearty laugh. "I'd be more convinced if it wasn't upside down, Gabe."

I look down. *Shit.* Sure enough, the book is upside down.

Nesrin's chuckle is so adorable that I can't help but join in. "Okay, you got me."

Sitting on one of the couches scattered throughout her newly finished bookstore, I feel her shoulder bump against mine. "So, what's going on?"

I drop the book with a thud on the table in front of us. "I don't know. My mind's just been all over the place lately."

"It wouldn't have something to do with a certain brunette and her young son, now, would it?"

I give her a side eye, and let out a breath. Lying to this woman would be pointless. She can smell lies like a superpower.

"Maybe."

Nesrin laughs. "Just go and see her, then."

"I don't want to scare her. I think she has been wronged in the past. She seems, I don't know . . . wary, nervous."

Nesrin makes a face. "I can go with you?"

I contemplate her offer. If I show up with a friend, it might help put her at ease.

"Come on." She jumps up with a bright smile on her face. A smile that I know promises trouble. I've come to know that look very well over the last nineteen months.

"I'll be your wingman." A wave of her magic moves around me, as if playfully nudging me.

I can't help but groan loudly at her antics.

"What?" she asks innocently.

"Nothing. Fine, let's go." I push to my feet.

Nesrin links her arm with mine, walking us to the door. "Oh, don't sound like that. It's not like I had to twist your arm."

We head outside and walk across the road to my car. "So, what else is bothering you?"

I quickly peer down at her. "What makes you think something is bothering me?"

"Come on, Gabe. We share a unique kinship. I can tell you've had an increase in your magic, and you seem even more distant than usual. You shouldn't let yourself get stuck in your head."

Opening up about my feelings or my past is unfamiliar territory for me. I'm quiet in nature, and am used to sitting back and observing, but I forgot Nesrin also observes, and she cares. It comes natural to her, to want to help. Furthermore, if she senses something amiss, her instinct to aid would be heightened as she can see the darkness that devours souls.

With a deep sigh, I stop and face her, my hands buried deep within the pockets of my jacket. "My grandmother visited me in a dream the other night."

"Wait . . . she did? You have a grandmother?" Nesrin's voice is soft.

"I do. She used the last of her life force to visit me before she took her final journey to Yomi."

Nesrin's eyes sadden, and she lays a hand on my arm. The touch of her magic fills me with a soothing warmth. "I'm so sorry, Gabe."

I give a slight shrug. "I wasn't even sure she was still alive. Her gift of dream walking passed on to me though, and I visited my family last night."

"Oh my god! Really!?" Nesrin shrieks, excitement lighting up her amber eyes.

"I didn't mean to do it, but somehow I ended up on the edge of the veil."

The light in Nesrin's eyes dims immediately. "Wait, what? You mean the veil of the dead?"

I nod, scratching my neck.

Nesrin's hand shoots out and her magic shocks me, making me jolt.

"Ouch!"

"What were you thinking?!"

"I just said I didn't mean to," I reply, rubbing my arm where she zapped me. Nesrin's gaze narrows, and I sigh. "Look, my soul was searching for answers."

"To what?"

"I don't know, but it led me to my parents."

Nesrin's eyes soften slightly. "I understand that need."

And she does. Nesrin's parents had a lot to answer for, but unfortunately for her, she isn't able to reach them in the Elysian Fields.

"After what happened to my parents, I assumed I was alone," I admit.

"You are never alone."

I give her a smile. "I know that."

"You'd better." Her tone is stern. "Because you're family, Gabe."

The moment we walk into the diner, my eyes immediately find Sara. She stands behind the counter, talking with an older couple, the scent of coffee lingering in the air. They say something, and she laughs, but it's just a polite laugh. It doesn't come close to reaching her eyes.

Despite the warmth inside the diner, I notice she has a cardigan on today. Perhaps for a touch of comfort or style? The cardigan drapes over her hourglass figure, concealing her curves. As I observe her, I can't help but notice the subtle shift in her demeanor. There is a hint of vulnerability in her eyes, a flicker of sadness that seems to weigh down her shoulders ever so slightly.

I feel Nesrin's hand lightly brush against my back, signaling that she is content to follow my lead. Moving toward her, I can feel the weight of her exhaustion in the air around us, and I notice how tired she looks. My feet move swiftly, bridging the gap between us in no time. Sara's expression changes abruptly when she sees me, first with shock and then with surprise. As her gaze moves past me and lands on Nesrin, her expression becomes guarded.

"Hey, Sara." I sit down on one of the stools.

To my right, Nesrin takes her place. Sara's eyes dart between the two of us, uncertainty etched on her face.

"Hi, Gabe. And Nesrin, was it?" She turns to face Nesrin, who is beaming at her.

Despite Nesrin's initial aversion to people, she has grown to love everyone she meets. But she tends to get stuck in her head, usually while trying to get a read on someone.

I cough into my hand. *'Stop being weird.'*

'*What?*' She quickly averts her gaze to mine, and her innocent eyes widen.

'*You know what.*' I fight back a smile.

Sara's smile wavers slightly, and uncertainty fills her eyes as Nesrin turns her attention back to her. "Yes, it's Nesrin. I'm so glad Gabe brought me here to meet you properly. He's been sulking around my shop the last two days."

Sara's cheeks turn pink, and I let out an exasperated groan. "Seriously, Nesrin, you just can't help yourself, can you?"

Laughing, Nesrin picks up a menu scanning it. "Nope." The word resounds with a pop.

Sara's chuckle is soft, but it immediately captures my attention, and I can't help but turn my gaze toward her.

"How are you? How's Tyler?"

Looking down, she wipes the counter even though it's already clean. "We are fine."

My gaze sharpens on her, detecting the lie. "That's good."

There is a beat of awkward silence as we just stare at each other. Sara fiddles with her pen. "Well, what can I get you?"

"I'll take the pancakes, please," Nesrin answers.

A cursory glance into the kitchen tells me that Tony has taken the day off. I feel the tension in my shoulders start to dissipate as relief washes over me.

"Make that two." I push the menus across the counter toward her.

"Okay, anything to drink?"

"Two coffees, please."

I'm staring at her, I know I am, and I can see it's making her squirm, but I can't seem to help myself. I enjoy watching the flush that creeps across her chest and up her neck at my attention. At least I know I'm not the only one affected. Nesrin's sudden jab in my ribs jolts me back to reality. I look at her and then back at Sara in apology.

Sara gives me a soft smile, tucking some hair behind her ear. "I'll put your orders in," she promises, and moves on to fill other orders.

My eyes follow her around the room. Occasionally, she will look our way, a thoughtful expression on her face.

"She likes you, but you're right," Nesrin interrupts my staring. "She's been hurt before."

"How can you tell?"

"She is doing her best to keep you at a distance, she also doesn't trust anyone. Her eyes never stay still. She is constantly scanning her surroundings." Nesrin's analytical mind is working overtime. I can practically see the gears in her head turning over. "Her movements are graceful, almost cautious, as if she is navigating the world with a delicate balance."

I frown, looking down the counter at Sara, then back at Nesrin. "She has customers, of course she would look around," I reply, my tone not quite believing.

"No, Gabe. She is always on edge. She is very good at hiding it though. I have seen her scan the parking lot at least twice in the last minute, she never has her back to the door. She is jumpy and standoffish with everyone. Her smile is never genuine, it's a practiced smile." Nesrin cuts into her pancakes which were just bought out by another waitress.

I look back at Sara and watch her interactions. Nesrin's right. How did I not see that?

'Because you were looking at her pretty face or her big boobs,' Nesrin mind-speaks. I send a glare her way and she shrugs. *'Just saying.'*

Commotion at the door has us both swinging around in our chairs as Tyler comes running in, tears streaming down his face. Before I know I've even moved, I'm crouched in front of him.

"Tyler?"

Through his tears, he launches himself at me, throwing his arms around my neck. I catch him, wrapping my arms around him as he buries his face in my neck, his tears soaking into my shirt. Each of his sobs feels like a knife twisting in my chest, causing my heart to ache. Within seconds, Sara is there, trying to get a good look at her son, but he has a death grip on my neck. Standing up, I take him with me, walking to the back of the diner, his tiny body weighing next to nothing in my arms.

I can sense Sara and Nesrin trailing behind me as I push into the office. Greta is seated at the desk, her wide gaze meeting mine in surprise. Her eyes go to Tyler, then to Sara as she looks around, trying to make sense of the situation.

"Take the couch." She motions behind me to the small couch hidden behind the door.

I sit down, pulling Tyler's arms from around my neck so I can get a look at him. Nesrin shuts the door, moving to my side as Sara kneels at my feet.

"Tyler, honey, please look at me," she begs.

Tyler hesitates for a moment, and then slowly pulls back so we can see his face. My eyes fixate on the growing bruise on his left cheek, and I feel a surge of anger rapidly surface. I look down and see his palms are grazed, like he's fallen over.

'*Calm down, Gabe, or you're going to shift. I can feel it,*' Nesrin warns.

Closing my eyes, I focus on the sensation of the air moving in and out of my body as I take deep breaths. Nesrin's hand on my shoulder is a balm to the fire in my veins, her calming energy washing over me with each passing moment. As I regain my composure, I slowly open my eyes again.

Sara holds her son's face, delicately brushing away his tears, her touch filled with love and concern. Realizing that there are too many tears, she promptly removes her cardigan to dry them up. My attention is drawn to a sizable bruise on her forearm that bears the unmistakable imprints of someone's fingers. It looks to be a day or two old, already turning a deeper blue. Sara is so absorbed in her son, that she doesn't notice me stiffen. The air becomes charged with tension as I slowly reach forward and trace my fingers over the bruise.

"Who did this?" I ask in a deathly calm voice.

Sara's body tenses, and her eyes lock onto mine, a crease of confusion forming on her face. Her eyes dart down to where my hand rests on her arm, and the color drains from her face.

"No one," she lies, cutting me a sharp look.

"Don't lie to me, Sara. Who did this?" I growl.

"It's been handled, okay?" she snaps, continuing to wipe her son's face.

"Tell me who did this?"

Her brown eyes flare in warning as she glares at me. "It's not important right now. Tyler is."

That seems to do the trick, snapping me out of my fixation. I move Tyler next to me on the couch and take in his bruised face. "Hey, buddy, can you tell me what happened?"

Tyler shakes his head. "I'm scared."

His eyes dart from me to his mother to Greta. Nesrin steps forward and crouches next to me, drawing his attention. I know what she wants to do, what she was born to do. Heal. Reaching her hand up, she cups Tyler's bruised cheek. I can see the pain fade from Tyler's eyes. She can't heal him outright without Sara and Greta noticing, but she can take his pain and stop further swelling.

"Hey, you have nothing to be afraid of. You remember my friend Gabe, the bodyguard. Well, I don't think he will let anything bad happen to you again, or me, or your mom," Nesrin whispers.

Sara looks at me and mouths, "Bodyguard?"

I give a nonchalant shrug, not feeling up to explaining it just yet. "She is right, Tyler, we are all on your side here."

Tyler is trembling, and I feel like ripping apart whoever did this. Tyler didn't deserve this. He is a smart, sweet boy.

"It was Tony," he whispers so softly. "He was at the bus stop. He started yelling at me about mom and went to grab me. I ran but fell over. Hit my face on the curb."

Greta curses, obviously hearing him just fine for an old lady.

Sara wraps her son in her arms. "I'm so sorry, honey."

I look over at Nesrin, but she is staring at Greta, her eyes seem to be conveying something to the older lady.

Greta rounds her desk. "That big oaf doesn't know when to let things be!" she huffs, storming out of the room.

Unable to stay still any longer, I rise from my seat and start pacing the room. I tightly ball my fists, feeling my heartbeat quicken, but then I consciously relax my hands, hoping to ease my nerves. My body trembles with the intensity of the fury I'm feeling. How dare he think it's okay to touch them? I knew it was him who left that bruise on Sara's arm. I want to crush him. Suddenly, Nesrin's grip on my arm brings me to an abrupt stop mid-pace.

"Gabe, calm down."

I go to snarl at her and catch myself. Nesrin's eyes widen in shock, obviously catching my near slip up.

I hang my head, immediately feeling guilty. "I'm sorry, Nesrin."

"It's okay. I understand," she brushes away my words.

"It's not." I sigh.

"Don't sweat it."

We turn and look at mom and son hugging on the floor.

"What are we going to do about this?" Nesrin asks.

I shouldn't be shocked by her words, but I am.

"Tear him to pieces and throw him in the river," I growl.

Nesrin laughs then covers her mouth, wide, accusing eyes swinging at me. *'You made me laugh during a serious situation. Jerk."*

"I meant every word," I reply.

I retie my hair and glance at Sara and Tyler one last time before turning and storming out the door, Nesrin right on my heels.

"Gabe, we could let the police handle this. Tony is human, and he assaulted a woman and threatened a child," she reasons.

I ignore her, pushing out the door. Using my enhanced sense, I easily detect the distinct scent of Tony. I quicken my pace down the street until I reach the door of the nearby bar.

Nesrin stops beside me. "This is a bad idea."

"Then why did you follow me?"

"Someone needs to be able to talk the cops out of arresting your ass when this all goes sideways."

"There won't be any cops called."

"We're really doing this, then?"

I give a quick nod, my hand instinctively reaching for the door-knob, ready to swing it open. "You stay out here."

With a strong grasp on my forearm, she brings me to an abrupt stop, and I turn to her.

A white glow surrounds her irises, giving her eyes an ethereal appearance. "I am your Luna. I don't take orders from you. I will be beside you as a friend, but I'm still your Luna," she growls.

The weight of her words hangs in the air, charged with a touch of magic. A subtle indication that she could easily compel me to leave this man alone. I dip my head in apology, feeling a rush of regret washing over me.

"This isn't smart," she whispers, her amber eyes returning to normal.

"No, it's not," I concede, "But he hurt what's mine."

As our eyes meet in stunned silence, I can't tell who is more taken aback by my unexpected words.

"Okay, then," Nesrin breaks the silence.

Clearing her throat, she adjusts her posture before confidently pushing past me and entering the bustling bar. Shaking off my surprise, I turn and follow her inside. As we enter, we spot Tony at the back of the bar, engrossed in a game of darts with two other men. Nesrin catches the attention of the men before they have a chance to see me. They start leering at her and calling out, and she confidently plays along, strutting over to them.

"Damn it, Nesrin. Lukas is going to kick my ass for this," I mutter. Just the thought of my Alpha finding out about this makes my skin feel uncomfortably tight.

It's too late to back out now, the wheels are already in motion. I follow Nesrin over, but they completely ignore me as they scrutinize her from head to toe. The way they lick their lips as they watch her makes my blood boil. Tony makes a move toward Nesrin, slapping her ass, and my reaction is immediate. I swiftly cross the space in an instant, ripping him around and forcefully pressing his face against the wall, my mouth inches away from his ear.

"You think you can just touch whatever you want, you piece of shit?" I snarl, my muscles trembling under the restraint not to break him in half.

"Fuck you, man!" he exclaims.

I can see he is trying to see where his buddies are, but I know Nesrin has my back. As I spin Tony around, I can feel the rough texture of his dirty shirt beneath my fingers as I forcefully press him against the wall.

"You go anywhere near Sara and Tyler again and I'll make you wish you were never born."

To his credit, Tony doesn't pale or tremble. No, the fucker laughs. The sound of his laughter is like a trigger, making me realize he is beyond redemption. That he will continue to do as he pleases. My forearm presses his neck firmly against the wall, pushing down with enough force that it becomes difficult for him to catch his breath. I draw up my magic, feeling it warm my chest as I lean in closer.

"There is nothing I wouldn't do to protect those two. If you go near Sara or Tyler again, if you don't change the way you treat people, this will be your fate," I whisper and I enter his mind, showing him exactly what I would do if he ever tries anything again.

From behind me, I can barely make out the sound of Nesrin gasping. I know she despises this aspect of my gift—the illusions and mental manipulations—but I need this worthless piece of shit to get the message. I release my grip on his shirt, allowing him to slide down the wall and collapse into a rumpled pile at my feet. Without sparing him a second thought, I turn, grabbing Nesrin's hand, and pulling her behind me as we leave the bar.

Chapter Eleven

SARA

Letting out a deep breath, I sit on the couch beside Tyler, who is immersed in the movie playing on the tv. I left work early to bring him home to rest. There was no way I could focus on work after that. Hell, it was only after I managed to calm him down that I noticed we were the only ones left in the office. I hadn't even heard anyone leave. Gabe and Nesrin had left, and I couldn't help feeling a little hurt that Gabe hadn't said goodbye. *Which is stupid.*

Nesrin was a surprise after the way our first meeting went. I would have thought she'd detest me. But only pure kindness radiated from her, and it was impossible not to feel a little uplifted in her presence. I could tell by the way she smiled at me, and the sparkle in her amber eyes when she teased Gabe, that there is nothing cold, ruthless or cunning about her, and I love that. I need that. It is the exact opposite of my father. And of Tyler's father, Kirk.

"Mom, why did dad hate us so much?"

The question catches me off guard, bringing my attention to Tyler. My mind goes blank as I try to come up with a response to the unexpected question. Tyler hasn't mentioned anything about our lives with Kirk since we ran. But looking into his sad eyes, I realize now that perhaps I should have taken the time to talk this through with him.

I take a deep breath, deciding to be truthful. "I don't know, Tyler."

I despise myself for not having the guts to leave earlier, and the regret consumes me. If I had acted as soon as I knew I was pregnant, we could have gotten away before things escalated to the extent they did. I was foolish, and my hopes that having Tyler would bring about a positive change actually worsened things. My life became an unbearable nightmare, a relentless torment that we both had to endure in our own way. I never should have laid that burden at his feet. I did my best to shield him from the brunt of it, but he saw more than I care to ever admit.

Tyler's hands twist the blanket nervously. "Was I a mistake? Is that why he didn't love me?" he whispers, and my heart breaks.

I scoot closer, grabbing his hands. "No, baby, you weren't a mistake, never a mistake. You were a miracle, my miracle. You were my shining star in the dark."

Tyler tries to hide his emotions by sniffing back his tears. The pain in my chest makes me feel like I'm being stabbed repeatedly as I watch each tear fall. Guilt floods me, filling up every bit of space in my body. I have failed as a mother. I have failed to protect him from this feeling of rejection and heartache.

"I love you so much, Tyler. We are a team, you and me. I will always be here for you. I can't change what has happened in the past, but we can make a better future." My words are soft as I run a hand over his head.

I know it won't make up for the damage done by his father, but it's all I can offer.

"You promise?"

The warmth in those big brown eyes as they stare up at me fills my heart with love.

"I promise. It's you and me against the world. There is nothing that could ever come between us." I pull him to me.

Tyler's small arms wrap around my waist as he burrows into my chest. So many emotions are battling for first place inside me. I lean back, resting on the couch, and stroke my fingers through his hair. We stay like that for a long time, both of us lost in thought as the movie plays in front of us.

"Do you think Gabe likes me?"

I look down at my son's profile. Is this what was worrying him?

"Of course he likes you. Why do you ask?"

"What if he hates me like Dad did? What if I do something wrong and he gets angry and leaves, or . . . " he goes silent, then mutters softly, "hurts you."

"No baby, Gabe isn't Kirk. He would never hurt us, and he could never hate you. I can't see Gabe ever getting angry at you, but people don't always stick around. I can't promise he won't leave, but it won't be because of you if he did."

"I hope he stays. Maybe it could be the three of us against the world?" he suggests.

My heart stalls in my chest, and I wish I could give him that, but Gabe isn't here to stay. I don't even know the guy, but for some reason he has had an instant effect on our lives.

I keep stroking his hair until I hear his breathing even out, and his weight slumps over me. I can't help but smile as I look down at him, his innocence shining through. A sudden sadness swells in my chest, growing like a living thing, consuming me.

Hurt.

Loss.

Regret.

Anger.

Each one fighting tooth and nail to claim the top spot. I feel my eyes burn as they fill with tears, the will to hold them back while Tyler is awake breaking. They slip down my cheeks, flowing freely, one after the other. A sob gets caught in my throat, and a hiccup follows as I look at my boy. He's my whole world, and the thought of losing him two years ago still haunts me. Maybe he deserves a better mother, one who isn't in hiding. He definitely deserves a better father, but he is gone now. He can't hurt us anymore.

One thing I'm sure of, I can no longer work with Tony. I will have to hand in my notice to Greta tomorrow, because going to the police isn't an option.

I'm still running my fingers through Tyler's hair absently as the tears subside. With a stuttering breath, I lean down and press a kiss to his head.

"I love you," I breathe.

With a great deal of effort, I move to lift Tyler into my arms and carry him to his bed.

"Geez . . . " I mumble. I forgot how big he is. The kid weighs a ton.

Making my way down the hall and into his room, I gently lay him in his bed and pull the covers over him, my finger swiping the hair from his forehead.

Quietly, I leave the room, shutting the door behind me. With a heavy sigh, I walk into the kitchen, and go about cleaning up our mess from dinner, and then walk around, checking all the locks on the door and windows.

Once I am sure the apartment is secure, I can finally hear the peaceful hum of silence, I make my way to the bathroom. With a gradual motion, I undress and enter the shower, where the hot water creates a soothing mist. As I stand under the hot water, I feel a persistent numbness creeping over my body. With my hands cupped in front of me, I tilt my head back, letting the stream cascade onto my chest. My mind clears as I stand there, rolling my neck from side to side, releasing all thoughts and worries from my consciousness.

I stand there for what feels like forever before I shut off the water and grab my towel. Robotically, I dry myself and apply my lotion before slipping into an old, torn, gray t-shirt and black shorts. I pull back the sheets on my bed and climb in, the silky material, cool against my legs, enticing me to move my legs back and forth in a soothing motion, a habit I've had since childhood.

I spend the night tossing and turning, unable to find the peace of sleep. I have gotten up countless times to check the locks, but still can't calm myself enough to sleep. I sigh as I sit up, flipping my pillow over and lying back down.

"Nope," I mutter, flinging my covers off me.

This isn't working. I silently make my way down the hallway, the only sound coming from my soft footsteps, and turn on the light in the kitchen. Moving about, I start making myself a cup of chamomile tea. I hate the stuff, it tastes like garbage, but I'm desperate to calm my nerves and maybe get an hour or two of sleep.

Tap, tap, tap . . .

I pause in my tracks, my breath held, straining my ears for the return of the sound. Another tap resounds, breaking the silence. With a quick motion, I spin toward the apartment door, feeling my heart start to race, as I grip the counter behind me. *Who the hell could that be?*

A sudden wave of dizziness and sickness overwhelms me as my nerves kick in. I maintain my focus on the door as I cautiously grab a large knife from the drawer and quietly make my way over the door. Resting my fingertips on the wood, I close my eyes tightly, and take a few deep breaths, waiting for my heart rate to calm down. Then I rise on my toes and look through the peephole. I feel a surge of relief wash over me, and I sway slightly on my feet. Carefully turning the key, I unlock the door and slowly pull it open. The shadows cast a veil over Gabe's face as he stands there, his hands buried deep in his pockets.

"Hey," he says.

I look past him into the night, then back at his face. "Gabe, what are you doing here?" I whisper. "It's three in the morning."

"I've been keeping watch over your place, and before you get angry, I know you don't need me here. I just couldn't go back home after what happened today."

Warmth fills me at his concern. No one has ever shown concern for our well-being like this before. With the exception of my mother, who passed away when I was five, and my best friend Mal, I have no one else.

"I'm not angry. Just confused," I reply honestly.

Gabe gives me a soft smile. "I saw your light come on and came to see if you're alright."

"I'm okay, just having trouble sleeping."

"And Tyler?"

"He is fine."

Gabe nods, his expression unreadable, as he takes a step back.

"Wait," I blurt. I'm not ready for him to leave yet.

Gabe turns back to face me, his eyes shining in the dim light. As I look up at him, my heart beating faster with sudden wariness. "Did you want to come in for a cup of tea?" I ask stupidly.

Of course he doesn't want a cup of tea, you idiot.

Gabe stares at me for several heartbeats, and I wrap my arms around my waist, beginning to feel slightly foolish. The way his eyes pierce mine makes my stomach twist and tumble. It is a feeling I'm unfamiliar with.

"I don't know about tea, but I'll take a coffee if you have any," he accepts at last.

I release a tiny sigh of relief, and step back, holding the door wide with a smile. "Of course."

Gabe moves past me into the apartment, his body brushing mine. I draw in a breath as he passes, which has my lungs filling with his scent. He smells clean and citrusy, as if he just stepped out of the shower, but he is still in the same clothes from earlier.

I close the door and lock it, peering through the peephole out of habit. When I turn, Gabe is watching me, a curious expression crossing his handsome face, causing me to blush in embarrassment. He looks at me, head slightly tilted, eyes serious.

"Are you sure you're, okay?" he questions.

Hesitating, I consider lying, but really can't be bothered.

"I don't know."

I head to the kitchen, trusting him to follow. Not that it's far. My apartment is tiny, but at least the kitchen and living room are separate.

"I dealt with Tony. He won't bother you or Tyler anymore."

My heart thunders in my chest as I spin around to face him. I lean my back against the sink for support as I will my heart to calm the fuck down.

"What do you mean, 'dealt with?'" I choke out, my hands gripping the counter on either side of me.

Stalking over to me, Gabe reaches for my hands, prying them from their death grip. He strokes the backs of my hands with his thumbs. "Nothing like what you're thinking, Sara. I just had a few words with him."

Relief swiftly sweeps through my body, but now I realize how close we are standing, and the gentle way he holds my hands. No man has ever touched me this gently before. My husband's touch was harsh and cruel, never gentle or kind. I can see the longing in his gaze. I feel it, too, but at the thought of my past, I freeze.

Gabe seems to sense me stiffen, and lets go of my hands.

"What just happened? What's wrong?" He reaches up to cup my face.

I flinch, jerking back in response, my stomach twisting with shame. Gabe immediately steps back, giving me space. Relief rushes through me, and then misery hits me, followed by guilt.

I want Gabe's touch.

More than I'm willing to admit to myself.

Worse is I know he isn't like my father or my husband, but I'm not sure I'm ready to open myself up to anyone just yet.

After being alone and distant from everyone for so long, I no longer know how to just . . . *be* with someone.

Chapter Twelve

GABE

Standing close to her, I feel a tug in my chest as I witness the panic in her eyes. It causes a deep ache to settle there, and I try not to reach up and rub the spot.

"I never want you to be afraid of me," I whisper into the silent space between us.

"I know," she whispers back. Her eyes don't leave mine, and I feel like she's trying to tell me something important.

I lean back casually against the table, crossing my arms over my chest, my movements slow and deliberate. Her eyes immediately track the motion, lingering on my arms before flicking back up to my face. I do my best to hide the smirk threatening to pull at my lips. She may be trying to play it cool, but the way her gaze follows me gives her away. She's nervous—her posture stiff, her hands fidgeting—but there's no mistaking the pull between us. I can feel it just as strongly as I know she does.

She's attracted to me, even if she won't admit it, and that knowledge lights a spark of satisfaction deep in my chest.

"What did I do wrong?" I ask.

When our eyes meet, her beautiful brown eyes widen in surprise. "Nothing, I'm just tired. I didn't mean to react that way."

She turns back to busy herself with the drinks. She is lying, and that pisses me off for some reason.

"I call bullshit," I challenge, unable to help myself.

She spins around so quickly that the mug almost falls off the counter, and she glares at me. "Excuse me?"

"You're lying to me. Something upset you. What was it?"

Fire burns in her eyes, overshadowing the fear from before. "It's none of your business, Gabe."

Pushing off the table, I step closer to her, slowly raising my hands. I give her plenty of time to see my intentions as I tuck a piece of hair behind her ear. To her credit, she doesn't jerk away or flinch, though she stiffens slightly.

"Maybe . . . I want it to be my business," I murmur. I watch her swallow hard before turning around, giving me her back.

"It can't," she whispers in reply, as she continues to make the drinks.

I want nothing more than to wrap my arms around her and pull her into my chest, protect her, shield her. But somehow, I don't think she would take that very well, so I move back a step. Then turn and make my way to the other room and sit down on the sofa.

I don't have to wait long before she is carrying our drinks in and sets them on the coffee table. Sara sits at the other end of the only sofa in the room, tucking her legs under herself, leaning back against the arm to face me.

"So, how long have you lived here?"

Grabbing her mug, she brings it to her mouth and blows on it before answering, "About a year."

"Where are you from?"

Looking up, her brown eyes lock with mine. "Why all the questions?"

I sense her apprehension, but I decide to push. "I want to get to know you."

"Well, I don't like talking about my past."

"Okay, that's fine." I reach for my coffee and take a sip before placing it back on the small table. "Look, I wanted to ask you if Tyler would like to come to the bookshop after school today. I'm watching my nephews as well, so maybe he can make some friends. Or if you're not working, maybe you'd like to come? I know you said before you weren't comfortable about me spending time with him, but I'm hoping you'll change your mind." I'm rambling and I can't seem to stop. Everyone who knows me would be shocked by the number of words spilling from my mouth right now. "Tyler is a great kid. It's not healthy for him to spend the afternoons alone at home or at the diner. He is in need of friends and things to do."

I watch her closely, hoping to read her, but her face is as guarded as it's ever been. We stare at each other in silence, and I try not to get my hopes up when she opens her mouth to speak. When she doesn't utter a word, I push some more.

"Look, I think Tyler would enjoy it, and I don't think after yesterday he should be alone after school, even at the diner. So maybe just a couple of times a week he can hang with me and my nephews. Liam and Noah are great boys."

I hope I haven't gone too far. Hope that she'll accept my offer. Sara's gaze becomes distant, and she brings her thumb to her mouth and starts biting her nail. That one action tugs at my heart. She looks so vulnerable curled up on the corner of the sofa, her mug resting on her knees. I reach over slowly and gently pull her hand away from her mouth. I can't help but get lost in her big brown eyes, which seem to hold the secrets of the world.

Her voice is soft when she finally speaks. "Okay."

"Okay?" I repeat, just to make sure I heard her right.

She seems like she is in a daze, her eyes glazed over, and I can't help but wonder what was in that tea.

"Yes, okay. Tyler would love that. I know he would."

"Okay," I murmur again, because I'm a little surprised she agreed. It is taking me a moment to get my thoughts up and running. "I can pick him up from the school, if you'd like?"

"Umm . . . sure." She draws the words out like she isn't so sure. "Are you working?"

"Yes, I finish at six, is that okay? I can come and pick him up."

"No, I'll swing by and pick you up and drive you both home."

"That's too much. I couldn't ask you to do that."

"You're not asking. I'm offering."

"Still," she mumbles, bringing her hand back to her mouth and biting her nail.

I reach over and take hold of her hand, feeling her fingers curl around mine in response. She looks up from our hands, and I can see the curiosity in her eyes. I wish I could read her thoughts to understand what she's thinking. I could if I really wanted to, but I'd never do that. There are some lines that should never be crossed, and if I want to build trust with her, that isn't the way to do it.

I let go of her hand and take a sip of my coffee, the warm liquid heating up my chest. "It's not a problem."

"Okay."

"Okay." Seems we were back to everything being *okay*.

Sara blinks slowly, her eyes appearing heavy. She is exhausted. It shows in the way she holds herself. I reach over, taking the blanket from the back of the sofa, and lay it over her. She gives me a tentative smile, pulling it up to her chest and resting her cheek on the back of the couch as she watches me. With all the details for tomorrow afternoon settled and Sara's eyes barely staying open, I should leave before she changes her mind. But maybe I'll wait a while longer. I can't say goodbye just yet, and she seems in no rush to kick me out. I will stay for as long as she lets me.

Chapter Thirteen

SARA

"Mom, Mom, Mom! Wake-up. I made you breakfast!"

I jolt awake, finding myself on the sofa, a blanket pulled over me. My neck is killing me, and I can't stop the groan that comes from my mouth as I push myself into a seated position.

When did I fall asleep? Did I fall asleep with Gabe here?!

Tyler's face lights up with a huge grin as he stands in front of me, his hair disheveled and messy. I smile at him, relieved to see that the bruising and swelling has significantly reduced. He seems to have a newfound energy as he practically bounces in front of me. It's enough to chase away the exhaustion clinging to me. The couple of hours of sleep I managed last night were restless. Though I seem to have slept deeply while on the sofa, seeing as I didn't even hear Tyler wake up.

I scrub my hands over my face, then pull my hair back, and make quick work securing it in a disastrous mom bun. "You did what now?"

Bouncing on his toes, he points to the kitchen. "I got you breakfast. Gabe showed me how to make coffee."

My eyes widen, and my heart rate increases as I stand up.

Oh my god, Gabe is still here?

That makes me move. I enter the kitchen with Tyler on my heels and see Gabe standing at my sink, his long-sleeve t-shirt rolled up his arms as he does the dishes. Tyler points to the table, but I can't tear my eyes from the man in my kitchen. With a quick glance over his shoulder, Gabe offers me a tender smile. My stomach freefalls as I stand here staring at him.

"Morning." The sound seems to rumble from his throat, sending a shiver through me.

"Morning."

Tyler tugs on my hand, drawing my attention. The aroma of freshly brewed coffee hits me, and I look at the table to see plates of pancakes and bacon, their steam rising in lazy spirals.

"Wow, Tyler. You guys have been busy. I don't know how I slept through all this." To say I'm astounded would be a massive understatement. I usually have trouble sleeping deeply, often waking up at the slightest disturbance. I must have been more exhausted than I thought.

Gabe dries his hands on a towel, then turns to us. "You needed sleep, and you knew you were safe," he replies, his eyes locking on mine.

I swallow roughly, not wanting to acknowledge the possible truth in that statement.

Gabe strides over to us, and I tilt my head back to meet his gaze as he stops in front of me. A smile stretches across his handsome face as he reaches up and tugs on some of my hair that has fallen from my bun. He stares at the piece of hair as if mesmerized by it, then his gaze moves to mine again, our eyes locking and holding. His hyper focus on me creates a sense of weightlessness, making my stomach do somersaults.

"You look beautiful."

My cheeks flush with warmth. I'm rendered speechless. No one has ever said that to me before.

"I have the most beautiful mom in the world," Tyler pipes in from his spot at the table.

I duck my head, embarrassed at the attention. I feel the tip of Gabe's finger under my chin, and slowly lift my face back to his.

"Beautiful and humble."

Clearing my throat, I step away before I do something stupid like kiss him. After my reaction last night, I think I need more time. I need to get used to having him around.

Shit. Am I really thinking of breaking my own rules?

"Are you staying for breakfast?"

"No, I'd better go, but I'll pick Tyler up today, and you when you finish work."

Tyler abruptly stands up from his chair before I have the chance to reply. "No, you have to stay for breakfast."

My son looks up at me, and I can't help but recall the conversation we had last night, and the pleading expression on his face.

I chew my bottom lip and face Gabe again. "You should stay. There is no way we can eat all this by ourselves."

I don't even want to recognize what his answering smile makes me feel. My god, he is gorgeous. When his black hair is tied back, his sharp cheekbones and chiseled jawline are more prominent.

Gabe playfully ruffles Tyler's hair, making it stick up in all directions. "Okay, I'll stay for breakfast."

Tyler jumps in the air. "Yes!!"

My son's happiness fills my chest, mending the cracks in my heart. Another tug on my hair startles me, and I turn around quickly.

"Thank you," Gabe murmurs, his expression showing warmth and tenderness.

"What for? You cooked all this, not me. You deserve to stay and enjoy it, too."

"For smiling. For letting me stay."

The blush creeps back over my skin again. This man is dangerous. My heart cannot handle a man like this. I can't help but feel unworthy of a man as kind as Gabe.

"Well, thanks for staying this morning, for cooking us breakfast. It was very sweet of you."

"I wasn't going to leave when there was no way I could lock the door behind me."

He has a point. I didn't even think of that. My heart overflows with gratitude. He really is a protector. That reminds me. "Nesrin said you were a bodyguard?"

"Guys, come and eat," Tyler excitedly brings our attention back to the table of food. "Mom, I want you to try the coffee."

I smile and make my way over to the table and kiss my boy on the head before sitting down.

"Thanks, baby." I take a sip and sigh at the way the warmth from the coffee heats my chest. "It's a great coffee, Tyler." My son beams, puffing out his chest with pride at the compliment.

Gabe watches us with a hint of amusement in his eyes. "You two are perfect."

Judging by the way his eyes widen comically after the words are out, I don't think he meant to say that out loud. My son's eyes light up. Gabe will never know just how much those few words mean to him. Tyler wants to know that he can be loved, that there is nothing about him that makes him unlovable. A mother's love is infinite, unwavering, but to have the love of another would mean the world to Tyler. I have prevented that from happening, with all our running and constant hiding. Quickly, I brush away my thoughts, wanting to keep my emotions in check.

"So . . . bodyguard?" I repeat my question before taking a sip of my coffee.

Gabe's gaze lifts to mine, and I swear he looks embarrassed. Diverting his attention, he piles our plates with food before he does his own.

"I'm not a bodyguard. I do help Nesrin out, and our group does . . ." he seems to mull over the words a moment, "a neighborhood watch type thing."

"Ohhhh, okay. What do you do for work?"

Gabe hesitates, and a wave of unease washes over me. This can't be good. Anxiety has me moving to sit on the edge of my chair. I knew he couldn't be perfect. No one is, but I'm not sure I want my vision of him shattered just yet.

"I own a small studio. I run classes there from self-defense to meditation."

Wait . . . That is not what I was expecting by the way he hesitated.

The tension melts away as I settle back into my seat. "That sounds great."

"Maybe I can take you there one day when you're free?"

"Sure, I'd love that."

Tyler's head swings back and forth between Gabe and me. "Can I come?" he chimes in.

Gabe looks over at him. "Of course. Maybe you can even join a class."

Tyler's eyes sparkle with excitement. "Really?"

"Isn't he a bit young?" I inquire, cutting Gabe off from answering.

Gabe shakes his head. "Not at all. I teach all ages. I have other instructors that work there as well."

"How long have you been running it?"

"It opened earlier this year. It's a fairly new business."

Taking a bite of my pancakes, my eyes fall shut. Oh my god, these are delicious, *so* soft and fluffy.

"These are amazing," I mumble around my mouthful.

Grinning, Gabe looks over at Tyler. "Glad you like it. Tyler did most of the work."

We keep the talk light over breakfast, Tyler carrying most of the conversation. A rush of excitement fills him upon hearing the news that he'll be accompanying Gabe to visit Nesrin's book store after school. When Gabe offers to drive him to school this morning, Tyler eagerly dashes to his room to get ready.

I can't help but smile at his enthusiasm, but my gaze drifts to the clock on the kitchen wall, the hands ticking steadily by. Time's slipping away, and I know I need to get moving if I don't want to be late. With a quiet sigh, I stand and reach for the stack of dirty dishes, intending to clean up before heading out. But before I can grab them, Gabe's large hand covers mine, his touch warm and steady.

"I've got it." His voice is calm but firm. "You go get ready for work."

I hesitate, chewing on my bottom lip as I look up at him. "Are you sure?" I ask, though part of me already knows his answer.

"Yes, now go." He lets go of my hand, grabbing the plates and walking over to the sink. I can't help but notice the way he casually pushes up the sleeves of his thermal, revealing his forearm tattoos. This man is getting harder and harder to turn away from.

Chapter Fourteen

GABE

I'm casually leaning against my car when Tyler emerges from the school gates. His footsteps echo on the pavement as he sprints toward me. His radiant smile stretches full across his face. Even from a distance, I can see his eyes sparkling with anticipation. His happiness is unmistakable. As he draws nearer, a palpable electric energy emanates from him, almost like a crackling current in the air.

"Hey, Tyler." I grin, opening the car door for him.

Climbing up, he gets seated. "Hey, Gabe! Thanks for picking me up and letting me hang with you."

"Not a problem." With a wink, I shut the door, then walk around the front of the car and quickly hop into the driver's seat.

"Ready to meet some new friends?"

His fingers fidget with the zipper on his bag, a clear sign of his nervousness. "Sure."

As I start the car and go to pull out onto the road, his tone causes me to hesitate.

"Hey, what's wrong?" My voice is filled with genuine concern.

Tyler takes a moment before finally turning to face me, his eyes meeting mine. "What if they don't like me?" he whispers, his voice tinged with vulnerability. His insecurity breaks my heart, knowing that he's worried about making a good impression on his new friends.

I take a deep breath, trying to find the right words to ease his worries. "Tyler, listen to me," I start, my voice filled with conviction. "You are an amazing person, and anyone would be lucky to have you as a friend. Don't doubt yourself. Just be you, and I promise you will have a good time."

His expression gradually softens, a small smile playing on his lips. The warmth in his eyes replaces the doubt, and I can see a glimmer of excitement starting to shine through.

"Okay," With a renewed sense of confidence, Tyler leans back in his seat, letting go of the tension that gripped him just moments ago. It's a small victory, but it fills me with joy to see him embracing the possibility of new friendships. As we continue our journey, I feel grateful that I can be there for him, offering support and encouragement every step of the way.

A short while later, and after having answered a hundred questions about Liam and Noah, we finally arrive at Nesrin's bookstore. Last year, the local coven's high priest lost his mind and set the bookstore ablaze. The incident left the pack in shock and disbelief. But Lukas, always the loving husband, came up with a brilliant plan to surprise his wife. Determined to bring back the magic of the beloved bookstore, he secretly arranged for a new location, and even gave it a new name. The Legacy.

We walk in, and are instantly greeted by Astraea as she dives into my arms. *'Uncle Gabe, I missed you!'*

With ease, I scoop her up into my arms. "I missed you too, Star."

Star, as everyone lovingly calls her, is the perfect nickname for Astraea—it suits her to a tee. At just four years old, she already shines with a warmth and brightness that can light up any room, effortlessly drawing people in. She's become a little beacon in our community, winning the hearts of everyone who meets her.

I ruffle her hair and gently lower her to the ground, facing Tyler. "Tyler, I'd like you to meet my niece, Astraea." I gesture toward her and then back to Tyler. "Astraea, this is Tyler, my new friend."

Tyler's shyness is clear as he gives a small, hesitant wave. "Hi."

Astraea steps up to him, her arms encircling his waist with a gentle embrace. A flicker of uncertainty and hesitation shows in Tyler's eyes, but he eventually musters the courage to embrace her back. Astraea pulls away, her toothy grin lighting up her face as her eyes dart back and forth between us. Grabbing his hand, she eagerly pulls him over to the kids' section, where small couches and bean bags await. I meet Tyler's anxious face and offer a comforting smile, hoping to ease any worries. I made him aware of Astraea's muteness and her individuality, and at the time, he appeared excited about meeting her.

"I'll be over in one second. I'm just going to go talk to Nesrin real quick. The boys will be here soon."

"Okay."

'I'll take care of him, Uncle Gabe.'

'I know you will, Star.'

Turning around, I go in search of Nesrin. Instead, I run into April, Nesrin's new employee. She saunters in my direction, her hips swaying gracefully. Her blonde hair rests just above her shoulders, in an asymmetrical haircut. Since she started a month ago, I've been gently turning down her advances. Her flirting is non-stop. Now is no different. When she sees me, her dark blue eyes sparkle with interest, and a seductive smile plays on her lips. Initially, I didn't mind the attention, but now that I've met Sara, it's beginning to bother me.

"Hi, Gabe," she greets coyly, eyeing my chest, as if she can see right through my clothes.

"Hey, April. Where is Nesrin hiding?"

"Are you not here to see me?" she pouts.

What am I supposed to say to that?

My eyes are drawn to movement as Nesrin rounds the corner, rescuing me from the need to respond. A wide grin spreads across her face and her eyes dance with excitement when she spots Tyler behind me.

"You made it!"

"Yes, we did." I grin.

"I can't believe she agreed. This is great," Nesrin says affectionately, her hand reaching out and squeezing my arm.

If anyone can read me well, it's this woman.

Nesrin's wearing her favorite leather jacket, so she must be intending to go out and meet her special clients later tonight. Ever since the events that took place last year involving Hera and the council, Nesrin is now free to openly provide her healing services to the supernatural community without being a part of the coven.

Previously, she had to discreetly offer her help, making sure the coven remained unaware of her activities.

My hope is that she won't have to go alone, and either Lukas or Zee will be going with her. Despite her best efforts to stay out of trouble, Nesrin has a natural inclination for finding herself in it. Although she belongs to a lineage of demigods, known as the legacies, she still needs to have her pack as a backup and for added security.

"Me either, to be honest," I reply, but I know she can see how happy it makes me that Sara has allowed this, has let me in.

The bell at the front door rings as two hyper boys run in, going straight for Astraea and Tyler. I don't even get a chance to make introductions. They do it themselves. Astraea is as silent as ever, so tiny among the boys.

"She'll talk one day, right?" Nesrin whispers to me.

I see the worry shining in the depths of her amber eyes as I lower my gaze toward her. Gently, I wrap my arm around her shoulders, and she leans into my side, seeking comfort, as she rests her head against my chest.

"I don't know," I say honestly. *'She seems content to communicate telepathically for now,'* I add through our connection.

We stand like that, our eyes fixed on the children, for a few silent moments. A cough from the side draws our attention, and we turn to April. A hint of accusation lingers in her gaze as she clears her throat again. I release my grip on Nesrin and take a step back.

Nesrin, however, doesn't hesitate. "Yes, April?"

April points to the two of us, then settles her eyes on my luna. "Aren't you married?"

Nesrin impatiently taps her foot, her arms crossing over her chest. "And?"

April shakes her head, her hair swaying in sync with her movements. "Nothing. It's nothing."

Only, it's not nothing.

"Nesrin is like the little sister I never had, April. She is happily married, and I'm–"

April cuts me off. "I get it." She waves a hand in dismissal.

"Mmhmm . . ." Nesrin hums, not convinced either.

Nesrin's phone dings with a message, and her face lights up. "I have a delivery out back. I'll be back soon." She darts off for her new arrival of books before either of us can speak.

Without fail, the woman's face will break into a wide smile as she opens each book delivery, inhaling the scent of fresh pages with delight. No matter how hard I try, I have never found a book that could captivate me; I always end up getting distracted by other things. According to Nesrin, the reason for my lack of focus is simply not finding the right book yet. She assures me that once I find it, nothing will be able to divert my attention from it. I highly doubt it.

"Are you sure there's nothing going on between you two? Because I've seen her husband, and he is huge."

I feel the vibrations building in my chest, but I suppress the growl before it escapes. "There is nothing between us but family bond. Her husband is like a brother to me, as she is like a sister."

"Oh, well, in that case, want to go out for drinks later?" A playful smile graces her pixie-like face as she leans on the counter, pushing her chest out to make her breasts strain against her tight top. My eyes don't drop to them like she wants, and I open my mouth to answer, only to be spoken over.

"Gabe is busy tonight. He has plans with my mom." Tyler's voice is hard as he scowls at April.

I try my best to conceal my grin as April swiftly straightens up. I don't have any plans tonight, but it seems Tyler has somehow managed to make his own claim on me. My eyes shift downward to Tyler, and I reach out, placing a hand on his shoulder, giving a gentle squeeze to grab his attention. His big, soulful brown eyes swing to mine, and I draw in a sharp breath at the uncertainty there.

"Tyler is right. I have plans tonight."

Just as April opens her mouth, I quickly intervene to prevent her from saying anything else that might upset Tyler or make me feel uncomfortable.

"I'm not interested in having drinks. There is someone else I want to get to know."

April gives a tight nod. "Okay, sorry."

"Don't apologize. You didn't know, but now I'm telling you."

Tyler's bright smile mirrors the happiness that fills me. I gently guide him back to the others, their laughter and chatter filling the air as they busy themselves with setting up a board game.

"You like my mom?" he asks in a small voice that is barely audible.

"Yes, is that okay?"

"Hell yes!"

I laugh quietly. "Okay, then."

"You won't hurt her, will you? If you make her cry, I'll be mad. She's the strongest person I know."

I lower myself to his level, crouching down in front of him so that our eyes are aligned. "She's not only the strongest person I know, but also the most beautiful."

A smile slowly forms on his lips, gradually spreading across his face. "She is beautiful."

"I won't hurt your mom, Tyler."

"Promise?"

"I promise."

With a quick nod, he eagerly dashes off to join the others in their playful activities. I sit and watch them all laughing, the sound of their joy echoing through the air.

Chapter Fifteen

SARA

I'm dead on my feet when I see Gabe and Tyler pull up at the diner. My fatigue hits me like a ton of bricks, and I extend my arm to retrieve my coat and bag from the counter, then wave to Greta before heading toward the door.

"See you Monday!" I call out.

Greta's brown eyes warm with her smile. "Have a good weekend, Sara."

Pushing out the door, I hastily make my way over to Gabe's car, the cool breeze caressing my face. By the time I get there, Gabe is already outside the car, extending his hand to open my door.

The word "hi" escapes my lips in a breathy tone, causing a rush of warmth to flood my cheeks.

Damn it, I am acting like a schoolgirl.

His smile is wide as he takes me in. "Hey, how was work?"

"Long."

He lets out a light-hearted chuckle. "That bad?"

I grin and climb into his Escalade, the soft seat enveloping me in a comforting embrace. I bite my lip to stop my moan, because damn if my body isn't aching right now.

"Yes," I mumble.

"Well, you're off for the weekend now. So relax and buckle in."

As he shuts the door and rounds the car, he sends me a mischievous wink that makes my heart skip a beat. The mere thought of him makes my stomach twist and turn, as if a swarm of butterflies are fluttering about, even though he has no idea of the effect he has on me.

"Hey, Mom." Tyler grins from the backseat.

Twisting in my seat, I reach my hand to squeeze his. "Hey, baby. How was your afternoon?"

"The best. Noah and Liam were so much fun, and then there was this little girl, Astraea. Mom, she is so beautiful. Like an angel."

My eyebrows raise, and I cast a quick glance toward Gabe as he gets in the car.

Tyler continues to talk for the short drive home, and I find myself disappointed not to have more time with Gabe. I hadn't realized how much I missed having a connection until Gabe came around. I was content with my own company and didn't feel the need for adult companionship. Now, tonight that is what I crave the most. Nevertheless, I can't bring myself to ask Gabe to stay. It's Friday night, and I'm sure he has plans. He likely has a long line of women competing for his attention. Women who aren't poor, guarded single mothers with enough baggage to fill a semi-truck.

With a sigh, I finally climb out of the car, the cool air hitting me as I shut the door behind me. My legs feel a bit stiff from standing all day. I'm not sure how long I'd been sitting there, just thinking, but seeing them both waiting for me pulls me back into the moment.

"Thanks for the ride, and for having Tyler today."

Gabe leans his back against his car, crossing one ankle over the other. His white t-shirt really emphasizes his tanned skin and dark features.

"Anytime. He was great." He looks to Tyler, who is already halfway to the stairs.

Dropping his schoolbag at the bottom of the stairs, Tyler spins, face lit up with joy, and races back over to us. It has been a while since I have seen him like this, and it is all thanks to Gabe.

"Thanks for having me today, Gabe." He beams at the man who is worming his way into our lives.

Gabe's eyes sparkle with amusement and affection, causing my heart to flutter. "Not a problem, Tyler." His eyes shift to me. "What are your plans for dinner?"

"Huh?" His question startles me. "Oh, umm . . . We'll probably just have, umm, noodles," I mutter, not wanting to admit my lack of cooking abilities or funds.

"What kind of noodles?"

I can't help but frown. *Is this a trick question?* He's seen how I live, right? "The quick and easy ones, the ones most people buy from the grocery store."

Gabe seems pained by my answer. "The instant ones?"

"Yes, the instant ones." I shrug.

I am a terrible cook. No matter how hard I try, my meals always end up tasting bland or burned. It's gotten me into trouble plenty of times in the past. Depending on Kirk's mood, the extent of my punishment would vary. But I never had anyone to teach me growing up. Now, most nights, I'm too tired from being on my feet all day to want to learn. I know I need to put in the effort for Tyler, but I'm lacking both the funds and the time to do so at the moment.

Gabe seems to be having some kind of internal debate as he stands there. He must come to a conclusion though because he turns for his car. "I'll be back!" he calls back to me.

My heart skips a beat as my eyes widen in disbelief. *Wait, what?*

"Why? You're coming back?"

"Yes, I'll be back. Don't make anything." Then he starts his car and pulls out onto the street while I just stand here dumbfounded for a moment.

What just happened?

"Mom, what are you doing?" Tyler calls from the stairs.

"Nothing." I take one more look in the direction Gabe went before making my way to the stairs.

If Gabe is coming back, I want to at least have a shower before he gets here. The only smells drifting from my body are coffee, grease, and sweat. Climbing the stairs, I unlock the door, and lock it behind me, giving Tyler strict instructions not to open it to anyone, even to Gabe.

Quickly, I make a beeline for the bathroom and turn on the hot water. As the steam fills the room, I strip out of my work clothes and step into the shower. I relish the comforting sensation of the hot water cascading over my body, washing the smell of grease and stale coffee from my hair and body.

Stepping out of the shower, my stomach chooses this moment to rumble. I realize then that I haven't eaten since 10 a.m. That was over seven hours ago. Swiftly, I dress myself, choosing a pair of black leggings, and slipping into a cute sweater dress with a deep v-neck in a delicate shade of pink. I love the way this dress hugs my curves and accentuates my figure, and the light color looks good on my darker skin. Not that I'm *trying* to look nice or anything like that.

Riiiggghhhttt . . . that little voice in my head says sarcastically.

There's a knock at the door just as I'm making my way to the kitchen. Tyler looks up from the TV and grins at me. "You look nice, Mom."

Smiling, I playfully tousle his hair as I pass. "Thanks, baby."

I check to see if it's Gabe first, before unlocking and pulling the door open. Gabe is standing there with two bags of groceries, his arms flexing as he shifts the bags higher. Man, his arms are so defined you can see every muscle. I'm not sure there is even an ounce of fat on him. I bet every muscle on his body is sculpted to perfection.

Oh no. I'm staring.

My eyes quickly lower, and I sidestep to make way for him. When he doesn't immediately enter, I slowly lift my head to glance at him.

Gabe is staring at me, his full lips parted slightly as he slowly takes in my dress, his warm almond eyes heating my body every place his eyes linger.

Nervous, I reach up, twisting my hair over my shoulder. "You can come in."

Gabe shakes his head, looking nervous for the first time since we met. What does he have to be nervous about?

"Sorry." He steps inside, moving toward the kitchen. "Hey, Tyler."

"Hey, Gabe. Are you cooking for us tonight?" Tyler jumps up from the sofa.

"Yes, is that okay?"

"Yeah, Mom doesn't know how to cook, but she tries."

Inwardly, I let out a groan of exasperation. I don't want Gabe to think any less of me. Yes, I am a terrible cook, but I am hoping I'm not the only woman out there who can't cook to save her life.

I follow Gabe into my small kitchen, halting Tyler. "Do your homework, then you can join us."

"But, Mom . . . "

"No. You have had all afternoon with Gabe. You need to do your homework."

Tyler's shoulders slump, and he turns for his school bag. I walk into the kitchen as Gabe pulls everything out of the bags. My stomach rumbles at the sight of all the fresh vegetables.

Amusement dances in Gabe's eyes, illuminating his face. "Hungry?"

"Yes."

"It won't take me long. I got wine, a red and a white. I wasn't sure what you preferred."

"White, please." I pull two glasses from the cupboard.

Gabe moves around my small kitchen with a grace and ease that I have never seen in a man before. He seems to know where I keep everything, and I'm a little embarrassed that I don't have much in the way of cooking appliances. As he works at chopping vegetables, his forearms flexing with each movement, I take a long sip of my wine. The flavors burst on my tongue, a fruity, floral aroma reminiscent of roses and peaches surrounding me and warming my body.

I watch in silence as Gabe cooks, the tantalizing smells wafting through the kitchen. It's like watching someone dance. He has me completely entranced.

"Did you need a hand with anything? I can chop."

"No, just sit there and relax. I want to cook for you." Gabe looks over at me, his lips tipped up on one side. "Plus, I like your eyes on me."

My cheeks heat, and I take another sip of my wine. *Holy shit.*

"I won't complain. I've never had someone cook for me before."

Gabe's eyes swing to mine in shock, but before he can say anything, Tyler comes bounding into the kitchen.

"It smells so good in here!" He peeks into the wok, then closes his eyes and takes a deep breath, his chest rising and falling in a theatrical manner. Laughter immediately bursts out of me.

Gabe chuckles, moving around Tyler to grab some bowls. "You remind me of my friend, Malachite."

"Malachite? That's an unusual name," I note.

"It is," Gabe replies.

But he doesn't elaborate further, which is perfectly fine, because he just placed a steaming bowl of noodles in front of me. The rich aroma hits me first, and my mouth waters instantly, excitement building as I pick up my fork, eager to dive in. As soon as the noodles hit my tongue, the spices bloom, filling my senses with a warm, savory burst of flavor. A low, involuntary moan escapes my throat, surprising even me.

I glance up, embarrassed, my eyes immediately finding Gabe's. His gaze is locked on me, with the kind of look that sends a warmth spreading through my chest. It feels intimate, like an unspoken connection between us, and my face heats under his scrutiny. I quickly avert my gaze, my cheeks flushing even more.

I focus on Tyler, his eyes wide with excitement as he shovels noodles into his mouth at an alarming speed. He chews with such fervor that it almost makes me laugh, his energy breaking the tension that filled the air just moments before.

"This is delicious, Gabe!" His enthusiasm is evident as he shoves another spoonful into his mouth.

"He's right, it's amazing."

A look of utter satisfaction takes over Gabe's face. "I'm glad you like it."

"Um . . . I love it," I clarify over a mouthful of noodles.

Just then, I feel the sauce dripping down my chin. *Great.*

Gabe snickers and passes a napkin. "I'll cook for you guys anytime."

Chapter Sixteen

SARA

"Hey, Mal."

"Girl!! I was beginning to worry. Where have you been?" Concern edges her teasing words.

A smile curls at the corner of my lips, as a rush of warmth spreads through me. Malory, my secret best friend from childhood, holds a special place in my heart. Growing up, she was the one who held me steady through the toughest of times, like an anchor in a stormy sea. When I'd all but retreated into myself, she was there, the light that pulled me from the dark recesses of my mind.

I vividly remember her sneaking into my room, the creaking floorboards betraying her presence as she gently tended to my wounds. The smell of antiseptic and the sight of colorful bandages comforted me, hiding the evidence of my father's anger. Malory, with her pleading eyes, urged me to escape my toxic environment when I turned twelve, but fear held me back, paralyzing my actions. It wasn't until much later that I got the courage to run, and I had to leave her behind.

Leaving her behind was a difficult pill to swallow, and the ache of missing her only grew stronger with each step I took. Mal had been helping me with my plans to depart for weeks, with the intention of joining me once the situation cooled down. Unfortunately, that never happened. Mal has been reluctantly tied to the clan for a solid two years, and the weight of guilt bears down on me, leaving a bitter taste in my mouth. Despite the fact that she has found a wonderful boyfriend, she still has to be accountable to my father, who, though he can't prove it, suspects her involvement in our escape. To ensure her safety, Mal and I communicate every other week using disposable phones, and she remains unaware of my current whereabouts. This way, if she is questioned, she won't be caught in a lie.

"I'm sorry, Mal. I lost track of the days," I apologize.

"Who is he, then?"

A surprised laugh escapes me. "What?"

"It has to be a man. That is the only excuse I will accept for you being a day late calling me."

My cheeks heat as thoughts of Gabe flood my mind. "Well, I have met someone, but we aren't dating. You know I can't."

"Why not? It's been two years. You deserve someone special."

I exhale heavily, letting out a sigh. For the better part of a year, Mal has been urging me to embrace a new life instead of just existing.

You're just going through the motions, Sara. You need to find a true place to call home.

But would I even recognize it if it was right in front of me? I have no idea what a true home is supposed to be like.

Hidden and ridiculed, my childhood was spent in the shadows, away from the cruelty of my father, and later, my husband.

"You know why, Mal. It's hard for me to open up. What if I have to leave and he asks questions? Or just questions in general about my life that I can't answer. I don't even know if I can physically let a man be that close to me. It would never work. Kirk ruined me," I whisper the last part.

Through the haunting echoes of relentless verbal assaults and the lingering ache of battered limbs, I hesitate in opening my heart to anyone. The sight of my father's face twisted with anger has been a constant nightmare since childhood. But after my mother's tragic demise when I was six years old, his torment grew exponentially, as though he held me accountable for her death. Trapped in a web of despair, he coerced me into marrying Kirk the moment I turned sixteen. Initially, Kirk's cruelty paled in comparison to my father's, and I clung to the hope that his heart would soften when I discovered I was carrying our precious Tyler. However, my naivety proved to be a cruel joke as the torment escalated beyond measure. Kirk's rage consumed him upon learning of my pregnancy, a seething anger that enveloped us like a suffocating fog.

"Not every man will be Kirk or your father, honey."

"I really like him," I admit, my throat closing up.

"I know you do," Mal takes a deep breath, blowing it out sharply before continuing, "so take a chance."

I want to. I really do, but I need more time.

"Let's talk about something else," I say brightly, hoping she will give me this.

I hear her sigh on the other end of the phone. "Okay, fine. I just want you to know, Sara, the life you're willing to settle for. You deserve so much more than that. It breaks my heart that you can't see it. I understand your reasons, I really do, but I don't like it. Just so you know."

My chest thumps wildly at her words, and I let those words sink into my soul. *You deserve so much more.*

"So, how's my boy going?" Mal relents.

Feeling relieved, a wide grin spreads across my face as I glance behind me to find Tyler engrossed in feeding the ducks by the lake. We're out for a walk to one of the many lakes in the area. We both love being outdoors. There is something about being in the woods that always leaves me feeling refreshed and invigorated.

"He's great, actually. He made a couple of friends. Liam and Noah. They're all close in age."

"That's so good. I'm so happy he's making friends. How's work? That creep Tony been leaving you alone?"

My smile dims slightly. Should I tell Mal what happened? It would only add to her worry. "Yeah, work is good. You know, as good as it can be. Tony left me alone after Gabe had words with him."

"Gabe? This is the guy you met?" Her tone is playful, and I let out an exasperated groan.

Shit. I basically threw her a bone by letting his name slip. "Yes, Mal. But there is nothing going on between us. He's just helping me out."

"Right," she drawls, earning an eye roll from me.

Tyler rushes over to join the conversation, his face brimming with anticipation to speak with Mal. I remind him again to tell her no details, not because Mal can't be trusted, but for her sake and ours.

After exchanging our goodbyes, Tyler and I spend the day meandering through the woods, soaking in the peacefulness and admiring the sunlight filtering through the trees. I packed a light lunch and plenty of water, ensuring we could stay out here for hours.

We walk through the many small trails, the dense canopy casting shadows on the vibrant green foliage. A symphony of chirping birds echoes through the air, their melodies intertwining with the soft sound of rustling foliage. The earthy scent of damp soil and decaying leaves lingers in the air, while a gentle breeze carries the sweet fragrance of wildflowers. The forest floor teems with life as small creatures scurry and dart about. Tyler eagerly points at each, trying to identify them.

I finally decide it's time to make our way back to the car. Reluctantly, Tyler follows, not wanting the adventure to end. Suddenly, a heightened sense of awareness envelops me, causing me to come to an abrupt halt. A chill trickles down my spine, and the hairs on the back of my neck stand on end. I can't shake the eerie feeling of being watched.

"What's wrong, Mom?"

Turning around to face Tyler, I muster a weak smile. "It's nothing."

Shaking it off, I begin walking again, but Tyler's gasp has me whirling around instantly.

He's pointing at a massive boulder jutting out to our left. My breath catches in my throat as my eyes meet the mesmerizing sight of a stunning red fox. Its vibrant red fur glistens under the dappled sunlight filtering through the surrounding trees.

Although red foxes aren't typically found in this area, there is no mistaking this majestic creature. It stands larger than most foxes, its body exuding a sense of strength and grace. The fox's thick, bushy tail sways back and forth in an elegant, rhythmic motion. Perched calmly on the boulder, it watches us with eyes that seem to hold a profound depth, as if it can see into our very souls.

Suddenly, with a slight tilt of its head, the fox sits back on its hind legs and emits a short, sharp bark. I jump and instinctively take a step back, my heart pounding in my chest. Without hesitation, I reach out, clutching Tyler's hand tightly, urging him behind me.

As if choreographed, the fox gracefully leaps off the boulder and begins to approach us, its movements deliberate and purposeful. Its golden eyes remain locked onto mine, intensifying the connection between us. A mix of excitement and trepidation course through my veins, as if I am on the verge of unraveling a mystifying secret.

"Mom, what do we do?" Tyler sounds slightly panicked.

"We will be fine. Just don't run or make any sudden movements. I think he's just curious," I reply, crossing my fingers.

I'm certain that foxes pose no threat to humans, so we simply have a curious creature in our midst. With each step the fox takes, my grip on Tyler tightens, instinctively drawing him closer to me. The fox tilts its head as it stares at us, then lifts its nose and sniffs the air. The adorable pointy ears twitch, adding to its unique charm.

"Hi, little guy." I keep my voice soft, not wanting to startle the creature.

Suddenly, the fox darts around our legs, its swift movements catching both Tyler and me off guard. In what seems like a playful manner, it comes to a stop right in front of us. With another bark, it quickly darts around our legs again, its velvety soft tail gently brushing against me. The tail has a white tip that looks like it has been carefully dipped in paint, just like its ears. In addition, it has a distinct white diamond shape of white fur adorning its forehead.

"Playful thing, aren't you?" I marvel, running my fingers through some of the fur on the tail.

"Can I touch it, Mom?" Tyler's little voice is full of awe.

I pause for a moment, a rush of alarm coursing through me, but the fox gently nudges my legs. "Sure. He seems friendly enough."

Tyler's hand trembles as he reaches out and sinks his fingers into the soft fur on the fox's back. His beautiful big brown eyes, wide and expressive, meet mine. Throughout all our hikes, we have never encountered an animal so eager to be touched as this one.

"This is amazing. I can't believe we're touching a fox!" he laughs excitedly.

I gaze down at him with adoration, a warm smile on my face, before shifting my attention to the fox. "It really is. Isn't it?"

I catch sight of movement from the side, and my attention is immediately drawn back to the boulder, where I spot a snow-white wolf watching us. The overwhelming sense of terror makes my entire body stiffen, causing my grip on Tyler to jerk.

Frowning, he looks up at me with a puzzled expression. "What is it?"

I swallow over the lump in my throat, my body trembling, unable to contain the surge of adrenaline. "Nothing, but I think it's time we go."

Please, oh please, don't be hungry, I beg in my head.

Carefully, I manage to detach Tyler from the fox and slowly start moving away.

With a dejected expression, Tyler pouts, "But I want to stay for a bit."

"No, it's time to go. It will be dark soon."

"Fine," Tyler huffs his disappointment.

With a quick glance, I notice the fox sitting there, its intelligent gaze fixed on us. My gaze instantly moves to the bigger threat, finding that the wolf hasn't moved from its spot on the boulder. I watch with bated breath as the wolf lowers itself. I don't know what to make of it. It's like trying to solve a puzzle with missing pieces. The creature settles down, gently placing its head on its massive paws. It seems to be trying to downplay its size, as if to appear less intimidating, but the effort is rather comical.

I'm debating whether it's safe to turn my back as a gentle breeze rustles the leaves, carrying a faint, mysterious sound from deeper in the woods. There is an oddity about it that I can't quite grasp. I frown and look in the direction the sound has come from. The sound rings out again, still a distance away, but still too close for comfort.

"What was that?" Tyler asks, now gripping my hand.

I don't answer. My attention fully focused on the fox and wolf, who have become incredibly aware. In a flash, they take off, leaving nothing but a blur as they disappear from sight in seconds . . . Together?

I shake my head in disbelief, unable to comprehend what I just saw.

What the hell?

Chapter Seventeen

Gabe

The sound of Malachite's rumble fills the air, and Nesrin and I instantly spring into action, worried that he has wandered too far from home once more. We can't take the chance of him being found by anyone. Humans pose a threat. They could either kill him or subject him to experimentation in a laboratory. The supernatural beings, on the other hand, present a different danger, as they would seek to enslave him and sell his blood. Not that we would ever allow any of those things to happen.

Nesrin has made significant progress in teaching him how to shield and cloak himself, but he still struggles to maintain it for extended periods of time.

It only takes us a few minutes to locate him. We skid to a stop at the edge of the massive lake, my eyes fixed on the majestic green and blue dragon as it gracefully swims, dives, and breaks the water like a dolphin. Malachite's mischievous playfulness and cheerful, shrill roars make it hopeless to resist finding him cute. In her wolf form, Nesrin lets out a breath and shakes her head before changing back into a human. She stands with her arms crossed, emitting a sharp whistle, while her eyes remain fixed on the dragon that has paused mid-leap upon hearing her.

It's impossible not to chuckle, and Nesrin's face betrays her own attempt to hide a smile. Malachite turns slowly, his wings flapping wildly to keep himself aloft. Flying is still new to him. Even though he appears as big as a large dog, he is still only a baby.

Malachite's head drops, his spirited demeanor fading as he lowers himself into the water. The moment he touches the surface, his bluish-green scales catch the light, creating a mesmerizing ripple effect that makes the entire lake shimmer. Swimming to the shore, his bluish green scales create a stunning wave effect as ripples spread outward.

Ever so slowly he emerges from the water in front of us, and opens his wings, shaking. Droplets of water spray everywhere. Malachite's big golden orbs look down at the ground before his head tilts up and his eyes lift in the perfect sad puppy dog expression. I stifle another laugh. He has that look *perfected*—a mix of pitiful and adorable that could melt anyone's heart.

Nesrin makes her way over to him. "Don't you give me that look. You know you're not supposed to be out here," she scolds, her hands on her hips, attempting to appear stern but failing.

Malachite's growl fills the air, a low rumbling sound which carries a hint of grumpiness rather than hostility. We have somehow grown to understand what he means with each noise. With time, he should be able to communicate telepathically with Nesrin, since she was able to communicate with his mother. And Astraea, who seems to be able to communicate with any creature these days.

"Don't sulk, it's not dragonly, Malachite," Nesrin admonishes, running her hand over his head, a smile breaking free. "I know you want to explore, but not on your own, and not till you can protect yourself. Okay?"

Malachite nods, his exhale creating a soft, weary sigh that escapes into the air in wisps of mist, eliciting another chuckle from me. I shift into my human form and walk over. The dragon's eyes light up when he spots me approaching. For some reason, he has taken a liking to me. We share a different bond. I seem to be the one he comes to when he thinks he is in trouble, like an older brother to hide behind.

"Hey there, Malachite. Enjoy your swim?"

A soft laugh works through me as he charges toward me, effortlessly sweeping my feet out from under me. With a thud, I find myself seated on the ground. Malachite, seizing the opportunity, scampers away and unleashes a spray of water from his mouth, leaving me completely soaked.

"Thanks, Malachite."

A cheerful giggle escapes Nesrin's lips, and a wide grin spreads across my face in amusement.

"So . . . race you home?" I challenge, getting to my feet.

Malachite's eyes flare in excitement as he bounces on the spot, mist pouring from his nostrils, and I see him look at Nesrin pleadingly.

"Yes, let's race," she chuckles.

Shifting into our animals, we dash off into the woods again, this time a dragon between us. The temptation to teleport ahead is tempting. With my increase in power, I've been able to teleport further, but I still have to be able to see where I'm teleporting.

However, when it comes to my water abilities, they are notably stronger. It takes little to no effort to hold a wall of water now. A bump from Malachite almost sends me sprawling on the forest floor. A not so gentle reminder that we're in a race.

The journey only takes us about ten minutes before we're breaking from the trees, the sight of Lukas and Nesrin's house coming into view. With a burst of speed, Nesrin shoots past me, leaving a trail of dust in her wake as she takes the lead. I'm about to teleport when I'm startled by Malachite's panicked screech. Glancing backward, I notice he is having difficulty slowing down, the fear in his eyes unmistakable.

'Nesrin!'

With a fluid motion, she shifts into her human form, her feet hitting the ground with a soft thud. Spinning gracefully, her hair whipping through the air, she spots the distressed dragon. Like radiant orbs, Nesrin's eyes gleam with an ethereal white light. The air crackles with energy as she raises both hands, her palms facing him. The scent of magic fills the air, a mix of earthy herbs and electric sparks. With a surge of power, her magic coils around Malachite, slowing him down in his tracks. The ground trembles as she plunks him unceremoniously in front of her.

"Geez, Malachite, we're going to have to work on your landing," she huffs.

I shift and stroll over to him, taking a seat on the grass beside him. "That was a little hectic."

Malachite's big golden eyes swing my way, then he's pushing my arm out of the way to try to sit on my lap. Laughing, I try to maneuver into a position where this can work. "Okay, okay. You're not a little dragon anymore," I tease.

"Remember when he used to sit on our shoulder? He was so tiny." A smile spreads across Nesrin's face, brightening her features.

Curled up between my legs, Malachite drops his head to my leg and huffs in annoyance, a stream of mist pouring from his nostrils.

"Dramatic much?" I chuckle.

"He's always dramatic," comes a deep voice behind us.

I twist, catching sight of Lukas and Zee making their way toward us. Lukas goes straight to Nesrin, pulling her into his arms and giving her a soft kiss.

I feel a sudden pang of longing deep within me.

I want that.

I want someone to hold and care for, to feel their warmth and embrace.

To find someone who needs me as deeply as I do them.

In an instant, my mind is overwhelmed with thoughts of Sara's smile and the warmth of her presence. I swear the air suddenly fills with her sweet cinnamon and vanilla scent, creating an intoxicating aroma that lingers around me. Seeing her in the woods today was unexpected; she seemed completely in her element. Despite my better judgment, an irresistible force compelled me to approach her, as if an invisible thread pulled us closer. Her scent is absolutely intoxicating, and her smile has the power to make my heart skip a beat.

I like her a lot.

But can I have more with her?

She is a human, and although it's uncommon for shifters to be with humans, it's not entirely unheard of.

Malachite shifts, drawing me from my thoughts, and I turn my attention to Lukas and Zee. "What are you guys up to?"

"Zee and I were just discussing the trip to Pittsburgh."

"What's happening in Pittsburgh?" I inquire, now fully alert.

Lukas sighs. "Finan has had a couple of his pack go missing. I was going to send Sander and one of us to assist."

"I'll go," Nesrin offers, but Lukas is shaking his head before she's even finished saying the words.

"It should be one of us," Zee answers, pointing between him and Lukas.

"Why?" Nesrin grumbles, her hands landing on her hips.

"Because we don't know what's going on."

"So?!" Nesrin snaps. "I used to live there. I know my way around."

Lukas's eyes flare in challenge. "I'll be leaving in the morning. I'll be taking Sander with me, and most likely someone from the coven. Marcus has offered to help."

Nesrin scowls at him, and that's my cue to hightail it out of here. I push Malachite off me and get to my feet, brushing the dirt off my pants.

"I'll leave you two to it then." I widen my eyes at Zee, who laughs, before giving Lukas a friendly slap on the back.

"Good luck, man."

"Wait, Gabe!" Nesrin calls out.

I turn back to her, and she tilts her head to the side, her eyes searching mine with a curious intensity.

Confused, I look down at my clothes. They are still wet, and I'm a mess, but it's nothing unusual for our runs. "What?"

"You seem . . . " she pauses, frowning. "Did you . . . " Then she shakes her head. "Never mind."

"Okay . . . " I reply, drawing the word out.

I turn to follow Zee, and even he seems perplexed by Nesrin's bizarre behavior. Zee and I casually make our way down to the bustling commune area. Zee's pace slows down, and I match his steps, sensing he has something to say.

"I heard you found yourself a human woman?"

With a grin, I think about Sara and Tyler laughing together during their hike in the woods. "I have."

They were perfect.

"Are you sure that this is wise?"

Recognizing that his worry stems from genuine concern, I hold back the bite in my words. "She is different. I can't explain it."

"Just be careful, okay?"

I can feel a growl building up in my throat as I narrow my eyes at my friend, who quickly raises his hands. "Look, all I'm saying is humans don't adjust well to this." His arms gesture around the clearing where shifters are milling about in their human and animal forms.

I sigh, running a hand through my hair, pulling it from the hair tie. "I know, but I really like her and her son."

"I'm not saying she'll freak, but maybe bring her around and introduce her slowly. We can have a small get-together. Meet her and her son. I want to see the woman who has you all distracted and shit."

"That's actually a great idea."

"She's already met Nesrin, so that's an opening. Plus Lukas will be away for at least a week, so the big, intimidating alpha won't scare her away."

I nod my head, pondering tactics that might sway her into agreeing to a cookout.

"Aren't you supposed to be teaching a class soon?"

I pull my phone from my pocket. "Shit."

Zee's contagious laughter rings in my ears as I sprint toward my car, adding a burst of energy to my hurried steps.

Chapter Eighteen

SARA

The bus stops only fifty meters from Gabe's gym, and Tyler practically bounces off as we step onto the sidewalk, his excitement endearing. Since we finished the hike early, I thought we could stop in and see Gabe. The cool breeze is especially sharp today, and I'm glad I brought my scarf. It's the soft pink one Greta got me when I first started working for her—super soft and comforting.

"Which way, Mom?" Tyler's eyes sparkle with anticipation.

I grin, running my hand over his head. "A bit eager, are we?"

"You know I am."

"Well, Gabe might be working, so don't get too excited. We're just here to take a look around."

Tyler grabs my hand and starts pulling me down the footpath. "He's going to be so happy to see us. He always comes to us, and this is our first time going to him."

I hum in response, biting down on my lower lip as nerves build now that we're so close. *What if he's angry that we came? That we showed up unannounced?*

My steps slow, and Tyler peers over his shoulder at me. "What's wrong, Mom?"

"Nothing," I mumble, trying to shake off my doubts.

I'm being silly. Gabe won't mind that we're stopping by. I'm just overthinking things.

My heart flutters the moment the gym comes into view. The words sprawled above the doors read: Yūsha Kan (□□□) – House of the Brave.

The sheer size of the building is astounding. Gabe definitely underestimated it when he spoke about his gym. Tyler releases my hand and eagerly rushes toward the doors, pushing his way inside. I follow suit, my eyes immediately drawn to the welcoming reception area. It's unlike any gym I have ever seen on TV, or even the one I briefly visited after my escape. With the abundance of natural light pouring in through the large windows, the space exudes a warm and inviting atmosphere. The walls are adorned with soft, neutral tones, beautifully complemented by luxurious accents such as deep red or emerald cushions scattered on cozy armchairs and sofas.

"Afternoon. Can I assist you with anything today?" A friendly voice draws my gaze to land on the polished wood reception desk. Behind the desk sits a young woman, her smile soft and warm, and I instantly feel at ease. Which is an odd feeling for me. My guard is always up when talking to people I don't know, but there is something about her that makes me feel safe enough to share my deepest, darkest secrets.

"Hi!" Tyler beams up at the woman.

Tucking her long brown hair behind her ear, she returns his smile. "Hi."

I walk over, my hand coming to rest gently on Tyler's shoulder, and exchange a warm smile with the woman.

"We're friends with Gabe, and were hoping to have a look around the gym. If that's okay?"

"Oh my gosh." Her green eyes dart between Tyler and me, her smile brightening. "You must be Sara and Tyler!"

My eyes widen, my mouth falling open. "Uhhh . . . yes."

"Gabe has told me all about you."

"He has?"

"Yes! I'm June. I run things front of house."

"Hi, June," Tylers interjects. "Is Gabe here?"

June's gaze drops back down to Tyler. "He is actually. He was late for a class today, so another instructor stepped in, but last I knew, he was in the Arcane Room. Come on, I'll show you."

She guides us through the gym, eagerly highlighting each section and rooms along the way. Passing a few people, I make a conscious effort to keep my eyes downward, ensuring no accidental eye contact. June stops in front of a set of wooden doors.

"Here we are. This is Gabe's private room."

The two intricately carved wooden doors quietly glide open, revealing a dimly lit room. As we peer inside, I can't help but inhale sharply, my eyes instantly fixating on Gabe's physique. He's standing there with his back to us, his top half bare, in a set of billowy pants. With a Katana gripped firmly in his hand, he gracefully executes a series of movements. The sounds of unfamiliar, soft music and the blade slicing through the air fill the room.

Tyler's soft "wow" barely registers in my ears as I continue to stare.

I am utterly captivated by Gabe. Every motion he makes seems as fluid and smooth as a flowing river. After that thought enters my mind, a strange sensation washes over me, as if I can almost hear the gentle flow of water circulating around the room. The glimmering sword catches the light, creating a dazzling display that sends shivers down my spine. *Oh wow . . . He's blindfolded.*

"Amazing, right?" June whispers.

My heart skips a beat as I jump, caught off guard. My cheeks heat with embarrassment as I flash her a sheepish smile.

"Just sneak in and watch. He usually does this for an hour every day, but he has already been at it for a while, so he shouldn't be much longer."

Tyler doesn't wait for me to agree before he ducks through the gap in the doors and takes a seat against the wall. Nodding my thanks to June, I step inside, noting the soft sound as she closes the door behind me.

Quietly, I take a seat on the floor next to Tyler, and we both sit, fascinated by the man in front of us.

I'm not sure how much time passes as we sit here in silence, but eventually Gabe comes to a stop and reaches up, removing the blindfold. I make a conscious effort not to openly stare at the way his muscles flex with every motion. Then, his eyes, warm and endearing, meet ours, and he smiles brightly, making a fluttering sensation move through my stomach.

"You came." It isn't a question but a statement, like he was hoping we'd visit, and just like that, all my worries and fears vanish.

"You are like a warrior!" Tyler jumps to his feet and rushes over to Gabe.

"It's good to keep your mind and body sharp." His eyes catch on mine. "You never know when someone might need a hero."

Swallowing hard to suppress the sudden lump in my throat, I push off the ground. "I hope you don't mind that we stopped by."

"Of course not. Did June show you around?"

"Yes. You really understated the gym. It's so peaceful here."

"And huge!"

"It is." Gabe grins, ruffling Tyler's hair. "It is also a haven, where individuals who have experienced trauma can come to heal and grow. I understand the pain and struggle that victims face, having gone through my own journey of healing. We believe in the power of connection and the importance of rebuilding one's sense of self-worth. Here, victims can find solace, understanding, and encouragement as they take steps toward reclaiming their lives and embracing their inner strength. Our ultimate goal is to empower each individual to stand tall, knowing that they are not defined by their experiences, but by their resilience and ability to overcome."

"You're amazing," I reply in awe. "I mean, this place is amazing."

Shit. Once again, I feel the heat rising to my face, a telltale sign that I'm blushing.

How can this man be real? How did I become so fortunate to cross paths with him? When will the ground crumble beneath my feet?

"I'll get cleaned up and I'll take you guys out for a milkshake."

"Yes!" Tyler accepts, jumping up and down.

Chapter Nineteen

GABE

At nightfall, I pull up in front of Lukas's house to pick up Nesrin and Jameson for our patrol. The moon hangs low in the sky, casting a silvery glow over the valley, and before I can even get out of the vehicle, Nesrin comes flying out the front door. She jogs down the stairs with an energy that seems boundless.

From the corner of my eye, I catch sight of Jameson cresting the hill from the commune housing area, his strides confident and determined. The younger shifter is always eager to prove himself, quick on his feet and sharper than most. He's been working his way up through the ranks with an almost obsessive focus, and it's no secret that he'll be leading his own patrol unit soon. He's hungry for the responsibility.

The passenger door opens with a soft click, and Nesrin slides in beside me, her grin as wide and bright as ever. Her eyes glitter with excitement, like she's already got some wild plan brewing in her head, and I can't help but raise an eyebrow in response.

"Well, someone's in a good mood," I note as the engine rumbles to life.

"Why wouldn't I be?" She buckles her seatbelt with a laugh. "Tonight's going to be fun. I can feel it."

Jameson jogs up the last stretch of the hill and reaches us, tapping on the window before opening the back door and sliding in, his expression as focused as ever. With a nod toward me, he flashes a smile in Nesrin's direction.

Lukas storms out of the front door and stops, standing on the porch stairs with his arms folded. It's too dark now to make out his expression, but he seems to be radiating annoyance.

"Do I want to know?" I inquire.

Her laughter dances through the air, light and playful. "Probably not."

"Did our alpha order you to stay home?" Jameson asks from the backseat.

"Yep," Nesrin replies, popping her p. Lukas leaves early tomorrow for Pittsburgh, so this is probably pay back.

Before I start down the driveway, I give Lukas a wave through the windshield. *'I will watch over her.'*

'You know what she's like.'

'Of course. I won't let her run off.'

I cut off our connection, glancing in the mirror at Jameson to see a glazed look in his eye. Lukas must be warning him to watch out for Nesrin through the pack bond as well.

"So, how are Sara and Tyler?"

"Good, I think. They came and saw me at the gym today."

"Really?" Nesrin beams. "Did you show her some wicked moves?"

I shake my head, pulling out onto the main road. "It was nice showing her what I do."

"Is this the human woman you've been seeing?" Jameson pipes up from the back.

"Yes."

"You planning on telling her what you are?"

His question doesn't catch me off guard, but it does make me stop and think. I want to tell her, of course, but will she believe me? Will she take Tyler and run?

"Maybe," I murmur, feeling Nesrin's gaze burning into the side of my head.

We drive into Portland, and I pull up at Washington Park. It's an ideal location to start our patrol—close enough to the heart of the city, but isolated enough for us to do our work unnoticed. Plus, the warehouse is nearby, a hub for the supernatural community, a place they frequent for supplies when the sun goes down. Usually, they provide their own security, but it's the kind of thing we like to keep tabs on. Trouble can spring up at any time, and we need to be ahead of it.

I cut the engine, and we climb out of the car. The crisp night air greets us as we move around the front of the vehicle, heading in the direction of the warehouse. Nesrin hunches her shoulders against the cold, tucking her hands into the pockets of her leather jacket. Jameson and I walk on either side of her, unconsciously flanking her as we make our way down the street.

Nesrin doesn't miss the subtle move. She raises an eyebrow, her lips quirking into a knowing smirk. "Lukas tell you to watch out for me?" she guesses, her tone light and laced with amusement.

I glance at her, keeping my expression neutral. "You tend to run off and get yourself in hot water a lot." That's a bit of an understatement. She has a knack for diving headfirst into trouble, no matter the situation.

"Yeah, you can't blame him," Jameson's voice is steady as he backs me up. His eyes are forward, his posture alert as always, but I can sense the flicker of amusement in him, too. Jameson knows Nesrin's ways just as well as I do. Hell, we've both had to pull her out of more than one tight spot.

Nesrin rolls her eyes, though the grin still tugs at the corners of her mouth. "I can handle myself, you know. I'm not some damsel in distress."

"We know," I agree, shaking my head with a small smile. "But someone has to keep you from turning every situation into a full-on disaster."

The sound of her laugh is light and carefree, but there's an unspoken acknowledgment between us. We watch out for each other. It's what we do. And even though she can take care of herself, it doesn't mean we'll stop keeping an eye out.

"Well, that was a boring night," Nesrin pouts, her voice breaking the quiet as we head up the hill toward the silhouette of my car faint in the distance.

"Yeah, but that's good." I cast a glance her way.

"After everything that went down with Suzy last month, we need some quiet," Jameson adds.

At the mention of Suzy, Nesrin's posture deflates. Her shoulders sag as the playful energy that filled her moments ago drains away. I can feel the shift in her, the sudden weight of sadness that settles over her like a cloud. Without a thought, I send a gentle wave of my magic toward her, an instinctual gesture to offer comfort. Her eyes snap to mine, and her gaze softens. I sense her longing, it's a feeling I know all too well.

"You miss Suzy?" I ask, my voice quiet.

Nesrin's lips press into a thin line, and she nods. "Yes. Since the dust settled, I've only seen her once. Now most of her time is spent at the estate by the ocean."

"Why don't you go stay there with her for a couple of nights?" Jameson suggests, casually kicking a rock that lies in the road.

Nesrin shakes her head, her brow furrowing. "I feel bad asking,"

"Why? You two are close. She'd want you there."

Nesrin's about to respond when something catches my attention. Movement in the trees. It's subtle, barely noticeable, and about a hundred yards out, but I can feel the energy shift. It's faint but unmistakable—a presence that's far from friendly. My instincts flare to life, magic simmering just beneath the surface as I tense.

Nesrin and Jameson immediately sense the change in me, their conversation stopping as they fall into a ready stance. Jameson's eyes narrow as he scans the trees, while Nesrin reaches for the dagger she always keeps tucked in her jacket.

"We've got company," I murmur, my voice low.

The whistle of an incoming object sailing through the air is our first warning. In a heartbeat, Nesrin's blue shield flares to life, shimmering like a protective dome around the three of us. Several arrows strike against it, bouncing off harmlessly as we shift our position, standing back to back. My eyes scan the darkened trees, searching.

"Who is it?" Jameson snarls, his mountain lion rising to the surface, the threat of a fight stirring his instincts. His voice is low, but there's a dangerous edge to it. I look over my shoulder to find his muscles coiled and ready to pounce.

"They're keeping to the shadows." Nesrin's gaze darts through the trees. The blue glow of her shield reflects in her eyes as sparks of white and yellow flick in them. Her white magic, inherited from her lineage of legacies, blended with the yellow energy of her shifter abilities.

Focusing my attention back toward the woods, I stretch my senses outward, feeling for anything unusual. There's a faint ripple in the nearby creek. The cool water pulses under my command, and through that connection, I feel it—the vibrations of heavy boots crossing the creek, the subtle splashing that gives them away. They're moving fast, retreating.

"They're leaving." I keep my voice steady as I follow their movements through the water, tracking their path as they disappear into the forest.

Nesrin drops her shield, the blue light fading as she bends down to pick up one of the arrows. A low growl erupts from her throat as she examines it, her fingers curling around the shaft. Her eyes flash, becoming unsettling white orbs, a clear sign of her anger.

"Hunters," she snaps, her voice filled with venom. She straightens up, holding the arrow like a weapon of her own. The look in her eyes is one of pure fury. Hunters are no small threat.

"Do you think we can catch them?" Jameson's voice is a low rumble beside me, his wolf straining to break free, eager for the chase.

I weigh the possibilities for a split second, listening to the fading footsteps in the creek, the quiet retreat of our attackers. "If we go after them now, we might," I answer. "But they've got a head start, and they're moving fast."

Nesrin clenches her jaw, her grip tightening on the arrow. "We'll tell Lukas. I won't act without telling him first."

"Turning over a new leaf then?" I tease.

Chapter Twenty

SARA

Dust particles dance in the sunlight streaming in through the front window. The guilt from avoiding cleaning overwhelms me as I sink deeper into the comfort of the couch. I really hate being sick, though as much as I hate Gabe seeing me like this, I can't say I haven't enjoyed him looking after me.

In the aftermath of my mother's death, nobody took any interest in my emotional or physical wellbeing. Having been left to fend for myself, it was during those moments of sickness that I yearned for her the most, craving the comfort of her gentle touch and soothing voice.

Gabe walks into the apartment, closing the door with a quiet click behind him. With each slow, deliberate step he takes toward the sofa, my anticipation grows, humming just beneath my skin. The steady sound of his footsteps on the hardwood floor echoes through the space, a calming rhythm that seems to match the quickening beat of my heart.

Finally, my gaze lifts as I let my eyes travel over his face. His handsome features pull me in effortlessly, and a genuine smile tugs at my lips. Everything about this man feels like perfection. The warmth of his presence fills the room, wrapping around me like a comforting embrace that I never want to let go of. His almond-shaped eyes—dark and intense—seem to hold the weight of the world, yet they radiate a softness, a gentle warmth that draws me closer, like a moth drawn to a flame.

"Hey," I murmur, adjusting the blanket around my legs.

Gabe's grin widens, as if he can sense my excitement. With a graceful movement, he settles himself on the coffee table in front of me, his elbows resting on his knees. The proximity allows me to notice the subtle flecks of golden hues dancing within the depths of his brown eyes. *How have I never noticed that?*

"Hey, how are you feeling?" His head tilts as he studies me.

Feeling self-conscious, I nervously run my fingers through my tangled hair, wincing as they get caught in the knots. But my eyes catch sight of the white box in his hands. My mouth waters, distracting me from any concern about my hair.

"Are they . . ." My voice trails off as I realize I completely ignored his question.

Gabe's smile transforms into a mischievous, knowing grin. Holding up the box, he gives it a little shake. "Are these?"

My hands reach out for the box, but he swiftly pulls it away, teasing me. A groan of exasperation escapes my lips, and I pout, jutting out my bottom lip. Gabe's eyes flicker down to my lips, and I can see the intense heat and desire pooling within them. I slowly draw my bottom lip in and run my teeth over it, feeling a tingle of awareness as a warm blush spreads across my cheeks.

"Gabe," Tyler's voice cuts through the silence, bringing us back to reality.

Gabe recovers quickly and turns to Tyler. "Hi, Tyler. How was school today?"

"School was . . . you know, the usual," he replies with a shrug.

Gabe raises an eyebrow. "Just the usual, huh? Anything interesting happen?" he probes.

Of course, I know how Tyler's day went, but I'm not about to say anything. If he wants to share the news, he will. I patiently wait, watching them both carefully.

Tyler hesitates for a moment, and quickly glances at me, before looking back to Gabe. "Well, actually . . . I got cast as the lead in the school play," he admits, his voice tinged with excitement.

Gabe's eyes light up with genuine delight. "That's amazing, Tyler! Congratulations!"

Tyler beams at Gabe's enthusiastic reaction, and I can see how much those words mean to him. He straightens, the surge of confidence he gets from them evident.

"Thanks, Gabe! It's the tale of *Peter Pan* by J.M. Barrie," Tyler explains, his excitement bubbling over.

Gabe nods approvingly, genuinely impressed. "Wow, Tyler. I didn't know you were into acting!"

Tears well up in my eyes as I watch Tyler's eyes light up with happiness and excitement, animatedly sharing all the details of his role with Gabe.

Only after he's finished does his attention go to the box that Gabe is holding. I notice an impish glimmer in Tyler's eyes, and raise an eyebrow at him as he casually sits down beside me on the sofa. Adjusting my position, I raise my legs and tuck them under myself, giving him more room while keeping a suspicious eye on both of them. Gabe's hair drapes over his face as he leans forward and places the box on my lap.

Excitement bubbles up inside me as I cautiously lift the lid. The irresistible scent of freshly baked cinnamon immediately captivates my senses, causing my mouth to water instantly. Nestled inside the box are six warm, golden cinnamon rolls, perfectly swirled and glistening with a delectable sticky glaze. The aroma wafts through the room, inviting and comforting. These have always been my ultimate favorite treat, but I haven't been able to indulge in them for quite some time due to financial constraints. As I take a bite, the soft, doughy texture melts in my mouth, and the sweet cinnamon flavor dances tantalizingly on my tongue. It's a moment of sheer indulgence.

"How did you know I loved these?" I cast a discreet glance in my son's direction. Of course. "Never mind," I tease, a playful lilt in my voice.

Gabe laughs, and I'm mesmerized by the sound and the sparkle in his eyes. He stands, reaching over to Tyler and messing up his hair before making his way into my kitchen. The playful gesture warms my chest and fills me with a sense of longing and need. My gaze drops, my focus shifting to the delicious roll as I place the box on the coffee table.

Damn it, I can't let these feelings take hold.

Why am I letting him into our lives?

Directing my eyes to Tyler, I am completely absorbed by the sheer happiness emanating from him, like a beacon of light shining brightly for all to witness. That's why I'm allowing this. To see the happiness on my son's face.

After a few minutes, Gabe returns with a warm cup of tea and gently sets it in my hands.

"Thank you."

Without warning, my thoughts turn dark, the small voice in the back of my mind whispering, *This won't last, it can't last. You're unworthy. Unlovable. When he finds out what you did, he will leave.*

The words burrow into me, wrapping around my heart like cold, constricting vines. No matter how much I try to push them away, they tighten their grip, squeezing out any hope I might have dared to feel. Gabe is here now, but the voice is relentless, reminding me of all the reasons why he shouldn't be, why he won't be for long.

I stare down into the tea, watching the tiny tendrils of steam curl upward, disappearing into the air. It's a small, delicate thing, this moment of peace, and the voice inside me is all too eager to shatter it.

Gabe's voice pulls me back to the present, cutting through the dark thoughts with a gentle, yet insistent question. "So, how are you feeling?" he asks again, his eyes searching mine for something—reassurance, truth, maybe just a sign that I'm okay.

Pushing the dark thoughts away, I blow on the tea, and peek up at him, entranced by the warmth radiating from his skin and the way his long black hair sits around his shoulders. Not for the first time, I wonder how soft his hair is.

"Much better. It must be this special tea you got me. What is it?"

"Nesrin is good with herbs and stuff. She made it for you." He shrugs like it's no big deal, when it totally is. This is a miracle tea.

"Oh, okay. Well, tell her I said thank you. I should be at full health by tomorrow."

"About that . . . I was going to ask if you wanted to come to a barbecue with me and my friends tomorrow afternoon?"

"Can we, Mom? Liam and Noah will be there!" Tyler excitedly bounces in his spot on the sofa.

Unease slides through my body. *Meet his friends?* "Oh, I'd have to speak to Greta to see if I can get it off first."

"I already spoke to Greta. She was more than happy to let you have the day off or switch your shift."

Anger burns my chest. How dare he go and ask Greta without even talking to me first?

Gabe senses my shift in mood immediately and holds up his hands in surrender. "Okay, why do you look mad right now?"

I place my tea down, shooting him a fierce glare. "You went behind my back."

"Sara, you can't stay so isolated from everyone. I hate seeing you so alone all the time."

I know he's right. I hate it, too, but what other choice do I have? No friends, no connections, no one who can get hurt. Those are my rules. I'm already getting too close to Gabe.

"I'm not alone." My stubborn side emerges, making me defensive.

"I don't count, Mom," Tyler pipes in.

I swing my head toward him and narrow my eyes. That isn't helping, little traitor.

"Yes, you do. You always count," I say with vehemence, making Tyler flush.

"Please, Sara. I want you there. I want you to meet my friends. I want them to meet you. Nesrin will be there, and you can meet Tyler's new friends."

"Yeah. Please, Mom?"

I can feel myself cracking under the pressure of both of them looking at me like that. Gabe is right and wrong. I don't want to be alone, but I also can't risk being found. I feel safe with Gabe, I always have, but if something were to happen to him because of me, or if I ended up having to leave, it would absolutely break me. I'm not so sure I could survive a hit like that. Pushing my blanket off my lap, I get up and start pacing the small space, my thumbnail going straight to my mouth.

"Tyler, can I talk to your mom alone for a minute?"

Tyler must have answered, because when I turn, there's no sign of him, he's vanished down the hall. My eyes shift toward Gabe, and in an instant, he moves toward me so swiftly that I find myself taking a few steps backward out of reflex. Suddenly, my back is pressed firmly against the wall.

Gabe's hands land on the wall on either side of my head, his arms forming a protective barrier around me. His piercing brown eyes capture my attention, and in that moment, time seems to stand still, as if the world is holding its breath.

"I care about you, Sara. It's not something I've hidden. I hate seeing you lock yourself away from life."

A lump forms in my throat, rendering me speechless. Moving closer, he lightly brings his nose to my neck, breathing me in. The slight touch sends a shiver down my body, awakening a primal desire that coils deep within me. On impulse, my hands gravitate to rest on his abdomen, intending to use my touch as a means to push him away. Instead, I grip the fabric of his shirt and pull him closer. Gabe pulls his head back, his gaze meeting mine. Those warm almond eyes trace a path over my face, lingering on my lips, which in turn has my heart thumping wildly in my chest. The desire to feel his lips pressed against mine consumes me.

Just one taste, one kiss. What could it hurt?

Before I realize it, my tongue darts out, grazing my bottom lip, as if it can already sense his lips lingering there. Gabe's eyes darken, even as they seem to emit a faint, ethereal glow. This man is constantly drawing me in closer and closer. It seems impossible to walk away from him.

The words are out before I can second guess myself.

"Kiss me." My whispered words are barely audible.

Gabe stiffens, his eyes flashing with heat. "Sara . . . "

"Gabe. Kiss. Me."

"Thank fuck," he mutters under his breath.

Gabe's head dips and his lips brush against mine, teasing and tasting. I can sense his internal struggle, his longing to be gentle with me, obvious in every movement.

But I don't want gentle. I want him.

I push up on my toes to deepen the kiss, and his arms drop from the wall to wrap around my waist, pulling me tight against his body. The moment ignites a fire that consumes us both. A rumble comes from his chest, sending a thrill of pleasure through my body, desire flooding my veins. My arms encircle his neck, while my fingers effortlessly glide through his velvety soft hair.

This is unlike anything I have ever experienced before. It's an intense experience, a mix of enthralling and disorienting sensations that leave me feeling consumed and dizzy. My mouth on an inhale and his tongue sweeps in, stealing my breath.

I groan, sliding my tongue along his, the sensations driving me wild. I've never been kissed before and it is amazing.

I can feel my body starting to thaw, the ice around my heart melting just a bit. I have never felt this before, this yearning to be touched, this passion, and a desire so strong I can't think or breathe.

In one swift motion, he hoists me up, my feet leaving the ground, wrapping around his waist. My heart pounds against my chest, a wild rhythm matching the chaos of the moment.

Before I am ready, Gabe breaks the kiss, feathering light kisses along my jaw. He nuzzles my neck again, taking a deep breath, like he's savoring my scent, and it sends more shivers traveling through my body. I angle my head to give him more room, liking the feel of him so close.

"You have no idea how long I've been wanting to do that," he murmurs into my neck.

I grin, running my hands down his extremely defined back, feeling the dips and swells.

"I can guess," I chuckle, warmth filling my chest.

"Does this mean you'll come to the barbecue with me tomorrow?" His fingers brush some hair behind my ear as he pulls back.

I sigh deeply, my exhale carrying the weight of my desire to create some distance between us, and I push him away gently. Gabe releases my legs, smoothly setting me down on solid ground as he takes a step back.

"I'm still mad you went behind my back. It wasn't your place. But yes, if Greta is fine with it, I'll take another day off."

"Yes!" sounds from behind Gabe, and both of us look to see Tyler peeking around the corner. I flush in embarrassment. *How long has he been there?*

"He just came back out," Gabe whispers, so only I can hear.

I look over at him. How would he know that?

Chapter Twenty-One

GABE

I can't get that kiss out of my head. Every time I close my eyes, I can vividly remember the softness of her lips against mine, the warmth that enveloped my entire being. The sensation lingers, like an intoxicating fragrance that refuses to fade.

I can still feel the gentle brush of her fingertips against my cheek, the electric current that surged through my body with each second I had her in my arms. It's as if her touch imprinted itself on my skin, leaving a trail of tingling sensations that danced along my nerve endings.

It was more than just a kiss; it was a moment of connection, of vulnerability, and of pure euphoria.

A moment I'd wanted to happen since she came storming from the diner that first day, her fiery presence filling the air.

I flick through the contacts on my phone and press Zee's name.

After a few rings, he answers, "Gabe, about time you called."

Unlocking my car, I climb in and shut the door. "Yeah, sorry."

"How's Sara?"

"Good. Nesrin's potion worked."

Zee chuckles. "That's great."

"Yeah . . . She said she would come this weekend."

Guilt worms its way through me unexpectedly. I went behind her back and talked to Greta. I was attempting to do something nice, and it hadn't occurred to me at that moment that she might take it the wrong way.

"That's a good thing, right? So, what's wrong?"

I shake my head, trying to clear the thoughts that are clouding my mind. "It's nothing. I need to train. You free?"

Lukas has become even more demanding with our training, particularly after the intense showdown last year. Every week, we are required to dedicate a minimum of two training sessions to hone our skills in our animal forms and hand-to-hand combat.

"I'm ready when you are," Zee replies.

"Okay, be there in forty minutes."

I end the call before the car can connect to Bluetooth, and the engine roars to life. Despite the energy coursing through my veins, I breathe a sigh of relief and feel my shoulders loosen up. I have my own piece of land, just a short distance away from Lukas's. I prefer it that way. I like my privacy and seclusion. But having spent the majority of this week attentively watching over Sara and Tyler, ensuring their well-being while she got over her cold, I have fallen behind in my training. And now that She's feeling better, I can start again. Plus, it will be good to get some of this newfound energy out.

Kyra and the boys are outside enjoying the nice weather with Nesrin and Astraea as I pull up to the house, parking out front. They all turn and wave when they see me.

I hold my hand up, waving back as I approach.

Astraea's eyes brighten, illuminating her face as they always do whenever she greets someone. Rushing over, she opens her arms for a hug. With a gentle motion, I lift her up into my arms, enjoying the sound of her laughter.

I would do anything for this kid, to keep that smile on her face. At least the high fae seem to have backed off. The constant pressure, the lurking threat of their presence have finally eased, leaving space to breathe. Nissa told us there's a war brewing in Faerie—something big enough to demand their attention. All high fae have been called back through the gates, summoned to their courts to fight whatever conflict is stirring on the other side.

Meaning that, for now, Astraea has been forgotten.

The relief that washes over me is bittersweet. I want to believe that she's safe, that this temporary distraction will keep their eyes off her, but deep down, I know better. The high fae never truly forget. They might pull back for a time, their priorities shifting with the tides of war, but they're like predators—patient, always circling, waiting for the right moment to strike.

Astraea pats my cheek with a massive grin that warms my chest. *'You ready to get your butt whoopsed?'*

"That doesn't sound promising, sweetie." I laugh quietly, putting her on the ground.

'S'okay. You will be fine.' Then she takes off after Noah and Liam toward the river.

A playful grin tugs at the corners of my lips as my attention shifts to Nesrin and Kyra. "Where's Zee?"

Kyra's brown eyes shine with amusement, and Nesrin wears a knowing smirk, as if she's holding in a secret.

"Why do I feel like I'm the main attraction here? What's with the looks?" I query.

Nesrin laughs, slapping me on the shoulder. "You know you're in for it today, right?"

"Nothing I can't handle."

"Mind if we watch?" Kyra's arms fold over her chest.

I'm starting to wonder if I should have skipped today. The sudden movement around the side of the house grabs my attention, and Zee storms over, his brows tightly furrowed.

"I'm glad you called. I need to let off some steam," Zee grumbles as he draws closer.

Shit. "Okay, then. What happened in the forty minutes since we spoke? Trouble in paradise?"

Zee grunts, his muscles flexing as he removes his shirt. I follow suit, throwing mine aside as Zee lunges forward without warning.

Fuck. Okay, not easing our way in today.

I block his initial blow, anticipating his follow-up attack and successfully deflect his punch to my stomach. Pushing us apart, Zee doesn't waste any time rushing at me again.

Leaning back, I narrowly evade his first strike, but the second lands with a glancing blow against my chin, sending a jolt of pain shooting through me. Gritting my teeth, I retaliate with a lightning-fast punch of my own, my knuckles connecting solidly with his jaw.

A trickle of blood escapes from the corner of his lip, but instead of faltering, Zee grins, his eyes alight with adrenaline-fueled excitement. "That's more like it."

Adrenaline surges through my veins as Zee's eyes flash and he launches a barrage of punches, each one a ferocious storm. I weave and dodge, the air crackling with the intensity of our battle. Sweat drips, muscles burning as we dance on the edge of chaos. Zee's right fist aims for my face, but I dodge left, pushing his arm wide, and land two solid punches to his ribs. Zee grunts and dances backward a few paces, and we circle again.

Zee's normally blue eyes are glowing yellow orbs as his shifter magic pulses to the surface. He's the first to attack, he always has been an impatient fighter. I avoid the hit, and spin around him, catching him in the back with a kick. Zee barely stumbles, spinning to deliver his own kick, grazing my shoulder. I jump back, muscles tensing, as he goes for another high kick, this time I grab his leg and hold it while I sweep his other leg from under him. Zee goes down, and surprisingly somehow takes me with him. We roll over the grass, each trying to get the upper hand. Being on the ground isn't ideal, especially because Zee is bigger than me.

His eyes light up with the need to shift, his muscles rippling as he fights off the urge. My fox is no match for his wolf, but if he shifts, I will have to shift as well. My magic is begging for use, but I push it back down and seal the lid. I have spent years training my magic, learning to control it, not letting it control me.

As Zee moves stealthily behind me, a rush of adrenaline floods my veins, swiftly sharpening my awareness. My heart thumps loudly in my chest, its beat reverberating in my ears.

Suddenly, Zee's arm encircles my neck, locking me in a choke-hold. Despite my attempts to resist by kicking out with my legs, he deftly avoids them all. With a quick tap on his arm, we disengage, both sprawled on the ground, gazing up at the sky, panting heavily.

"Someone piss in your cereal today?" I mutter between breaths.

Zee chuckles. "Fuck."

"Yeah, fuck," I reply.

Two shadows fall over us—Nesrin and Kyra looking down at us, grinning.

"Is that all you guys got?" Nesrin taunts.

Zee sits up, pushing the hair off his face. "Go away, woman."

With a quick flip, I stand up and offer a handout to Zee, who promptly takes it and stands.

"Another round?" he offers, his blonde hair in disarray around his head.

I let out a hearty laugh, fully aware that this is going to be a lengthy affair. "Of course."

We take up stance, and I manage to block most of his hits, catching him with a few kicks. After a while, we are both still trading blows at a rapid pace when Nesrin whistles. Pausing, we glance in her direction.

"Looks like it's lunchtime," I say, shaking Zee's hand. "Thanks for the workout."

"Anytime." His smile is infectious. I'm glad to see his mood has improved.

Quickly grabbing my shirt, I make my way over to the house, feeling the cool breeze against my sweaty skin. Jogging up the stairs, I place a kiss on Nesrin's head.

"Any word on when Lukas and Sander will be back?"

Nesrin frowns, clearly still pissed at being left behind. "No, I haven't heard from him in twenty hours. He seems fine through the bond, though it's muted considerably from the distance."

Kyra twists her hair nervously. "You think they're okay?"

"You haven't heard from Sander either?"

Kyra shakes her head, her teeth digging into her bottom lip.

Pulling my shirt on, I wrap an arm around her shoulders. "I'm sure they're fine. They have Finan, Roan, and Alex there. Finan's pack is trustworthy. If anything were wrong, they'd let us know."

Zee just grunts his agreement, digging into the sandwich Nesrin brought out.

"I'm having Sara and Tyler over tomorrow for the day. I was planning on having a cookout, and I want you all there."

Kyra's eyes widen, her shock clear. "You're introducing her to us? This must be serious."

"It is," Nesrin confirms.

I look over at her as she takes a seat. There's a honey-like quality to her eyes today, and a knowing twinkle resides within them.

"This is good. I'm in. Though Leila is busy, so she won't make it," Zee adds.

Nesrin narrows her eyes at Zee. "Why, where is she?" she demands.

Zee grumbles something under his breath before answering, "Something about Hades and Milinoe, I don't know."

Nesrin nods her head, her eyes filling with understanding. We all settle onto the porch, the creaking of the wooden chairs filling the air as we dig into our meal and the kids run up to join us. From then on, the conversation continues to be easy-going and relaxed as I mentally prepare a checklist of everything I will need for the following day. I want every detail of the day to be perfect.

Chapter Twenty-Two

SARA

Sitting by the fire pit, I watch the shadows dance across the faces of those around me. They laugh and eat, the plates on their knees wobble but remain steady. I drop my eyes to my empty plate in disbelief that I've devoured every single bite. Gabe's cooking is truly remarkable.

I lift my gaze and meet Zee's eyes. He gives me a gentle smile before turning to say something to Kyra. When Gabe introduced me to Zee, I initially felt intimidated by his towering height and imposing broad shoulders. My eyes were nearly popping out of my head, but he was so charismatic that it wasn't long before I felt more at ease.

Then there was Kyra, Liam and Noah's mom. She is so sweet and kind, her boys a reflection of their mother, and they have such good manners. Her husband, Sander, is away at work with Nesrin's husband, Lukas, so I've yet to meet them. I've heard a mention of Zee's wife, Leila, but no one's said where she is. I did manage to learn she is Nesrin's sister.

Nesrin shines like the sun in the group, drawing everyone toward her with her warm presence and quick wit. She seems to always be one step ahead of everyone in their constant bantering.

It has been fun to watch, especially the back-and-forth between her and Zee. The two of them got into a heated debate about the perfect chicken marinade. Both are stubborn, neither willing to back down, and everyone else in the room paused to watch the showdown.

At one point, Zee, clearly frustrated, tried to end the argument with a sharp, *Would you just stop arguing already?* But her response was quick and so matter-of-fact that it was hard not to laugh.

I'm not arguing, Zee. I'm simply explaining why I'm right, the words left her lips with such confidence that Zee could only throw his arms in the air in exasperation. Without another word, he stormed off to grab a round of drinks, muttering under his breath as everyone else in the kitchen exchanged amused glances. A battle of wills over something as simple as chicken marinade, but with all the passion of a serious debate. I'd never experienced anything like this before.

Suddenly, laughter fills the air, and my eyes immediately find Astraea. Nesrin's daughter is gorgeous, a ray of sunshine. Her infectious smile seems to radiate a celestial charm, as if she were from another realm.

Gabe shared with me that her name, which means star maiden, was inspired by the Greek goddess of innocence, a daughter of the titans. The goddess had resided on Earth for a short time, but when the Iron Age dawned, bringing along agony and wickedness, Astraea abandoned the Earth and went to the skies where she transformed into the constellation Virgo. According to the myth, when Astraea returns to Earth one day, she will once again bring the utopia that was there during the Golden Age, bringing an end to human suffering. As he spoke, his voice resonated with a soothing and captivating tone. I had been so entranced by the story I hadn't heard anything else.

Cracks have begun to appear in the armor I built around myself. Slowly but surely, Gabe is chipping away at those cracks. If I'm not careful, I could easily find myself falling in love, not only with him, but also with his friends. It would be so easy to forget about my past and start a new life. And yet I can't shake the fear of it all being ripped away from me at any moment.

There is an urgency inside of me to put as much distance between my future and my past as possible. *A future that holds a promise of healing and growth.*

How I'm going to do that, I'm not sure, but I know it is going to be hard to walk away from Gabe if it comes to that. For now, I want to see where this goes. I will have to confess my past to him soon. See if he will be willing to take the risk and stay by our side, or if he will wash his hands of us. The heaviness in my chest is much stronger than it should be when that thought crosses my mind.

Shit, I have already become emotionally attached.

"Sara?"

I blink, looking toward Nesrin. "Sorry?"

"That's okay, I was asking how long you've been in Portland?"

Shit, the questions are going to start, and why shouldn't they? I'm getting closer to Gabe, and they are his family. Of course, they will want to know who I am.

The panic builds up inside me, causing me to clear my throat nervously. "I have been here for around a year." I blow out a breath. That wasn't so hard.

"How'd you come to work at Greta's?"

I freeze, my fingers spasming. I blink several times, as if that could change the question, but Nesrin's warm smile and kind eyes put me at ease. I find myself relaxing slightly.

"Greta found me one night when Tyler and I were at a woman's shelter. She helped me. Set me up with an apartment and a job." That was way more than I meant to share.

"A shelter?" Nesrin frowns and the others fall silent.

All eyes are on me, but I can't bring myself to meet their curious faces, and instead focus on my plate. I can't bear to witness the pity that will be directed toward me. I've come a long way since then.

"Yes, I had nowhere else to go at the time. I'm forever grateful to Greta for giving me a chance."

"So am I." Gabe's deep voice resonates next to me as his hand covers mine, providing warmth and comfort.

My eyes are drawn to our hands. I can feel every finger resting on my hand, the feeling of safety and protection wrapping around me from that one simple touch. I peer up at him, and a tender, apologetic expression marks his features. I give him a reassuring smile, assuring him I'm okay and that his friends are only looking out for him.

"What about your family? Friends?" Kyra tears a piece of lettuce from her burger and puts it in her mouth.

A sharp pain pulses in my chest at the question, and I absently rub the spot, trying to ease the ache. Zee's eyes catch the movement, and I quickly drop my hand back down. "I don't have any family or friends. It's just Tyler. Just the two of us."

"That's not true," Nesrin's voice cuts in, her tone firm, almost insistent.

My heart skips a beat at her words, a sudden rush of fear sending a jolt of adrenaline through me. "What?" I breathe, my voice barely audible.

"You've got us now," Gabe chimes in, his words gentle but certain.

Zee shifts forward, leaning his forearms on his knees as he locks eyes with me, his gaze unwavering. "You're one incredibly strong woman, Sara. You've got the heart of a lioness—protective, loyal, fierce."

His candidness takes me by surprise. I can't help but respond softly, "You've just met me."

"So what?" Zee shrugs, his expression resolute. "I can tell you're a good person. A good mom."

His intense stare dares me to disagree, and my throat tightens, emotions threatening to spill over. "You're going to make me cry." My laugh catches in my throat as the tears start to rise.

Zee's eyes widen in panic, and Nesrin bursts out in hysterics, doubling over as she points at him. "He *hates* it when women cry. He can't handle it. Tough man's kryptonite," she manages to say between cackles, which only makes me laugh.

Kyra joins in, giving Zee a teasing slap on the arm. "Wuss," she jokes.

"Whatever," Zee mutters with an exaggerated eye roll, but he winks at me playfully, his lips twitching into a smile.

I grin back, warmth flooding my chest. There's a lightness, a sense of connection that's entirely new to me. Slowly, but surely, I feel something I haven't felt in a long time—a sense of belonging.

Chapter Twenty-Three

GABE

From a distance, I notice Tyler sitting alone on the balcony, lost in his own world. Excusing myself from the lively group below, I climb the stairs with a sense of foreboding clawing at the edges of my consciousness. As I approach him, I can't shake the feeling that something is amiss.

"Everything okay?"

I take a seat next to him, but Tyler doesn't look at me. His eyes instead remain fixed on his mom down by the fire, laughing with Nesrin and Kyra. She looks so at ease, so happy. Her radiant smile lights up her face, casting a warmth that reaches the darkest corners of my heart.

"She likes you," Tyler murmurs, his voice barely above a whisper.

Taken aback, it takes me a moment to reply. "Good. I like her, too."

"She looks happy and healthy," he continues in a faraway voice.

That's an odd thing to say.

"She used to be so skinny."

With a frown, I look down at Tyler before I lower my gaze to Sara. The flickering flames from the fire pit dance across her skin, creating a soft glow that almost gives her an otherworldly aura.

"What do you mean?"

"They never let her eat a proper meal, only gave her scraps, if there was any. I tried sneaking her food once, but it only got her punished. They were so mean to her."

I stiffen, my muscles coiling with tension the more he speaks.

"Mom deserves to be happy and loved." His words hang heavy between us.

"Who did this? Who hurt her?" I demand, trying my best to keep my voice calm and level.

"My dad, my grandfather, the others. Everyone treated us differently. Everyone except Aunt Mal."

Closing my eyes, I take a deep breath, the primal urge to protect and avenge roaring to life within me. The tingling sensation of magic surges through my veins, begging to be unleashed.

"Don't say anything to Mom, please," Tyler pleads, a note of panic riding his words.

I shake my head, but keep my eyes closed to prevent my magic from being revealed in their reflection. "I won't."

Sensing Sara approaching, I take several deep breaths and release my magic, letting it sweep over the area discreetly before opening my eyes. I give Tyler a reassuring smile. "I promise, it stays between us."

"What are you two talking about?" Sara comes to stand in front of me.

"Just boy talk," I assure her, reaching out and wrapping an arm around Tyler and giving him a gentle squeeze.

Tyler smiles briefly before focusing on his feet. Which I'm guessing he does because he is a terrible liar, his emotions always give him away. I catch Sara's eye and respond with a smirk and a shrug. I extend my hand toward her and gently guide her onto my lap. I'm surprised when she willingly sits down. Despite the abundant space on the bench, she chooses to follow my lead. Strangely, that sensation gives me the same exhilaration as winning a race. Glancing at Tyler, I give him a wink, letting him know that everything will be alright.

With a smile on his face, Tyler leaps up. "I'm going to find Liam and Noah." His words come quickly, then he's running for the stairs.

My arms tighten around Sara, soaking in her soft skin and warmth. I will allow what Tyler told me to settle in my mind for a while before taking any action. I promised I wouldn't say anything, so I will patiently wait and see if she chooses to disclose the information to me.

Sara's arm wraps around my neck, and she leans her head against my shoulder. The sensation of her breath against my skin, so warm and intense, is pure torture. With my arms around her waist, and her body pressed against mine, a sense of intimacy rises that makes my pulse pick up.

Earlier today when I went to pick them up, Sara came down the stairs wearing a white dress with bright yellow flowers on it. It has a low vee dip that shows off a hint of her cleavage, and flows down to her ankles. I had waited at the bottom of those stairs just admiring her as the long, wide sleeves flutter with her motion. When she got to the bottom, I wrapped an arm around her waist and touched my mouth to hers without thought. Now I want nothing more than to see this dress on my bedroom floor.

"Thank you for tonight," she mutters softly, her fingers running up and down my forearm.

"No. Thank you." There is a moment of silence as I hesitate, then ask what I've been wanting to all night. "Will you stay the night?"

My question hangs in the air, and I feel a surge of nerves in my gut as I await her response.

Pulling back, Sara's searching eyes lock onto mine, as if she's trying to read my mind. "I don't know . . . "

She trails off and begins chewing on her bottom lip, a nervous habit I try to alleviate by gently pulling her lip from between her teeth.

"Nothing has to happen, Sara. I just don't want you to leave yet."

As she looks out at the people below, her brow furrows in deep thought, considering my words. It's comforting to know that she is taking her time to think before giving me an answer instead of immediately shutting me down.

Reaching up, I grasp her chin in thumb and forefinger, bringing her face back to mine. "I'll go at your pace, baby. If you want me to take you home, I will."

A mix of emotions flicker in her big brown eyes, leaving me on the edge.

"I want to stay," she whispers.

"You sure?"

Sara nods in return, and I let out a slow breath.

"Okay," I reply, leaning in to give her a gentle and lingering kiss.

Pulling apart, I lift her off my lap before she can notice the bulge in my jeans, and stand. I reach up, unable to stop myself from touching her, letting my fingers gently stroke her cheek.

How could anyone hurt her?

Feeling my anger resurface, I clasp her hand and turn swiftly to lead her toward the stairs. The others turn as we approach. Nesrin's eyes follow us, twinkling in the light of the fire, her coffee held between her hands.

"Everything okay?" Curious, as always.

"Perfect," I reply and look at Sara, who ducks her head, letting her hair cover her face from view.

We settle down side-by-side on a log by the fire. I push some of her hair behind her ear, before leaning in and whispering, "Don't hide that beautiful face."

Zee and Kyra both rise to their feet.

"We are going to head back." Zee looks at Nesrin, raising an eyebrow.

"Oh, right, yes. We are going to head off." Nesrin jumps up.

Chuckling, I stand up and see Astraea and the boys running over to me. I lift Astraea into my arms, feeling the weightlessness of her tiny body.

'I like them,' she whispers in my mind.

'I like them, too, Star.'

'Can we keep them?'

My laughter erupts. She is just like her mother. Sara's curious gaze meets mine, and for a moment, I forget that she is unaware of our ability to communicate through our minds.

'*I plan on keeping them.*'

'*Good,*' Nesrin and Astraea say together.

My eyes dart to Nesrin, and her joyful grin stretches from ear to ear. Zee approaches Sara and wraps his arms around her, embracing her tightly. Her body tenses up for a moment, but she hesitantly extends her hand around him and gently pats him on the back.

"Was great to meet you, Sara," he says, then turns to Tyler. "And you too, Tyler."

Sara and Tyler's cheeks turn a shade of pink, and my chest tightens as I witness the genuine surprise on her face when Kyra steps forward and wraps her in a hug. Nesrin is next in line, and when it's her turn to say goodbye to Sara, she holds her a little longer, their whispered conversation hidden from the rest. Sara tightens her grip on Nesrin and relaxes into the hug. I can faintly sense Nesrin's magic lingering in the air, a comforting presence that eases something unseen.

Pulling apart, Nesrin turns and reaches for Astraea, and I give them both a kiss on the cheek.

"See you later," I say out loud, then in her mind. '*Thank you.*'

Nesrin nods, a small smile forming on her lips as they turn and start walking toward the cars. We wave goodbye to the boys, watching as they pile into the car, laughter and banter echoing through the night. Kyra waves goodbye and leaves first, with Zee and Nesrin following behind. Once the last car disappears around the bend, we stand there in the quiet aftermath. The only sounds left are the rustling leaves.

"Right. Tyler, want to pick a room?"

"Wait, we're *staying?*"

Sara grins. "Is that okay?"

"Hell yes!!"

We burst into laughter as he playfully sprints back to the house.

While Sara gets Tyler settled in, I pack away the leftover food. But I feel her presence, and turn to see her standing in the doorway, wearing a thoughtful expression. The warm glow of the kitchen lights highlights her beautiful, soft brown skin.

Finishing up, I toss the dish cloth into the sink and walk over to her. With a blink of her deep brown eyes, she snaps out of her reverie, and her vibrant energy fills the room around us.

"I'm going to make sure everything is good outside, then I'll be back. Make yourself comfortable."

What I really need is some fresh air. Having her in my home, her scent drifting in my space, is driving me crazy.

I do a swift check of the perimeter, and ensure the fire is completely out before returning inside. Sensing that Sara is still in the kitchen, I make my way there.

"What do you think you're doing?"

Locks of hair, woven with every imaginable shade of brown, tumble in soft waves down her back, catching the light. Her dress clings loosely to her body, the delicate sleeves slipping down her arms, leaving her bare shoulders exposed. There's something captivating about the way she moves so effortlessly, as though unaware of just how much attention she commands.

Every coherent thought stutters to a halt the moment she shifts, turning just enough to peer back at me. Her deep brown eyes, usually so guarded, hold a softness I'm unfamiliar with—a warmth that seems to melt the space between us.

"The dishes." The playful smile tugging at the corner of her mouth sends a jolt through me.

A low growl rumbles from my chest, and I inch forward a step, bringing me to within two feet of her. "I think the question is *why* you're doing the dishes."

Her teasing grin drops and her demeanor dips into something sincere. "Because you and your friends took care of me all night, and I thought it would only be right to return the favor."

"It's not a favor to be repaid. That's just what friends do."

Friends.

What bullshit.

Nothing about this is *friendly*.

It feels as if I'm teetering on the edge of a cliff. It's like reaching an intersection and making a turn that has the potential to completely redefine your existence. Or looking out over a stunning valley and finally feeling a sense of belonging.

Chocolate eyes swim, searching mine where I tower behind her, so close that I can feel the energy crackle between us. One step closer, and I'm afraid it might pop.

"I just wanted to return the kindness," she murmurs.

"I don't want you to ever feel like you have to pay me back, or you owe me. I do things for you because I want to."

Confusion clouds her face, and she rinses the last plate, placing it into the dishwasher. Slowly, she turns, drying off her hands with a dish towel before she sets it aside, her eyes full of questions and intent. "Why? You don't know me or owe me anything. I'm not–"

"Bullshit." I move so fast that I don't even realize I'm there until my hand gently tangles in the silky strands of her hair, and the sweet scent of her shampoo fills my senses. With tender precision, my fingers expertly knead into the soft base of her skull, her eyes falling shut. I press her firmly against the cool, marble counter, the sound of our breaths mingling in the air.

"I might not know all the details about you, Sara, but there's something about you I recognize here." I gather up her hand and press her palm flat on my chest where my heart is beating. "Something I feel. And the problem is, I care too fucking much."

Her chin trembles as she stares up at me, and my hand slips down to grasp her by the nape of her neck. Her lips part, and the air vibrates around us.

"I can't stop thinking about you. Like there is a constant craving deep inside me, an insatiable desire that never seems to fade when it comes to you."

Her eyes seem to glaze over, and she runs her tongue across those plump, tempting lips, and my gaze dips to capture the action. My mind goes to the kiss we shared the day before in her apartment, and my body tightens.

"Tell me to kiss you." The words are desperate. The last thread of my restraint.

I can feel her fingers wrapping around my shirt, clinging to me. The inch of space between us is alive with a wild, frenetic energy.

A second.

An eternity.

"Kiss me."

And that thread snaps.

My mouth drops to hers, and her lips part on a gasp. I sweep my tongue into her mouth, devouring her completely.

Without stopping, I bend, grabbing her behind the thighs and lift her into my body, her legs wrapping around my waist. Her arms drape over my shoulders, her delicate fingers teasing my hair, as I turn and head toward the stairs. Walking into the bedroom, I slowly drop her feet to the ground, my hands skimming her body as I do. The combination of the soft fabric of her dress against my palms and her alluring scent creates an intoxicating, intimate moment.

I step away from her, running a hand through my hair, and let out a breath. "My shirts are in the top drawer. I'm going to the bathroom." To splash some cold water on my face.

In that moment, our eyes connect, and a wave of electricity passes between us. Sara's eyes then wander around my room, her bottom lip anxiously trapped between her teeth. I stifle a groan, rubbing my hands over my face. It's going to be so hard to hold myself back. Perhaps this isn't the wisest decision. Putting her, my sweetest temptation, in my bed, in my shirt, in my space.

Quickly, I turn on my heel and walk to the bathroom, shutting the door behind me. *Holy shit*. I need to let her set the pace. I turn the tap on and cup the cool water in my hands and splash it on my face. When I look in the mirror, my eyes are shimmering gold. Fuck.

With each deep breath I take, I can feel a sense of calm washing over me, soothing my mind. When I open my eyes again, they are back to normal. Grabbing a pair of sleep pants from the shelf, I quickly change out of my jeans. Then pull my shirt over my head and toss it aside, feeling the cool air against my skin.

As I walk into my room, I see Sara lounging on her stomach on my bed, her eyes fixed on a book. She has changed into one of my t-shirts, the fit accentuating her figure. The moment she hears me approaching the bed, she pushes herself up and onto her side, leaning on her elbow and cradling her head in her hand. She has let her hair down, allowing the long strands to cascade around her shoulders and onto the pillow. I want to run my fingers through her hair, tug on it, wrap it around my fist as I slide my cock inside her. Lust overwhelms me, and I slow my steps so I don't frighten her.

Sara's eyes travel along my chest and down to where my sleep pants sit low on my hips. I notice her dazed look, and a small smile tugs at my lips as I climb onto the bed and lie next to her, matching the way she is positioned, our bodies aligned. She gives me a soft smile, her lips curving gently upward.

"You're beautiful." My fingertips caress her hair.

Her response is breathy and soft. "Thank you."

I move forward, sliding closer to her so we are lying face to face. Without breaking eye contact, I reach over, gliding my hand down, hooking it around her waist and pulling her into me. I move my hand further down, to the curve of her ass and down her leg. Slowly, I grab behind her knee, hiking her leg over my hips, making it so our bodies press tightly against each other. Throughout this, her eyes remain fixed on mine, our breaths mingling in the stillness of the room.

My heart is beating so damn fast right now. I've never had this reaction to a woman before.

Taking my time, I let my hand glide slowly over her silky, soft skin, starting at her knee. I savor every second, the warmth of her body beneath my fingers as I trace a deliberate path upward. My hand travels over the curve of her hip, and I continue the journey across the fabric of her t-shirt, feeling the contours of her waist and ribs. As my fingers skim lightly along the side of her breast, I can feel the tension building in the air between us.

I love the way her breath catches, the quiet, involuntary gasps that escape her lips with every soft, teasing touch. Each sound fuels my need to keep exploring, to savor every reaction I elicit from her. My eyes never leave hers. There's something electric in her gaze, a mixture of anticipation and desire that mirrors my own.

As my fingers trail up the delicate column of her neck, I watch her swallow, her pulse quickening beneath my touch. My hand finally finds its place, fingers tangling gently in her hair, pulling her just a little closer.

"May I?" My eyes drop to her lips.

"Yes," she breathes.

Gently, I fist her hair, and tilt her head, my mouth dropping to hers. This kiss is fierce and passionate, devoid of any sweetness or gentleness. This kiss is claiming.

I want her to know she is undeniably mine, and I have no intention of letting her go. The electric connection between us pulsates through the air, filling the room with tension. The faint scent of her perfume mingles with the sweet aroma of roses, intoxicating my senses. With every beat of my heart, I hold her close, feeling her warmth radiating against my chest, knowing deep inside that I'm never letting her slip away.

I will cherish her and keep her safe. Always safe. Both of them.

Chapter Twenty-Four

Sara

God, his hands on me drive me crazy. I never knew it could feel like this. So intense and magical. It's so addictive, and I never want it to stop. I can feel his touch seeping into my skin, leaving a lingering sensation that I never want to fade away.

Gabe's tongue playfully traces the edge of my lips, coaxing me to part them. The moment his tongue brushes against mine, a rush of desire floods me, leaving me breathless and wanting more. My moans escape into his mouth, and in response, his grip on my hair tightens, igniting a tingling sensation that spreads throughout my body.

I mold myself against him, aching to feel the warmth and closeness grow even stronger. The need to rip this shirt off my body and feel his skin against mine is overwhelming. With a slight movement of my hips, he lets out a deep groan, and I'm left breathless as I feel the undeniable hardness against me. My mind momentarily freezes, but then I take a deep breath, and am instantly surrounded by the comforting scent of Gabe.

Gabe's touch caresses my body, his fingers sliding beneath the fabric of my t-shirt. The touch of his fingers against my bare skin makes me gasp, feeling a rush of electricity. His warm hand covers my breast, plucking and teasing my nipple. The heat is instant, and a pulse of pleasure throbs in my core, stealing my breath away.

Gabe's hands continue to move over me, and I can tell he's gauging my reactions. We are still lying on our sides, our faces only inches apart, our bodies pressed together. I want to explore the various tattoos that cover his torso and arms, but I don't want to stop what we've started. I lean back just enough to pull the t-shirt over my head, leaving me in only my panties. Gabe doesn't waste any time pulling me back to him, our chests pressed against each other. His kisses trail down my neck, then he's moving lower, taking my nipple in his mouth, and I arch into his touch. This is like nothing I've ever felt before. My brain is buzzing with desire.

Is this what it's meant to feel like?

I push Gabe's pants down with my feet, feeling his cock brush against me when it comes free of the fabric. I reach down, wrapping my hand around the shaft, gently stroking. I feel his body tense up as a small groan slips from his mouth. Nervousness courses through my body, and my stomach flutters with a swarm of butterflies as I soak in his reactions.

"I want you inside of me," I breathe against his lips.

Gabe's eyes are molten as he stares back at me. "Are you sure?"

"I'm sure."

"I promise there's no pressure. If you want to stop, we will stop."

I know he'll back off if I ask, but that is the last thing I want.

Gabe leans closer, his lips brushing my ear. "And if you just want to ride my tongue tonight until you come, I'm happy to oblige."

His words send a shiver cascading down my spine, making my nipples hard, as liquid fire flows through my veins.

He bites down on the spot under my ear, and I moan, loudly. Before he can say another word, I lunge for him. This time, I am kissing him, desperately. I break the kiss, my lips trailing down the column of neck, as my hands roam his chest.

"Gabe?" I pant, completely breathless.

"Yes."

"I want to feel you moving inside of me."

Without a word, he reaches behind for the nightstand and produces a condom, ripping it open with his teeth as he hands it to me.

"Put it on." His voice, deep and demanding, makes me shiver in the best of ways.

My hands shake as I take it from him and watch as my fingers roll it over his length. There is barely any room between us as we lie here facing each other. The moment I release him, Gabe grabs the back of my panties, shredding them. My eyes flare in shock.

"I can't wait," he lifts my leg, hooking it in his arm before sliding inside of me in a slow, torturous stroke. His mouth finds mine again, and I groan. My mind floats somewhere outside of my body as heat coils in my belly, spreading outward.

"Ohhhhh . . . fuck . . . " I moan, my nails digging into Gabe's shoulders.

He moves at a slow, steady pace, drawing out each thrust. My head spins with a lust that stokes a fire deep inside me, something I've never felt before.

Letting go of my leg, Gabe's arms encircle me, and his hand finds its way back into my hair, holding me against him.

He adjusts his angle, moving up onto one arm so he can pick up the pace. My nails drag down his back, gripping his ass as he plunges inside of me over and over. My pleasure grows in waves, and I arch my back, my hard nipples rubbing against his chest, setting sparks alight.

"Oh. O– Oh . . . g– god, Gabe," I stammer, my words becoming incoherent.

My core tightens, and Gabe's answering groan sends me toppling over the edge of the cliff. Leaning over me, he captures my mouth with his in a passionate kiss, drowning out the cacophony of uncontrollable sounds. As he growls into my mouth, his strokes become erratic, matching the intensity of our shared climax. That sound rumbling from his chest is the hottest I've ever heard in my life. His weight presses down on me, his body still intertwined with mine, and he remains there for the longest time, his presence pressing against me like a reassuring anchor. Holding him close, I can feel my throat tightening as I try to suppress my overwhelming emotions. The fear of losing him consumes my thoughts.

I need to tell him about my past.

Chapter Twenty-Five

SARA

I slowly blink my eyes open, the soft morning light filtering through the curtains. I smile, feeling a sense of warmth and contentment wash over me. Snuggling into Gabe's chest, I breathe in deeply, delighting in the citrusy scent that clings to him. His chest rises and falls in a steady rhythm. Memories of the night before flood back to me—the connection we shared was . . . I can't even explain it. But there was an undeniable spark that ignited between us.

Opening my eyes, I pull back just enough so I can see his face. A smile of wonder tugs at my lips as I trace the contours of his face with my fingertips, marveling at the way his features seem even more handsome in the early morning light. Gabe's eyes flutter open, revealing a face that is tender with a hint of mischief.

"Good morning." His voice is husky with sleep as he presses a gentle kiss to my forehead.

"Good morning." My heart flutters in my chest when I meet his gaze.

"I could get used to this."

"What?" I whisper.

"Waking up with you in my arms."

My pulse kicks up and Gabe leans in, brushing his lips over mine in a teasing manner. The world outside seems to fade away, leaving only the two of us in our own little bubble of intimacy.

"Me, too," I purr, our lips barely a breath apart.

Yesterday felt surreal, an experience beyond my wildest imagination. But as the morning sun illuminates the world, reality sets in, with vibrant hues painting the sky and the chirping of birds filling the air.

"I didn't get a chance to explore your body like I wanted to last night." Gabe reaches to lift the sheet, but I hug it to my chest, a feeling of self-consciousness coming over me.

He grins. "Baby . . . "

My heart swoons, and I instinctively relax my fingers, letting go of the sheet.

Gabe's eyes shift to the door, his warm smile brightening his face, as he leans in and gently kisses my forehead. "We'll pick this up another time. Tyler's awake."

Before I can question him on how on earth he could know that Tyler is out of bed, Gabe gets up from the bed, and all thought focuses on his naked body on full display. *Oh, wow . . .*

Gabe tugs on his sleep pants and ties his hair up into a bun, then snatches a t-shirt from the floor before heading to the door. He glances at me, his eyes traveling over my body covered by sheets. Desire darkens his eyes, and I try not to fidget under his perusal.

"Take your time. Have a shower. I'll start the coffees," he finally says, and I release a breath I've been holding.

As he slips from the room, I fall back onto the pillow and grin up at the ceiling. Butterflies fill my stomach, and all I want to do is call Mal and tell her all about Gabe. My eyes dart nervously to my bag, and I anxiously chew on my lip.

Screw it.

Sitting up, I gather the sheet around me, and secure it tightly. I reach for my bag and grab the burner phone, switching it on. While I wait, I nervously chew on my thumbnail, feeling a mix of excitement and anxiety.

Before I can even reconsider, I quickly dial Mal's number and press the call button. One ring. Two.

"Hello?"

"Mal, it's me."

Her voice drops to a whisper. "What the hell, S? Is something wrong?"

"No, nothing's wrong. I just wanted to talk."

"Girl, are you trying to give me a heart attack?"

Guilt surfaces, and I look toward the window. "I'm sorry."

Mal lets out a sigh, and I can hear a door being shut in the background. "Don't apologize. You just scared me."

"I was just excited to talk to you."

"Why?" She's clearly curious.

"I stayed at Gabe's last night."

The silence on the other end of the line is so pronounced that I instinctively move the phone away, wondering if we have been disconnected.

"Mal?"

"Are you serious?"

"Yes."

"Oh, my fucking god, that's awesome!" she squeals.

A burst of laughter escapes me, and I rest the back of my hand against my cheek, feeling warmth rise to my face.

"How was it?"

"Amazing . . . He is so . . . He is incredible."

"Where are you now?"

"In his bedroom."

"Where is Tyler?"

"Downstairs cooking breakfast with Gabe."

Mal sighs dramatically, giving off an air of daydreaming. "I'm so happy for you."

"Thanks," I whisper, my voice barely audible as a surge of emotions overwhelms me.

"Are you going to tell him?"

"I kinda have to." Dread coils deep in my stomach.

"It will be fine."

I hum, not sure I believe her.

"It will be." Her voice is so strong, so sure.

"Talk soon."

"Talk soon," she agrees.

Hanging up, I drop the phone into my bag and slide off the bed, stretching out the tension in my muscles. Without delay, I make a beeline for the bathroom and step into the steaming shower, allowing the water to wash away the remnants of sleep.

Once I'm out, I reach for my dress from yesterday, slipping it back on, minus the underwear, thanks to Gabe shredding them last night. A little smile plays on my lips at the memory. As I finish getting dressed, the tantalizing aroma of fresh coffee wafts through the door, cutting through the air and pulling me toward the kitchen like a magnet.

Chapter Twenty-Six

GABE

The sun dips below the horizon, casting a warm glow over the city streets. Sara and Tyler lead the way out the door of the restaurant where we have enjoyed a cozy dinner. The air is crisp, and the scent of rain lingers in the breeze. We are due for a storm any day now.

I slip my hand into Sara's, noticing the soft smile playing at the corners of her lips. "I had a wonderful time tonight, Gabe. Thank you," she purrs, her voice warm with affection, and her cheeks flush with a rosy hue.

My heart flutters with contentment, an answering smile spreading across my face. "Me, too. I want to tell you something."

Sara's steps falter momentarily as she looks up at me, her eyes full of apprehension. "Oh?"

"Nothing bad. But . . . " I hesitate, feeling stupid. "No one knows this besides my best friend, but my real name—my Japanese name—is Makoto."

Sara stops walking, pulling me to a stop beside her. I'm caught off guard when she steps closer and reaches up, pushing some hair from my face. As her fingers glide across my jaw, my eyes fall closed for a moment.

"Makoto," she tests out the name.

My heart thunders, my eyes snapping open. "Say it again," I whisper.

She smiles, pushing up on her toes, her lips brushing across mine. "Makoto."

My arm sweeps around her waist, pulling her curvy body flush with mine. She lets out a soft sigh as my lips descend on hers. It's as if she's been waiting for this moment all night.

Tyler's giggle echoes in my ears, and I hastily distance myself from Sara, feeling a wave of embarrassment wash over me, and I look away with the heat rising to my cheeks.

Shit.

I rub the back of my neck and tilt my head to meet Sara's beautiful brown eyes.

Clearing my throat, I close the distance to Tyler, ruffling his hair. "Sorry, bud."

"You can kiss my mom whenever you like. It makes her happy," he urges with a bright smile.

I shake my head, a small smile playing on my lips.

The three of us continue toward the car, our footsteps echoing on the pavement, and Tyler hums a tune. The street lights blink on, one by one as the darkness settles in around us. Suddenly, Tyler's humming transforms into a whistle. The notes floating on the evening breeze like delicate petals dancing in the wind.

However, I falter at the sound of his whistle, a flicker of unease flaring to life in my chest.

"Tyler, perhaps it's best not to whistle," I warn softly, unable to hide my cautious tone. "In Japanese folklore, it's said that whistling at night can invite unwanted attention from spirits."

Sara frowns slightly, her brow furrowing in confusion.

Tyler turns a shade pale. "I'm sorry."

My head shakes as I offer him a reassuring smile. "It's okay. I know you meant no harm. But it's better to be cautious, especially when it comes to matters of superstition."

With a nod of understanding, Tyler falls silent. It's a relief when they don't question it more. I'd rather not tempt fate any further. Together, we continue to the parking lot, the soft glow of streetlights casting long shadows on the pavement.

Chapter Twenty-Seven

SARA

Bad weather in Portland is nothing new, but it means fewer customers and less tips. That's always a downside of being a waitress. I could always rely on my base wage, but the tips make life a little less hard. The rain pours relentlessly outside, tapping against the windows of the diner. The gloomy atmosphere mirrors my own feelings as I scan the empty tables.

Leaning against the counter, I watch the rain streak down the windowpane, creating a mesmerizing pattern. I'm on closing shift, and from the looks of it, we'll be closing an hour early tonight. With a smile on my face, I wave farewell to the last couple of regulars leaving early. I clear their table before walking over to flip the sign and lock the front door. The rain intensifies, coming down in sheets that pelt the front windows with even greater force. The sound is thunderous, drowning out any other noise, including my thoughts.

With a heavy sigh, I begrudgingly begin the task of cleaning. The new cook in the kitchen already started shutting down parts of the kitchen over an hour ago and is eager to leave by the looks of it.

"Hey, Bill, you can head home. I'll finish up here," I call out, catching the older man's attention.

"You sure you're good to lock up?"

With a smile on my face, I turn to face him and dismissively wave him off. "I'm fine, Bill, go home to your wife. I have a lift coming soon."

"I don't like leaving ya here alone."

"I'll be fine. Have a good night, and say hello to Ginna for me."

"Okay, then. Take care, and I'll see you on Monday!" Bill heads toward the back of the diner.

My mind drifts as I clean, captivated by the vivid memories of the past couple of days I shared with Gabe. The images of our nights together replay in my mind, accompanied by the distant hum of Tyler's laughter and the clinking of pans in the kitchen. The smell of Japanese dishes filled the air as Gabe patiently guided me through the art of cooking. We haven't spent the night together since that first night, but tomorrow we both have the day off, so he is staying at my apartment tonight. Gabe is planning to take me hiking in the morning after we drop Tyler off at Kyra's. He mentioned that there's something important he wants to show me.

In my own world, I clutch the bag of trash and slip through the creaking back door, emerging into the dimly lit alley. The rain has dwindled to a gentle drizzle, but I quicken my pace, my footsteps echoing against the damp pavement. A sudden sense of foreboding overwhelms me, causing my heart to thud painfully in my chest.

With a sense of urgency, I raise the lid of the grimy dumpster and deposit the discarded items within.

I pivot to make my way back, my attention drawn to a distant figure at the end of the alley, and a chilling wave of terror paralyzes me. Our eyes lock, and in this fleeting moment, time seems to suspend. Panic surges through my veins, and I instinctively spin toward the diner, only to find another man blocking my escape, effectively trapping me in this nightmare.

They found me. How did they find me?

While I can't see their faces clearly, their stance and clothing unmistakably identify them as hunters.

"You look good, Sara."

My heart pounds with a mix of fear and adrenaline, causing my entire body to tremble. I quickly spin back around and find myself face-to-face with the man in the dimly lit alley. The voice and eyes are familiar to me. I know them well. It is the voice that stars in my nightmares.

No, no, no, no, no, no.

As my hand instinctively pats my side pocket, a sinking feeling settles in my gut when I realize my phone is in my bag.

Fuck.

Sharp pain steals my breath as a fist grips my hair, ripping my head back sharply. Startled, I let out a yelp as my hand instinctively shoots backward, desperately seeking the person who has me in their grasp. I'm roughly dragged into a hard body, a knife poised at my throat. Amidst my panic, I didn't hear him approach, his footsteps muffled by the pounding of my heart.

My eyes widen on the approaching figure. With each step my father takes, the tension in the air grows thicker. "Where is my grandson?"

"Like I would tell you," I choke out, the grip on my hair tightening painfully.

Tears spring to my eyes from the sharp pain along my scalp. My father steps forward, and without hesitation throws a punch to my ribs. All the air escapes my lungs, and I gasp desperately, but the air refuses to enter my lungs, leaving me breathless.

I'm forcefully thrown to the ground, the pavement biting into my palms and face. I lay there, desperate for oxygen, as the figure of the other man materializes above me. My blood freezes at the sight of my brother-in-law, Sam.

"Bet you didn't expect to see me," he sneers.

I am so screwed.

Squeezing my eyes shut, I desperately try to escape the suffocating grip of fear that threatens to consume me. I refuse to succumb to it, determined to resist its grip. I can feel the adrenaline coursing through my veins, my heart pounding in my chest, and something foreign growing and expanding.

"Open your fucking eyes, bitch!" Sam yells.

A powerful blow strikes my ribs, the sharp crack echoing in my ears. The pain that follows steals what little air I have. My eyes snap open, and I take in the sight of my father standing there, his face devoid of any emotion, as Sam lands another kick to my midsection.

What have I ever done to deserve his hatred?

The knowledge that Tyler is at home with Gabe tonight brings me a profound sense of relief. I can't bear the idea of him seeing me die. Another forceful kick lands directly on my thigh, causing a sharp jolt of deep, intense pain. My brother-in-law, though not physically imposing, possesses the same cruel nature as my father. I don't understand why, but my entire clan has an intense animosity toward me. Beyond that. They treat me with contempt. Not a single person ever came forward to aid me during my childhood, leaving me feeling abandoned and helpless. Except for Mal. Even though I know some didn't agree with how I was treated, they were too afraid to speak up or help. Mal's grandparents harbored a deep dislike for my father, yet they never intervened to prevent his actions.

"You think you can just kill my brother and disappear? Did you? Did you think we would forget?" Another kick lands hard in my side, and I instinctively fold my body inward to shield myself from the blow. I will never forget that night two years ago; it left an indelible mark on my soul. I won't ever regret it, though. Kirk got what he deserved, and I can feel the satisfaction coursing through my veins, knowing his evil was wiped from this earth.

As anger, pain, and fear intertwine in me, I feel a tingling sensation ripple from deep in my chest and gradually radiate outward. The pain becomes a distant whisper as I lie here, feeling a gentle warmth enveloping my body. Summoning all my strength, I struggle to rise, feeling the strain in my arms and legs as I lift myself onto my hands and knees. I struggle to maintain my balance on shaky legs, and my eyes lock onto my father approaching from the side. In a split second, his hand intercepts Sam's fist, halting another blow from landing.

"Not until I know where my grandson is," he growls.

"Why do you hate me so much? I'm your daughter," I whisper hoarsely.

Striking out, he hits me across the face. The sting burns like fire as tears well in my eyes. I stagger backward, my hand instinctively reaching up to touch the spot where his blow landed. The pain radiates through my cheek, pulsating with fierce force. His sneer deepens, his lips curling into a sinister smile that sends shivers down my spine. Malice and contempt emanate from his piercing blue eyes. The coldness in his steely gaze strikes me harder than his physical assault. Tears well, a mixture of both physical and emotional pain.

"You are no daughter of mine!" he snarls with so much venom it is like a physical blow.

With a sudden start, I recoil and take a step back. "What?"

Stalking toward me, he pulls out a dagger, one that identifies our clan. A hunter's dagger.

"Your whore of a mother had an affair. You were the product of that affair, and not just with anyone, but a fucking filthy mage. I killed him in front of her. I wanted to kill you outright, but they put a protection spell on you. The best I could do was make your life as miserable as I could. I told everyone what you were. That the very thing we hunt was in our clan. They hated you as much as I did." His words spew forth like acid, eating away at me.

My heart is pounding so loud that all other sounds cease to exist. A rhythmic drumbeat of fear and determination. Blood rushes through my body as my brain begins piecing together my whole life. Everything makes so much sense.

Taking a menacing step forward, the man I've called father poises his dagger at the ready. I'm so stunned by this information that I'm slow to react. So many emotions crash through me, as he swiftly grabs me by the throat and sinks his dagger into my stomach. My eyes widen in disbelief, and I suck in a sharp breath.

At first, all I feel is the impact as my brain tries to catch up with what's happening. Then in an instant, a strong, electrifying sensation courses through my body, akin to a severe electric shock, as my body realizes that thousands upon thousands of circuits have just been severed. An intense heat radiates from the stab wound. It's a heat like nothing I've ever imagined.

Without thought, my hands shoot out in front of me, shoving him away with an unexpected strength. And judging by the surprise on his face, he didn't expect it either. My vision tunnels on the man I thought was my father. I can feel adrenaline pumping through me, numbing the pain. I grip the dagger and pull it from my stomach, dropping it to the ground. The sound of it hitting the cement reverberates through the air, but it sounds so far away. I enter a state of autopilot, moving my hands in a fluid motion as if guided by an invisible force.

The man who is not my father steps back, and his eyes widen as a gust of wind comes out of nowhere, whipping around me. The wind howls its fury, tearing at my clothes, pulling my hair in streams on both sides of my face. A surge of courage courses through me as I feel the magic swirling around and through me, making me feel strong.

With a growl, I add more force. The wind lifts him clean off his feet, throwing him hard into the brick wall. A loud crack sounds upon impact. The sound resonates within my head, echoing and lingering. I watch detached as his eyes roll into the back of his head, and his lifeless body drops to the ground in a heap. I won't allow myself to feel relief though, not when Sam is still here. The wind dances around me, carrying with it a weightless sensation as my feet leave the ground. I turn to Sam, his eyes widening in shock as the wind begins swirling around me like a tornado. Sam's eyes dart nervously between my father and me, before he abruptly spins around and runs off down the alley.

"Fucking coward!" I scream, but my voice is carried away by the wind.

I can feel the magic slipping away from me, like sand through my fingers. My energy drains from my body, leaving me weak and exhausted. At least now I know what it is . . . *Magic.* I am half witch. The man I called my father all these years had killed my real father, and possibly my mother. The ground greets my feet with a gentle touch, and then I sink to my knees. I stay there for a moment, feeling the roughness of the ground beneath me. I deliberately avoid acknowledging the man I forcefully propelled into the wall. The sound of his impact still rings in my ears. My hand clutches my middle tightly, feeling the warmth of my own blood seeping through my uniform and staining my hand crimson.

I need to get home. I need to see Tyler. I need Gabe.

Stumbling to my feet, I cautiously make my way from the dimly lit alley onto the street. The pain in my ribs intensifies, gnawing at me as my adrenaline and magic wanes. I have only made it a block when I slide down the wall of a building, feeling the rough texture against my back, desperate to catch my breath. Every part of me is hurting. Despite my efforts, my wound continues to bleed, and I grow increasingly lightheaded. Wrapping my other arm around my ribs, I wince in pain and let out a hiss. My palms and knees are marked with scrapes, and tiny rock fragments are embedded in the wounds. My face throbs with pain, and I can only imagine that it mirrors the battered appearance of my hands.

Taking short, shallow breaths, I attempt to regain my composure. A sudden noise catches my attention, and I turn my head to the side, rolling it on the wall. Looking down the street, I see someone approaching. *Damn it.*

I try pushing to my feet, but the pain from my ribs catches my breath, making me slide back to the ground. When I look up again, the figure is crouched down in front of me.

"Sara?" The voice is light, calm.

I raise my gaze, and I'm met with the sight of a middle-aged man, his tousled brown hair framing his face, and his eyes radiating warmth as they meet mine.

"Do I know you?" I gasp, the effort of breathing too hard.

"No, we haven't met, but Nesrin has told me all about you. I've been waiting to officially meet you. I'm Merve."

"Nice to meet you," I whisper.

"You're hurt, let me call someone. Get you to a hospital."

"No! Please, I live about four blocks away. Can . . . Can you help me home? I need to see my son," I grit out through clenched teeth.

He considers for a moment, but relents, "Okay."

With a swift motion, he reaches down and effortlessly lifts me off the ground, his strength surprising me. I let out a sharp yelp, the sound echoing in the empty street as he tenderly cradles me against his chest. The pain washes over me, overwhelming my senses, and leaving me gasping for air. His embrace is firm yet gentle, providing a slight comfort amidst the agony.

"Sorry," he mutters, sounding upset.

"It's . . . It's . . . fine . . . " I gasp.

With a nod, he starts down the street, and I can feel something off about the way he is walking. The pain clouds my mind, and a swirling feeling of confusion takes hold of me. Is he hurt? Or is he disabled?

Feeling bad, I try to wriggle down, but he tightens his hold. "It's okay, Sara. Try to relax. We will be there soon," he says in a soft, soothing voice.

I try my best to relax, feeling the weight of my head rest on his shoulder. Much to my surprise, we reach my apartment in less than a few minutes. I don't recall telling him where I live, but I must have. My adrenaline spikes when I see the stairs leading to my apartment. I scramble down from Merve's arms and almost land on my knees, but Merve grabs me just before I hit the ground.

"Easy there, little one," he mutters, but I'm already up, and staggering my way toward the stairs.

Chapter Twenty-Eight

SARA

My ribs . . . I can't stand straight as I climb the stairs, my muscles straining with every step. I trip and land hard on my knees, the shock and pain causing me to cry out in agony. My hands are slick with blood and slip on the rails as I try to pull myself up.

The door opens above with a sudden bang, causing me to jump in surprise. Gabe is standing at the top of the stairs, his tall, lean body tense, clad only in sleep pants. Gabe's eyes flash with fury, revealing the intensity of his emotions. They begin to give off a soft glow, but I must be hallucinating from the blood loss. Gabe descends the stairs in a blur of motion. Just watching him leaves me breathless. He scoops me up and races back up the stairs, bounding over multiple steps at once. If I wasn't in so much pain, I'd be totally turned on and impressed by the ease and swiftness of his movements. Perhaps a little jealous, too.

Before I can catch up to where we are, Gabe places me on the sofa, the soft cushions molding to the contours of my body as he gently lays me down. Then his face hovers above mine, and he softly brushes my hair away from my face.

"Baby, tell me what happened?" The soft glow in his eyes is still there, only brighter than before.

"Your eyes are beautiful," I whisper.

Gabe's eyes soften, and tiny golden flecks dance and flicker within the depths of his brown irises. Out of the corner of my eye, I detect a brief flicker of movement near the door. With a sudden motion, my head jerks to the side, and an involuntary gasp escapes from my mouth.

"Shhh . . . it's okay, it's just Merve. He's a friend," Gabe's soft voice captures my attention once again. "Can you tell me what happened?"

With trembling hands, I tentatively reach up and brush my fingers across his face, feeling the slight stubble and the warmth that radiates from him. My eyes instinctively snap to my hands, where the crimson stains of my blood stand out starkly. I'm at a loss for where to even start. Merve steps up and places a towel in Gabe's hand, who immediately applies pressure to my stomach, covering the stab wound. Stars burst behind my eyes, and I continue to stare at Gabe, drawing strength from him.

"I've called Nesrin. She is on her way."

"Thanks." Gabe doesn't take his eyes from mine.

"What? No!! It's late. You can't just call her. Why would you anyway?" I try to sit up.

Gabe's hands lightly land on my shoulders, pushing me back down.

"Nesrin can help heal your injuries, baby."

Confusion sweeps over me like a tidal wave. Is she a doctor? I don't think so . . .

"Tell me what happened. Who did this to you?"

I close my eyes and see that body hit the wall over and over. Violent tremors course through me. No matter how hard I try, I can't make myself stop.

"She is going into shock, Gabe," warns a faint voice from somewhere in the room.

A warm hand encloses mine and gives me a gentle squeeze, followed by a kiss on my head. "It's okay, baby. We will get this sorted. I promise."

"My ribs," I breathe out, and feel Gabe reach for the buttons on my uniform.

He hesitates. "May I?"

I nod my head, needing the restrictive clothes off. Merve walks over with an ice pack wrapped in a towel. He places it in my hand, moving it to my face where I fell earlier and hit the pavement. "Hold it there, okay?"

"Okay," I whisper, tears welling in my eyes at his kindness.

I gaze up at the older man, his face etched with deep lines and wisdom. His eyes, a gentle shade of brown, reflect his genuine kindness. I'm grateful he found me. Otherwise, I'm not so sure I would have made it.

Gabe's fingers graze lightly over my ribs on my left side, and I hear him suck in a sharp breath.

"Fuckers!" he swears.

With a loud bang, my front door bursts open, startling me. Gabe's gentle touch steadies and grounds me in the moment.

"It's okay, it's just Nesrin."

"Holy shit! What happened?" Nesrin rushes in, followed by a very large male, his shoulders almost taking up the width of the door. His eyes, a captivating shade of deep green, survey every corner of my apartment before connecting with mine.

I immediately avert my gaze, avoiding the piercing intensity in his eyes. Nesrin pushes past Gabe and Merve, making her way to my side. Gabe moves to stand, but I reach my hand out, quickly grabbing his arm.

"Stay," I beg.

I need his comfort and reassurance. Gabe nods and settles next to me with Nesrin. I look at her and gasp as her eyes light up. They are no longer a warm amber color, but pure white orbs. Static crackles along her skin and she removes the towel and places her warm hands on my wound. My eyes are glued to her as I sense my body tugging, the muscles and skin seeming to be weaving back together. Then her hand moves up, landing on my ribs without hesitation or warning. I draw in a breath as I feel my pain recede and my breathing becomes easier. I can feel my bones fusing back together. Like a curious explorer, a gentle warmth moves through my body, leaving a trail of comfort in its wake. Nesrin leans closer, her hands gently cradling my face, her touch warm against my skin as she glances down at me with a soft smile.

"There. Like new again." She exhales, falling back on her haunches.

I reach my hand up, feeling the smooth texture of my skin. The swelling on my cheek has faded, and overall? I feel refreshed and rejuvenated. Inhaling deeply, I am met with a blissful absence of pain.

"How?" I whisper.

Nesrin has to be a witch, like me. I stare at her, my eyes wide, my mouth hanging open. Then I'm scrambling to sit up. My dress falls open, but modesty is the least of my concerns right now. When Nesrin's eyes land on the mark just above my hip bone, she gasps audibly, her gaze swiftly returning to meet mine.

Gabe curses under his breath, positioning himself in front of Nesrin, as if shielding her from harm. From me. My chest fills with hurt as uncertainty swirls inside me.

"You're a hunter?" In a swift motion, the man with the piercing green eyes steps forward and pulls Nesrin up, positioning her behind him despite her protests. Frowning, I look down at the mark Kirk and my father branded me with. The mark of the hunters was seared onto my flesh, becoming a permanent scar. They pinned me down while they did it, Kirk muffling my screams with his hand. Unlike everyone else who got it tattooed on their arm, mine was burned into my flesh. I remember the excruciating pain, the smell. It was absolutely horrendous.

I remember them saying that I would never find contentment. That I would never be one of them, and this mark would make me a traitor to others who would think to take me in. That I wouldn't be a part of either world.

I never understood what they meant.

Not until now.

I know the hunter's clan are ruthless and hunt magical creatures, with no exception. They are a source of fear for everyone in the magical community. The weight of the realization leaves me breathless. I am in a room of magical creatures: the glowing eyes, the speed, the strength, and the healing. *I haven't been imagining it all.*

In front of me, Gabe crouches down, his eyes level with mine. "Tell me you're not a hunter, Sara?" His voice is pleading.

My hand extends toward him, but he flinches, causing me to abruptly pull back. His reaction stings, and I instinctively tuck my hand into my chest, desperately trying to protect myself from further emotional harm.

"No, I'm not a hunter. I swear."

"Then how did you get that mark?" Green-eyes asks sternly.

"My father and ex-husband did this to me. They held me down and marked me with their symbol. Calling me a traitor, saying I'd never find peace. I never understood their hatred for me until tonight," my voice trails to a whisper.

"Your father is a hunter but you're not?" he challenges.

And I don't like it, I immediately find my fire, and shake my head. "I will never be like him. He is a monster!" I snarl.

To his credit, the big guy just blinks slowly at me, then moves his gaze to Gabe. "This is the first time you're seeing this mark?"

I blush and once again, my mouth runs away with me. "We've only been naked together once!" I snap. "Not that it's any of your business."

Those green eyes flicker yellow as they swing back to me, and I swallow over the sudden lump in my throat.

Gabe takes a seat next to me. "It's okay, Sara, I believe you. I need you to tell us what happened. Who did this to you?"

"I killed him," I blurt, my anger fading.

The weight of my actions settles heavily on my conscience. I killed Kirk and my father. Well, the man who wasn't really my father. I'm a murderer. I have to leave. They will come after me, they'll take Tyler. Hysteria bubbles up, and I frantically look around.

"Who?" Nesrin's voice, so calm and steady, is a stark contrast to the inner turmoil I am experiencing. Without me noticing, she has swiftly maneuvered past the men and positioned herself in front of me.

"My father. No, not my father. The person who I believed was my father was not my actual biological parent." As I found out tonight. "Why did he keep me around? Why not send me away?" I'm upset by the wobble in my voice, and I'm rambling. I'm not upset I killed him. He deserved it and more. I'm upset this keeps happening to me. What have I ever done to deserve such pain and misery?

Everyone in the room wears a mixture of expressions, shock, anger, and disbelief.

"Mom?" Tyler's voice sounds from the hall.

I jump up, scramble over the top of the sofa, and wrap my arms around him. I hold him tightly, squeezing him against my chest.

"Mom, what happened? You're covered in blood."

"I'm fine. I'm not hurt, but I need you to pack your stuff now, only what you need. We need to leave."

Confusion fills his face as he takes a step back, and determination coats his next word, "No."

I can't do this now. He has to listen. "We need to go, Tyler. Now."

"No, I want to stay here. I want to stay with Gabe. Gabe will protect us!" he yells, turning and running to his room, slamming the door behind him.

My heart sinks staring at Tyler's closed door. I suddenly feel a comforting warmth on my shoulder—a touch that can only belong to Gabe. "Sara, just take a seat and tell us what's going on. We can help."

My mind races like a speeding train as Gabe leads me back to the familiar comfort of the sofa. It is at this moment that I notice Merve's absence from the room. My gaze goes to the large man who is leaning against the wall with his arms crossed over his chest, a thoughtful look on his face.

Gabe notices me staring. "Sara, this is my good friend Lukas."

"My husband," Nesrin chimes in.

Lukas's mouth twitches, a mix of affection and adoration evident in his eyes as he looks at his wife. That is something I can never have. I'll never be free. I notice that my dress is still undone, and quickly fumble to button it up, my cheeks turning red with embarrassment. As soon as I'm done, I notice the expectant looks on everyone's faces.

Right . . .

"Tonight was quiet. The rain had kept everyone away, so I was closing up early. I told Bill to leave and that I would be fine to finish up. I had to take the trash out, and as I walked through the alley behind the diner, I was cornered by my father and one of his men. There was an . . . altercation. I killed him, and the other ran." I bring my eyes up and look at Gabe. "I've been on the run for two years now. This is the first time they have found me."

How did they find me?

My knee starts bouncing as my mind races over everything. I killed another man. Sitting beside me on the sofa, Nesrin places her hand on my leg, silently conveying her support. "Why are you running?"

I'm hesitant to reveal too much, but I don't care anymore, I'm tired. "I killed my husband."

The silence is so profound that I almost wish I didn't say anything.

"It wasn't her fault. My dad didn't love us. He hated us, just like Grandpa. He tried to hurt me, and Mom was protecting me," Tyler's voice cuts through the silence.

Spinning in my seat, I see Tyler standing in the doorway, tears streaming down his face.

"Tyler, baby?" I choke out as tears fill my eyes at his distress.

Rising to my feet, my muscles coil with tension as I begin to approach him. Instead of embracing me, Tyler positions himself in front of me, as if shielding me from the rest of the room. My heart thuds painfully as his little voice rings out, "I won't let you hurt her, she has been hurt enough."

Tears flow freely down my face as I tightly embrace him from behind, pulling him into my body. "Tyler, it's okay," I whisper into his mess of shaggy brown hair.

I lift my gaze from my boy to study the expressions on the faces of the other people in the room. Tears well up in Nesrin's eyes, and she instinctively places her hand over her mouth, as if desperately trying to suppress her emotions. Lukas remains completely motionless; his face devoid of any hint of emotion. Gabe's eyes bore into us, a mix of sadness and fury etched across his face. As before, his eyes are aglow with the unmistakable shimmer of magic.

With determination in his eyes, Gabe strides over to us and crouches down, meeting Tyler eye to eye. "Remember that night at my house when I swore to you I would protect the two of you? I would never hurt your mom, Tyler." Then looking up at me, those brown eyes soften further, making my stomach dip. "I love her."

My heart soars and my eyes widen in surprise, and then I feel like I'm free falling. *He loves me?*

Tyler breaks free from my grasp, lunging for Gabe. Without hesitation, Gabe catches him, his powerful arms wrapping around my son in a firm hug. I bring my hands to my face, trying to hide the evidence of my tears.

Could he really love me? I am marked as an enemy. I have killed people.

"You mean it?" Tyler's voice asks meekly.

I steal a quick glance through my fingers, meeting Gabe's eyes for a fleeting moment before he redirects his focus to my son. "I mean it. I love you, too, Tyler. I won't let anything happen to either of you," Gabe promises.

Letting go of Tyler, he rises to his feet and steps in front of me. Reaching up, he grabs my wrists, moving my hands away from my face. Gently, he cups my cheek, guiding my eyes to meet his. As his thumbs caress my face, I feel my tears being tenderly brushed away, leaving behind a sense of warmth and affection.

"I love you, Sara. I think I've loved you the moment you stormed out of the diner, eyes full of motherly fury, and confronted me."

My laughter catches in my throat, and I quickly reach up, gripping onto his wrists tightly, seeking some form of anchor. "You don't hate me?"

Resting his forehead against mine, he shakes his head, his breath warm against my skin. "I could never hate you."

Warmth bursts through my chest. "I love you, too," I breathe against his lips.

Pressing his lips more fully against mine, he kisses me, and my heart swells. I wrap my arms around his neck, returning his kiss. His arms go around my back, squeezing me tightly against him. As we break apart, I become aware of the curious eyes watching us.

"Sorry," I mumble, looking at the ground, letting my hair cover my face.

"Don't apologize. That was the sweetest shit I've seen in months." Nesrin smirks at us, her arms crossed over her chest. I can't help but let out a slightly choked laugh.

"So, what's next?"

Lukas pushes off the wall and comes to stand closer. "We need you to start from the beginning and tell us everything."

Nesrin moves into my line of sight, blocking Lukas from me. She tilts her head, her eyes assessing me.

"You're a witch, aren't you?"

Her words hit me like a lightning bolt, causing me to instinctively take a step back. With my father's confession, I know I am, but how did she guess?

"That's why they hate you so much," she continues. My brain recalls her glowing eyes and the healing. I don't know how I forgot, except that the last hour has been full of so many revelations.

"Yes, my father admitted as much."

"Is that how you . . . " Nesrin trails off.

Gabe and Lukas stand off to the side, their eyes fixed on our interaction. I have a feeling Lukas still doesn't trust me. And why would he? I have the mark of the hunter on my body. Even though I wasn't allowed to truly be one of them, I was raised by them.

"Yes, I used my magic, though I didn't do it knowingly. I was somehow able to lift my so-called father up with wind and send him flying into a brick wall. Magic only manifests unintentionally for me during moments of extreme danger. It feels as though my actions are driven by an involuntary defense mechanism that I have no power over. It's unpredictable."

Nesrin nods. "That makes sense, you weren't brought up to learn and nurture your magical side. It's understandable it appears during times of stress. You said you killed your husband. Was that the first time you used your magic?"

I'm surprised by the bluntness of her question, but I know deep down she only wants to help me. "I don't think so. I used it twice before then as well, but I don't remember the first time very well. I was young. I thought it was a dream."

"Can you tell us what happened when you escaped?" I understand the unspoken words. *When I killed Kirk.*

I look at Tyler. "You should go back to bed, Tyler."

I don't want him to relive that night two years ago.

Tyler shakes his head, his eyes narrowing. "I'm staying, mom."

I go to argue, but Gabe's gentle touch on my arm silences me. "Let him stay."

"I don't want him to hear this," I argue, narrowing my eyes. Yes, he knows, to some extent, what I endured, but not all of it.

"Mom, please. I need to know, too," Tyler begs, his little shoulders pulling back.

"Are you sure, Tyler?"

He nods, taking a seat in front of the sofa on the floor, pulling a pillow onto his lap. Okay, then.

I can't do this seated, so I make my way to the window. Pulling the curtain aside, I peek out, keeping my focus on the parking lot outside as I begin this story.

"I have a vivid memory of when I was six. The image of my mother that day is crystal clear in my mind. Maybe because it's the last time I ever saw her, but whatever the reason, I remember her getting ready to leave on a mission. She was nervous. She tried her best to hide it, but I could tell she was worried. It appears she had a valid cause for concern. Her team was ambushed, and she lost her life in the attack. The news of her death devastated me, shattering my heart into a million pieces." I pause, taking a breath. My voice drops lower. "My mom was my protector, the only one who ever talked to me, wiped my tears, and even fed me. My father never once looked at me or spoke to me, his demeanor was always cold and distant. I was basically invisible, but when my mother died, that changed. His attention that I had craved so much became a nightmare, and I hid myself away to avoid it."

A lump forms in my throat, and pressure bears down on my chest as I force myself to swallow. "As soon as she was gone, he started lashing out at me. Without my mother to play interference, I was fair game. I wasn't allowed to talk, eat, or be seen. If I disobeyed, I would be punished. I knew he wanted me gone. He hated me so much, and I never understood why. For a long time, I prayed for death so I could once again be with my mother."

I hear Nesrin's intake of breath behind me.

"That was, until Mallory showed up when I was around ten. Without her, I would not be here today. I'm sure of it. She selflessly gifted me clothes that no longer fit her, ensuring I had something to wear. Among the clan, she was the sole person who showed me kindness. It infuriated her to witness the mistreatment I suffered. We'd fantasize about the world and plan to run away together. Then one day, my father came to me saying I wasn't his problem anymore, and I was going to marry Kirk. His most ruthless hunter."

My voice drops to a whisper. "I was only seventeen. I knew nothing of men or marriage."

A low, guttural growl fills the room, and I instinctively shut my eyes, aware that it is Gabe and that my words are causing him pain.

"The idea of escaping my father's cruelty filled me with a glimmer of hope, like a tiny bud ready to bloom. I was stupid and naïve. I went from one viper's nest to another. Kirk was okay in the beginning. I thought maybe it wouldn't be so bad. I was wrong." I swallow over the tears. "It was nothing like our time together, he was rough, brutal. Then I fell pregnant, and some stupid part of me thought he would have been happy, that maybe having his baby would somehow make him love me." I shudder, taking a deep, shaky breath at the memories that come flooding back, so sharp and clear.

I feel a warm, very large hand land on my shoulder, squeezing in comfort just for a second. With a slight turn of my head, our eyes meet, and a brief but meaningful exchange passes between Lukas and me. The unexpected comfort he's offering takes me aback. Throughout the night, he has kept his emotions hidden behind a cool and distant facade. But now, his eyes seem to soften and ask. *Are you okay?*

I give him a watery smile, feeling a lump forming in my throat, and quickly look back out the window.

Clearing my throat, I continue, "That night, when he found out I was pregnant? He tried to kill me," I whisper hoarsely.

I can feel my body shaking, but I can't stop it. Tyler barrels into the back of me, his arms hugging me tightly around my waist. I reach behind, wrapping an arm around him. I didn't want him to hear this, but he has to know he wasn't the one everyone hated. It was me.

"He got a few hits in, but things got hazy after that. Somehow, he ended up unconscious on the floor, and I ran to Mal. We made plans that night to get me out, but I wanted to go back to the house and get some of my mother's stuff. When I got there, he was awake, and my father was there. I was trapped, like a caged animal, within the walls of my own house. It took a whole year for me to be granted permission to venture outdoors again. Mal had to slip notes under my door." I let out a humorless laugh. "When Tyler was born, I always had a guard on me. The first chance I got to run was on Tyler's sixth birthday, two years ago. Tyler was upset Kirk forgot his birthday . . . " I trail off, not wanting to voice the next bit.

Memories come rushing back to me, each one filled with vivid details and intense emotions. My mind is filled with a symphony of screams, crashing sounds, and the haunting howl of the wind. Above it all, Tyler's desperate cries echo in my ears. And there, in front of me, lies Kirk's lifeless body, a sight that shakes me to my core.

Tyler looks up at me. "It was my fault. I got mad and started throwing things. I was so angry at him, then he hit me, and a crazy wind started. It was all my fault," he cries.

I bend down, taking his little face in my hands. "Tyler, you saved us. You got us out of there. You gave me the strength to fight," I say vehemently. "I stayed longer than I should have. I messed up and put you in danger. Despite knowing that we weren't loved, I stayed. I should have run the night I found out I was pregnant. I never should have gone back to the house. I was so, so stupid."

Regret washes over me as I realize that was exactly what I should have done on that fateful night when I learned I was carrying a child.

Suddenly, Gabe materializes by my side. "You weren't stupid, baby." He wraps both of us in his arms, and I slump into him, letting him take all my weight.

"Tonight was the first night I've seen any of them since the night we ran," I say into Gabe's chest.

Lukas pushes off the wall, bringing his phone to his ear. "Zee. Greta's Diner. Get there now. We need a clean-up. Send the patrol out. I want to know if there are hunters lurking in the area." He hangs up, turning to look back at me. His hard eyes soften slightly. "My pack will take care of it."

I let out a long exhale, my body sinking with relief. Gabe tugs me toward the cozy sofa, urging me to take a seat. Tyler sits next to me, his face red and blotchy. I wrap him in my arms, burying my face in his hair.

It isn't even five minutes before Lukas's phone rings, breaking the silence and catching me off guard.

"What? Okay, search the area. I'm staying here with Nesrin. Okay, thanks Zee." Hanging up, he looks to me.

Not enjoying his level of intensity, I cringe. "What?"

Running his hand through his hair, he curses under his breath, looking away. "There's nobody in the alley. Could he have been alive?"

"They must have come for him," I mutter. "I don't think he got up and walked away." That crack I heard when he hit the wall. No way was he walking away from that alive. "I can call Mal and find out what she knows."

All heads turn to me. "You're still in contact with her?" Nesrin's words are drenched in surprise.

I'm confused. Do they think that Mal betrayed me? She would never do that. She's my friend.

I straighten my spine, looking at each of them. "Yes, I talk to her every other week."

All three look at each other.

Lukas walks over and extends his arm, offering me his phone. "Call her. Put it on speaker."

"Okay," I mutter, my fingers trembling as I dial Mal's number.

"Hi, you've reached Mallory. Please leave a message, but only if you're awesome."

I look up at Lukas in question, should I leave a message? Reading me perfectly, he nods. "Hi, Mal, it's Sara. Call me back as soon as you can on this number."

I hand the phone back to Lukas, tucking Tyler into my side, my fingers running through his hair. We don't have to wait long. Lukas's phone lights up, and he answers, putting it on speaker on the coffee table. I open my mouth to answer, but don't get a chance to speak.

"Oh my god. Sara. Are you okay? I heard they found out where you are, but I didn't have your number to warn you. We didn't think that little detail through. Fuck, please tell me you're okay. Please tell me that you and Tyler are okay. That you're safe."

My relief is swift. I knew there was no way my friend would betray me.

"Mal," I choke out past the tears. It is so good to hear her voice, and my emotions surface hard and fast.

"Are you okay?" She sounds frantic. I need to get my shit together before she loses it.

Gabe's hand reaches over, squeezing mine, giving me the strength I need to answer her. "Yes. Yes, we are okay, Mal. I'm with Gabe and his friends."

"Oh, thank god. I was so scared."

"What have you heard? How did they find me?"

"Not much. I don't know how they tracked you down. Mike left earlier in the week. I knew something wasn't right. He was hiding something from me, so I followed. I saw him meet with your father and Sam and a couple of others. I heard them say your name. After they left, I followed them. But I lost them when they got to Portland. Where are you? I can meet you. Are you still in Portland?"

I open my mouth to answer, but before I can speak, Lukas interrupts, "That's not a good idea. We don't know you. I don't trust you. All you need to know is Sara and Tyler are safe, and we will keep them that way."

I glare at Lukas, then turn to Gabe, but his expression gives nothing away. Nesrin is anxiously chewing her lip, her eyes concentrating on the phone.

"She can be trusted," I assure them, feeling the need to defend my friend.

"Is this Gabe?"

To anyone else, Mal might sound normal, but I can hear the underlying hurt in her voice.

"No, this is Lukas Black, Alpha of the Pacific Northwest Pack in Portland. Sara and Tyler are under my full protection. She is family, and we protect our family here," Lukas growls, his voice deep and terrifying. His green eyes glow yellow around the edges, as power rolls through the room.

I inhale a sharp breath in disbelief, my eyes flaring with shock. I see Nesrin move to his side, her slender arms wrapping around his waist as he pulls her closer. My jaw drops, and I quickly glance back to Gabe for confirmation.

"Alpha?" I stammer.

My heart rate picks up. *The fucking alpha.*

I can hear Mal's breathing on the other end, but she is as speechless as I am. I hadn't actually asked any of them what they were yet. It felt rude to ask. For some reason, I thought all of them were like me. I have a feeling I'm going to be getting a few surprises soon.

"We need a photo of Sara's father. He isn't where she left him," Lukas adds when no one speaks.

"Sure, I'll send one now."

The phone dings a second later. Gabe steps closer, tilting his head.

"Do you hear that?" he asks no one in particular.

We all go silent, and Nesrin and Lukas growl in unison, their eyes flashing.

"They are tracing the call," Lukas explodes, the sound sending the hairs on my arms on end.

His words hit me like a punch in the gut, and I panic, frantically reaching for the phone and pressing the button to end the call. With my hands shaking uncontrollably, I become acutely aware of the heavy, audible breaths of those surrounding me. Gabe steps over to me, helping me stand. "Go pack some clothes, whatever you need. We need to leave now."

Chapter Twenty-Nine

GABE

"Fuck!" I growl.

This has been the longest night ever. I storm over to my bag in the corner, only just realizing I'm still not wearing a shirt. What a fucking mess.

Sara doesn't deserve any of this, neither does Tyler. I want to tear all those hunters apart for what they did to her, the way they treated her, for something that wasn't her fault. She is half human, half witch. I didn't expect that. I really wasn't prepared to see the hunter's mark on her, either. It knocked the breath from me when I saw it. My heart sank so deep I wasn't sure if I'd survive hearing the truth from her.

I pull the shirt over my head, feeling the fabric settle against my skin as I turn to see Lukas and Nesrin both focused on the phone in front of them. Their expressions are tight, and a tension fills the air that sets my nerves on edge. My steps are deliberate as I close the distance between us, my hand already extended toward Lukas.

"Let me see the man I need to kill, if he isn't already dead." My voice is low, steady, but the edge of menace is unmistakable.

Lukas hesitates, his eyes meeting mine for just a second, but it's enough to trigger the frustration simmering in my chest. A low growl rumbles from deep within my throat. But the instant I hear it, I taper the growl back. Lukas is my alpha. I will never challenge him. Never.

His eyes flash, a clear warning in them that makes my pulse quicken. My gaze immediately lowers, my head dipping in deference as instinct takes over. My neck is exposed to him, a gesture of submission, and though it's automatic, it doesn't sit easily. The primal part of me rebels against being kept in check, but my loyalty to Lukas is absolute.

With a deep sigh, Lukas reluctantly passes me the phone, his hesitation clear. The weight of what I'm about to see presses down on me like an invisible hand around my throat. My fingers close around the phone, and as my gaze drops to the screen, my world suddenly narrows, tilts, and collapses in on itself.

The image staring back at me is like a blow to the chest, knocking the air from my lungs. My vision tunnels, the edges blurring as if the ground has disappeared beneath me. Then, out of nowhere, a sharp tone blares from the phone, jolting me like a live wire. Startled, I release my grip, the phone clattering to the floor as if it were burning hot.

The sounds around me fade into a distant murmur, muffled like I'm submerged underwater. It can't be. It just can't. But it is.

"Gabe! Gabe!" Nesrin's voice cuts through the fog, but she feels so far away, her words barely reach me. My heart pounds erratically, my mind spiraling back to a place I thought I'd buried deep—back to that horrifying day in the woods when I was just a child. The day my family was ripped away from me.

Everything around me spins violently, and I can't focus on anything. Nesrin's hands grip my shoulders, trying to anchor me, but I shake her off, staggering as I lock eyes with Lukas. My breath comes in short, shallow bursts, fury and despair warring inside me.

'It's him. He killed my family,' I whisper in his mind.

Lukas's expression falters for a brief moment, but then he rises to his full height, towering over me. A fierce, inhuman growl rumbles from his chest, the sound so primal and raw that it rattles the windows. His anger is palpable, mirroring the storm brewing inside me.

"What is happening right now?" Nesrin's voice is laced with worry and distress, her eyes darting between me and Lukas, searching for answers.

But I can't answer her. I can't explain the maelstrom of emotions threatening to consume me whole. My mind is trapped in the past, reliving the terror, the helplessness, the blood. My body feels disconnected, like I'm floating through a nightmare I can't wake up from.

I stumble toward the door, desperate for air, for anything to break the suffocating grip of the memories clawing at my mind.

Nesrin quickly steps in front of me, her hands firmly pushing on my shoulders. "Gabe, talk to me!" Her magic crackles through the room in response to mine.

"I can't." I try to push past her, but she holds her stance.

"Gabe, your mate needs you right now. You can't just leave!" Her words are harsh, her white eyes blazing.

I stare into her wide eyes, trying to comprehend what she just said.

I blink. "Mate?" I stammer.

Nesrin shakes my shoulders, and I can feel her irritation radiating through her touch. "Yes. I was wondering when you'd notice, but you're taking too long. She is your mate. From the moment we spotted her hiking in the woods, I could tell there was a shift in you. The connection between your souls and magic is already strong. You chose her, and her soul accepted."

I recall the day vividly, and the way Nesrin gave me a strange, lingering gaze. It was as if she knew something I didn't, but I dismissed it as nothing. Nesrin is known for her odd quirks.

Desperate to escape the suffocating confines of this apartment, I shake my head vigorously. The apartment feels suffocatingly small, as if the walls are closing in.

"Nesrin, let him go," Lukas urges, making her head snap toward him.

The sound of Sara's hurried footsteps fills the hall, her suitcase scraping against the floor with each step. My anger resurfaces, feeling like a volcano about to erupt, as I realize her entire life is reduced to a mere fucking suitcase. That man robbed her of a complete life, leaving her with a childhood void of the happy moments that should have filled it. Constantly looking over her shoulder, ready to run at any given moment. I won't let her live like that any longer.

"Gabe, what's wrong? Why is everyone yelling?" she questions, seeing my face.

She takes a step toward me, but I abruptly raise my hand, halting her in her tracks. I shake my head, hoping to dispel the scattered thoughts swirling inside my head.

I need to go.

"I have to go." My voice sounds strange to my own ears.

Lukas nods. "I've got them."

"Wait!" Sara cries, running for me, but I'm already gone.

Adrenaline courses through me, heightening my reflexes and sharpening my instincts. Magic infuses every inch of my body as I shift, leaping down the stairs. Lukas will do what needs to be done. He will get them to the pack house where they'll be safe.

I need some space so I don't do something I'll regret forever.

I run blindly in the direction of home, memories of that fateful night flooding my vision like a torrential downpour. A deep ache throbs relentlessly in my chest, a visceral manifestation of the regret and helplessness that gnaws at my soul when I think about my parents. I can almost feel the weight of it, pressing against my ribs, as if trying to crush my spirit.

I vividly recall the overwhelming feeling of powerlessness that washed over me like a tidal wave when the cruel reality set in—I couldn't save them. All I could do was stay hidden, keep myself safe, no matter the cost.

It was days since we'd started running in hopes of outwitting our pursuers amidst the labyrinthine forest. However, because I was still young, my magic hadn't fully manifested, preventing me from shifting with my parents. Not only that, but the previous night, under the cloak of darkness, my father had fought off a couple of hunters, suffering injuries in the process. The memory of his fierce determination lingers, mingling with the scent of blood that clung to the air, a bitter reminder of the dangers that followed us.

Realizing that we couldn't outrun the situation, my father urged my mother to take me and escape. He made the decision to sacrifice himself so that we might safely get away. I will always remember the intense fury reflected in my mother's dark, nearly ebony eyes. The depth of her love for my father made it impossible for her to walk away. They stood together, always. So instead, they concealed me within the hollowed-out trunk of a scorched tree, ensuring my safety. Cautiously, I scaled up the tree, staying hidden, while my parents erased any evidence of my presence. I climbed until the darkness enveloped me, but a sliver of light seeped through a minuscule opening, which allowed me to cautiously peer outside. From that vantage point, I witnessed the heart-wrenching sight of my parents desperately pleading for their lives. Fear gripped my chest as the three hunters encircled them. The leader, who I now know was Sara's captor, cruelly reveled in my parents' desperate pleas for mercy. A palpable aura of pure hatred emanated from all of them. The intensity of that hatred was beyond my comprehension. Until now.

Fire burns hot in my blood, demanding retribution for what he had done.

The shimmering silver net he ensnared them with crackled with a faint electric hum, draining what little magic they possessed.

However, their pleas fell upon deaf ears that fateful day. My parents, though weakened by the silver's touch, tapped into their dwindling reserves of magic to ensure my concealment. The kitsune possess the uncanny ability to manipulate minds and create illusions, though the strength of this power varies between individuals.

That man ruthlessly took the lives of my parents, their crimson blood carelessly scattered across the forest floor. Their anguished cries echoed in my ears, forever etching them into my memory. From my hiding spot, I could see the flickering flames as they set the bodies of my parents alight before departing, leaving behind a haunting scene.

It is a memory that forever haunts me, leaving a lasting imprint on my soul.

Chapter Thirty

SARA

I'm frozen to the spot, my hand gripping the front door, as I stare out into the darkness where Gabe disappeared. Gabe, who I just watched turn into a fox. The fox we saw in the woods. I'm sure of it. I sense someone approaching, and Nesrin comes to stand beside me.

"Gabe will be back. He will meet us at the pack house." Sympathy laces her words.

I let go of the door and face her. "What happened?"

Nesrin turns to Lukas, her gaze begging for understanding. I want to know what happened while I was packing. I was only gone for five minutes.

"You need to grab your stuff, now," Lukas says instead of answering my question.

Anger surges through me, disregarding the fact that he is the alpha. I want to understand the reason behind Gabe's sudden departure. Why he looked so haunted . . .

"No, damn it! Tell me why Gabe left? Why did he look so upset?" my voice cracks with emotion, and I hate it.

Nesrin looks at me with a hint of sadness in her eyes, gently placing a hand on my arm. "It's not our place." She turns for the hall. "Come on, I'll help you get your things."

I want to unleash my rage and let out a piercing scream, but I hold myself back, knowing I am better than that. Reluctantly, I follow the sound of my footsteps echoing through the room as we hastily pack the last of my belongings into the bags. I glance down and grimace at the sight before me. Two suitcases now hold the entirety of my existence, an improvement on the single one I had when I first started running.

With a heavy heart, we make our way back into the front room. Tyler's bags stand by the door, waiting to be taken. Lukas effortlessly gathers all of Tyler's belongings and moves toward the door, his footsteps steady and determined. The heavy silence hangs in the air like a suffocating blanket as we descend the stairs. Waiting for us outside is Lukas's massive black dual-cab Ford F150, its engine idling softly, filling the air with a low rumble. Lukas places Tyler's bags in the tray with a thud, and reaches for mine. I hand them over as a crisp breeze sweeps over the parking lot, cooling my anger somewhat.

"Where is Gabe?" Tyler asks timidly, looking at each of us.

Nesrin answers, "He has gone ahead to let the others know what's happening. He will meet us at my house."

"Your house?" I inquire.

"Yes."

"You're a witch, too?" I don't want to assume, but I have a feeling Lukas's pack isn't the normal pack.

Nesrin looks back at me and pauses before speaking. "Kind of, yeah."

"But you're married. I mean, mated to the alpha?"

A dreamy smile spreads across her face, making her eyes sparkle. "Yes, we are. I'm a hybrid. Like you, only I'm half shifter."

"You were the white wolf," I say with awe. That had to be Nesrin.

"She's much more than that, she's just modest, but we can fill you in later. We need to leave." Lukas ushers us along.

"Don't listen to him. But yes, that was me."

Lukas opens the door for Nesrin. "We need to move now," he demands, helping her into the car.

The urgency in his voice makes my pulse race. Can he sense something? I open the back door, helping Tyler in.

The car ride is silent, each of us lost in our own thoughts. My nerves start to kick in, and Tyler, with his observant eyes, notices the tremble in my hands. Reaching over, he interlaces his fingers with mine, filling my heart with tenderness. When I glance down at our hands, I realize I'm still in my torn work uniform, stained with dirt and blood. In the midst of my panic, changing slipped my mind. I'll make sure to clean up as soon as I have the opportunity.

Nesrin and Lukas share a look in the front seat. The fact that I'm in a car with the alpha of one of the largest packs in the country, on our way to his house, should fill me with fear. Surprisingly, though, I feel calm. Nervous, yes. Scared, no. Unlike other hunters, I was never raised to harbor hatred toward magical creatures. I wasn't raised to think anything of much really. That would've required them to care what I thought, outside of knowing how much they *didn't* care about me.

The drive takes us past Gabe's property, and further down toward the river. Lukas and Nesrin's house is a sprawling masterpiece, with intricate architecture and elegant details. As we approach the house, I marvel at its distinctive design. A large sweeping staircase leads up to a wrap-around porch with large windows. The house itself is two stories with what looks like enough space for an attic or loft at the very top.

Lukas stops the truck, and we all climb out, making our way inside. As Nesrin shows me to a cozy room where Tyler and I will be staying, the soft scent of fresh linens fills the air.

It is well past midnight when I finally have a moment to shower. Tyler is fast asleep, which is surprising. The steam from the shower fills the room, and I go about washing off the evidence of the night. I slip into a pair of comfortable jeans and throw on a cozy, lightweight sweater. There is no way I can even attempt to sleep, so I make my way down the stairs and into the kitchen. Nesrin and Lukas turn their heads my way as soon as I enter.

"Coffee?" Nesrin offers.

"Yes, please."

Nesrin nods. "I just need to go to the bathroom, then I will make you the best coffee you've ever had."

"Okay. Thank you."

With a heavy sigh, I sink into the chair at the kitchen table, the anticipation of seeing Gabe making me feel on edge. *Where is he?*

Lukas's phone rings, breaking the silence, and he quickly answers. I watch as he paces the room, his voice barely audible as he speaks with whoever it is on the other end in a hush tone. Hanging up, he puts the phone down, then places both hands on the counter. Leaning over, he hangs his head, his face hidden by a curtain of dark hair. He looks like he has the weight of the world on his shoulders.

"Thank you for helping me," I whisper, guilt slithering into my heart.

Looking up, his stormy green eyes meet mine. "I meant what I said, Sara. You and Tyler are family now. You are under my protection."

"I don't understand."

"You are important to Gabe. That makes you important to us. Nesrin loves you already. In this pack, we are all family, so with a bunch of new brothers and sisters at your back, if you need anything, you call one of us. Okay?"

I'm so overwhelmed with emotions that all I can do is nod. Lukas's eyes glaze over for a second, and he excuses himself. Being left alone in my own thoughts may not be the best thing; the silence feels suffocating. My heart feels heavy as sadness swells within me, like a living creature ready to overpower me. I feel a pulsating ache in my chest, as if it's being crushed by the weight of hurt, loss, and regret.

I blink away my thoughts, my eyes fixed on Lukas's phone resting on the counter. I quickly spin to view the empty space he disappeared through, my heart racing. Getting up, I reach out and grab the phone, its surface smooth against my fingertips before it slips into my pocket. I walk to the back door on the other side of the kitchen. Carefully, I twist the knob, my senses heightened as I strain to catch any sound of an approaching presence. Nothing. Holding my breath, I slip out the door, the cool breeze brushing against my face. I take a shaky breath and retrieve the phone, fingers trembling as I search for Mal's number and hit call. Just as my feet hit the last step, on the third ring, she answers the phone.

"Mal?"

"God, Sara. What's happening?"

"I love him," I gasp out over a sob that has been building in my chest. I rub at the throbbing pain, trying to soothe the ache. I miss Gabe, his absence has left a void within me.

"Oh, hun, I know you do."

"Mal, he took one look at me tonight, pathetic and damaged on those steps and he leaped down them like a superhero. He scooped me into his arms, and he held me like I would break. He didn't hesitate."

There's silence on the other end. If it wasn't for her breathing, I would have thought she'd hung up. "Mal?"

"You really love him?" she breathes, her own emotions getting the better of her.

"Yes."

"I'm so happy for you."

I can feel the weight of worry pressing down on me, suffocating and relentless. I don't know where he is. The others said he was meeting us here, but he's not here. "He disappeared. I don't know where he is, Mal."

"What the–" Mal stammers, shock and surprise coating her voice.

There's a commotion on Mal's end.

"Mal?"

I hear a grunt and the sound of flesh hitting flesh.

"How could you? You betrayed me!" Mal cries, though it sounds muffled.

"Mal?" I whisper harshly, desperate for her to answer me and tell me she's okay. Who is there with her?

I can only just make out another voice.

"Fuck you!!!" Mal screams.

Another thud resonates through the phone, accompanied by a low groan. My stomach sinks, and waves of nausea wash over me. My friend needs help, and I'm unable to do anything.

I hear the phone being picked up. "Sara?" the deep male voice says.

"Yes," I growl.

"Ah, the voice of the woman who has corrupted my girlfriend." His tone is filled with disdain.

My heart turns to ice, and a fiery hatred courses through my veins. "You hurt her," I snarl. It isn't a question, it's a statement.

"Irrelevant. Listen, we have your lover boy here, and are willing to trade. You for him."

Before I can respond, Mal growls, "Sara, don't you do it!"

"Shut the fuck up!" Another thud sounds and Mal falls silent.

My hands shake uncontrollably as my vision swarms with flickering light.

He is going to pay for this. No one hurts the people I love, ever. I need to face my past, accept who I am. I'm half witch. I am stronger than I was before. The old me would have cried and begged, but she's gone. I killed her when I killed Kirk. I am a survivor, my resolve burning bright. I have to be stronger for Tyler, Gabe, and Mal. My determination strengthens, and the air crackles with urgency, filled with the sound of my resolute breaths. I am prepared to confront the past head-on. I feel a surge of strength, ready to rise above the pain, and refuse to be weighed down any longer.

I grit my teeth. "Where?"

Mike's soft chuckle resonates through the phone. "Knew you'd see reason."

"Just tell me."

"Down at the wharf. We are in an abandoned ship on the east side near the lookout."

I hang up without saying a word and look around the endless backyard. I should tell someone what's just happened. They would help, I know they would, but I can't put any more people in danger. I need to do this alone.

I put Lukas's phone in my back pocket and make my way over to his truck. No, that would create too much noise. *Shit . . .*

Frantically, I scan the area, my heart pounding as my eyes dart around in search of a means of escape. Suddenly, a glimmer catches-es my attention, drawing my gaze toward a compact hatchback nestled next to the barn. Its polished surface gleams under the moonlight, casting a mesmerizing reflection. Determined, I quicken my pace, the sound of my hurried footsteps blending with the rustling of leaves as the wind picks up. I reach the vehicle, and a surge of adrenaline courses through me, fueling my urgency. With agile movements, I climb into the driver's seat, the smooth leather embracing my body.

"Please, please let the keys be here somewhere," I mutter to myself.

I reach out, my fingers blindly searching for the keys. Grabbing the visor, I instinctively pull it down, the sound of the hinges creaking in the silence. A set of keys falls into my lap, their weight pressing against my thighs.

"Yes!" I hiss, the urgency evident in my voice.

With trembling hands, I fumble to insert the keys into the ignition, silently pleading for the car to start, while desperately wishing that nobody will come searching for me in this moment. The car starts immediately, the engine's roar breaking through the stillness, and I send a quick thank you to whoever is listening. I speed down the driveway, the rush of adrenaline coursing through my veins. Only once do I glance back, feeling a mix of guilt and determination. I hope Tyler will forgive me, that he'll understand I need to end this.

Chapter Thirty-One

SARA

The salty scent of the ocean hits my nose as I get out of the car at the wharf. I can't see anyone, at least not yet. Slowly, I make my way into the harbor, and feel the first drops of rain hit my face. Lightning flashes in the distance. I've always loved rainstorms. They always seem to pick me up when I'm down, giving me strength, making me feel alive. Maybe it's the raw, uncontrollable power that I'm drawn to. I'm not sure, but I know I can draw strength from the storm.

As I approach the ships, a heavy weight settles on my chest, constricting my breath. The air is thick with anticipation, every step increasing the pressure. I know I can't rely on my magic this time; it's too unpredictable, and I don't have the slightest clue how to summon it. In order to save Gabe and Mal, I have to make a trade, and then find a way to escape.

Drawing closer to the ships, the one Mike described materializes before me, its presence growing more imposing. The sight of its towering figure sends a shiver down my spine, not made easier by the knowledge that I can't swim.

The sound of shuffling footsteps draws my attention to my surroundings. Fear heightens my senses, and my breathing accelerates. Out of the dark, several dark figures emerge, creating an eerie atmosphere. The tension in my muscles grows as I clench my hands at my sides, ready for whatever may come. Turning slowly, my gaze sweeps across the crowd, searching for a familiar face amidst the sea of strangers. The scent of anticipation hangs in the air, mixing with the faint aroma of the ocean.

Finally, my eyes lock onto Sam, a mix of anger and frustration flickering across my face as I bare my teeth at him. But before I can fully process his presence, a new figure comes from the shadows, stepping forward with purpose. He stands tall and lean, his imposing frame casting a shadow over the scene. His face, chiseled and emotionless, reveals nothing of his intentions.

In a deep, commanding voice, he speaks, his words echoing through the air. "Glad you could make it, Sara. Your father will be happy to see you." With each word, my heart skips a beat or two, the weight of his statement sinking in.

"He's alive?" My disbelief is clear as I blink the rain from my eyelashes.

A feral grin spreads across his face, and the sound of laughter fills the air. "Yes, and he is very eager to see you. He has something extra special planned for you."

A flash of lightning suddenly illuminates the area, revealing several daggers, gleaming and ready for action.

"You promised to release Gabe and Mallory if I showed up," I remind him. "I won't go with you unless I see them set free, alive." My voice remains surprisingly steady and resolute, despite the fact that I feel neither of those things right now.

"What makes you think you have any say in how this will go?" the leader's voice cuts through the sound of the rain as he raises it to be heard.

Just as I am about to respond, he gives a signal to the men surrounding me. In response, one of them swiftly rushes forward, attempting to grab hold of me. Acting quickly, I duck under his arm and twist around, feeling the rush of wind against my face.

My eyes quickly scan the group of men, and I realize with a sinking feeling that I am severely outnumbered. Just as I process this, another figure separates from the group and charges at me, their dagger ominously glinting in their hand. On instinct, I step away from their attack, my heart pounding in my chest. But in my evasive movements, I stumble sideways, unintentionally bringing myself closer to the rest of the group.

Taking a deep breath in through my nose and exhaling through my mouth, I focus on controlling my breath while skillfully avoiding several more attempts to grab hold of me.

I push away another swipe of an arm, feeling the force of it as it grazes past me. With quick reflexes, I block the follow-through hit, the impact reverberating through my arm. Somehow, my feet are taken out from beneath me. I grunt as my back hits the ground. I'm soaking wet now, my hair plastered to my face, but I waste no time jumping to my feet. Ignoring the pain shooting through my shoulder, I dodge another attack, this time knocking a shorter man to the ground. As his grip falters, the dagger slips from his fingers and hits the ground. I lunge forward to seize it, but a powerful blow sends me careening off course once more. A sharp pain shoots through my shoulder, causing me to let out a groan. I glance down, wincing at the gash there, blood flowing freely down my arm. My gaze zeroes in on the leader, and I feel a surge of adrenaline course through my veins, my hand trembling slightly as it covers the wound.

"Where are they?" I grind out, feeling the blood leaking through my fingers.

"Mal is taking a nap, and your lover isn't here. He never was."

His words slam into me, and I sag with relief. *Gabe isn't here. He is safe.* This is a trap, of course, and I am totally screwed, but at least Gabe and Tyler are safe. I will try to get to Mal, and if luck is on our side, we will escape. I won't accept any other fate.

A kick lands to the back of my legs, and I fall down hard on my knees, water sleuthing down my face and body. My clothes are soaked through, and the cold is seeping in. I narrow my eyes and fix a piercing stare on the men standing around me.

"You can all go to hell," I growl, proud of how fierce I sound. That timid little girl is gone. I will not revert back to her. I'm determined to stand tall and confront whatever challenges come my way.

"Where's your magic now?" he taunts, his voice dripping with sarcasm.

All around me, the air is filled with taunting and cruel laughter. Undeterred, I grit my teeth, feeling the tension radiate through my clenched jaw. I hold my tongue, refusing to let myself be provoked by their taunts. As I lock eyes with the leader, his gaze is filled with an unsettling malice, making me question my next move.

"Get her inside," he growls at the men, his tone filled with a commanding authority.

Two of the men come toward me, but I won't make it simple for them. Recalling my self-defense training, I quickly maneuver, spinning to the side while lifting my leg in a powerful kick that connects with one of their stomachs. He doubles over in pain, but the second man charges at me. The moment he tackles me, his sheer strength overwhelms me, pinning me to the ground and stealing my ability to breathe.

"You're wasting time," a male voice says from above.

"Fuck off!" I wheeze out, struggling to push the guy off me.

With a well-placed knee to the groin, he grunts and loosens his grip, allowing a chance to kick out forcefully this time. I scramble backward, but the others are already there, waiting and moving forward, grabbing my arms and hauling me up. I bite my lip to stifle the cry of pain shooting through my shoulder as they roughly tug me toward the ship. Once inside, I'm dumped on the floor of what I believe to be the bridge deck. I locate Mal, unconscious and handcuffed to a desk on the opposite side of the room. I push myself to my feet, adrenaline coursing through my veins. My damn heart is pounding fiercely in my chest. I take a deep breath and begin to make my way over to her. But my progress is halted as Sam steps into the room with the leader of the men. I stop abruptly, feeling the tension in my jaw as I clench it tightly shut.

They wear smug smirks on their faces. As I look around, I realize that there are only two other men monitoring us.

"So, all this fuss over you. I thought you said she was dangerous, Sam."

Sam looks uncomfortable. "Don't let her fool you. She killed my brother and seriously injured the boss."

The man stands there, arms crossed and legs apart, studying me. "You and Mal thought you were so clever, thought we didn't know about your calls. But we knew."

I tilt my head, studying the man in front of me. He towers over everyone with his impressive height and strikingly dark features. His hair is meticulously shaven in a military cut, emphasizing his disciplined appearance. Despite his rough exterior, there's a surprisingly slight softness in his eyes when he looks toward Mal.

"You're Mal's boyfriend. Mike?" I gasp.

With a face as cold and hard as stone, his words echo with a biting harshness. "Yes, I was."

With every ounce of self-control, I resist the temptation to attack him, though my muscles are tense and ready to strike.

"You're a piece of work," I seethe, my voice dripping with anger.

Mal must be heartbroken. She believed Mike wasn't like the other hunters.

"Thank you," he replies as if I've given him a compliment. Then he turns, grabbing something from the desk behind him. Turning back to me, he throws me a first aid kit. "Patch yourself up. Can't have you bleeding out before the boss gets here."

Both of them turn, leaving me and Mal alone with two guards, one stationed at each exit. I drop the kit and run over to Mal, gasping when I see her face. Both her eyes are swollen, her face and neck coated with bruises. I can only imagine what she is going to look like under her clothes. Her short brown hair hangs loosely around her face.

"Mal. Mal, wake up." I give her a gentle shake, desperate to rouse her.

Grumbling something, she slowly opens her eyes, the once-vibrant blue now appearing dull. As soon as she realizes it's me, she jerks upright, her hands desperately pulling at the handcuffs.

"Sara, what are you doing? You can't be here." She's frantic as her eyes move around the room.

"It's okay, Mal. I've come to get you out of here."

"No, you need to go. I will be okay."

I shake my head. "I'm not leaving without you this time."

"But they will kill you!"

"They can try."

Her eyes widen as she looks at my arm, the color draining from her face at the sight of all the blood. "What happened? You're bleeding!"

Standing up, I swiftly reach for the first aid kit and settle down beside her, ready to help. "It's nothing," I mutter, rummaging through the bag for supplies to clean and dress my wound. I need to figure out how to get these cuffs off Mal and escape the guards. Before *he* gets here. My brain can't seem to wrap around the fact he is still alive.

Chapter Thirty-Two

GABE

"Where is she?"

I may have finally run enough to clear my head, but now I feel guilty for leaving when Sara and Tyler needed me. Tyler I found sound asleep on a mattress on the floor in Astraea's room upstairs. However, Sara seems to have vanished without a trace.

Nesrin looks worn out as she paces the room, her hands trembling with anxiety. "We don't know. She went outside to call her friend Mal, and then when I went out to see if she was okay, she was gone."

Frustrated, I run my hand through my tangled hair. This can't be happening. Why would she leave? She didn't run, that I'm sure of. There is no way she would ever leave Tyler behind.

"We need to find her," I murmur.

Lukas strolls in, his eyes instantly drawn to his mate, and he pulls her into a tight embrace. "I have a tracker on my phone. If she still has it, we can find her. I've already called Sander."

Sander's our computer expert. Tracking Lukas's phone will be a breeze for him.

"I've also called Stephan and left a message. He'll know where the hunters are hiding," Nesrin chimes in.

How did I not think of that earlier? It seems like the vampire has eyes everywhere, always aware of what everyone's doing.

"Why would she leave?" Nesrin queries. "It doesn't make sense."

"Maybe Mal set a trap. Lured her away," Lukas suggests.

I shake my head. I didn't think so. Sara was so sure that her friend wouldn't betray her. "I don't know."

"I agree. I don't think it's the friend." Nesrin sighs.

I run both hands over my head. "I promised Tyler I would protect them."

The front door swings open with a bang, and Sander storms into the room. His unkempt dark blonde hair would suggest he just woke up, but his eyes are wide awake and focused. "I have a hit. She's at the wharf."

Suddenly, Nesrin's phone rings, and she answers it immediately. "Hi Stephan. Yes. Okay." There is a slight pause. "Really? Thank you. We'll meet you there."

As she hangs up, her gaze meets mine. "Stephan confirmed the hunters are at the wharf at an abandoned cargo ship on the east side. He's going to meet us there and provide backup."

I grab the back of the lounge, my fingers curling around the soft material. "He's going to help us?"

"Yes." Nesrin starts for the front door, all of us on her heels. She looks back at us thoughtfully. "Should we call Marcus?"

Lukas shoots her a look. "We can handle it."

"But Sara is half witch, the coven–"

Anger surfaces and I interrupt her, "Can know if she chooses that path."

A blush spreads across Nesrin's face as she gives a nod. We make our way outside, deciding to take separate cars. She and Lukas go in one car, while Zee pulls to a stop in front of me. Sander and I quickly jump in. My body trembles with the surge of adrenaline. I never should have run away.

We make it to the wharf in record time, my knee bouncing the entire way. I could sense Zee shooting glances my way every now and then. But they know I'm desperate to get to Sara, so no one commented on my agitated state. We park next to Nesrin's beat up little VW. That must be what Sara took when she left earlier.

"Okay, what's the plan?" Zee rubs his hands together, bouncing on his toes. His hair is pulled back, but some strands have come loose, probably from all his bouncing. Zee lives for this shit. And usually so do I, but all I can think about is getting to Sara.

Lukas's eyes start glowing as he surveys our small group. I swear, when he's this angry or close to shifting, his human body appears bigger, as if straining to keep his beast of a wolf contained.

"Right, I want everyone to be on the lookout. The goal is to get Sara out. Anything else isn't important right now."

Nesrin steps forward, her white-orb eyes glowing in the darkness, a slight aura shimmering around her body. "I can feel her on the main bridge." Tilting her head, she breathes out slowly.

My heart thumps painfully while my body twitches with the need to get to Sara, but we need the information Nesrin is providing. "There are twelve men on board, and only two are guarding her. No, three." She frowns, closing her eyes. "The third doesn't seem conscious, so maybe that's not a guard."

Stephan suddenly appears at my side. A growl slips out, and I scowl at the vampire. "Don't do that, man."

Running his hands down his suit jacket, he smirks at me, his eyes flashing magenta. "There is a car approaching, in case you wanted to know. Three occupants, eight minutes out."

Lukas shifts immediately, his black wolf emitting a bone-chilling growl. *'Nesrin, Gabe, you are with me. Zee and Stephan, I want you to come from the back of the ship and work your way to us at the bridge. Create a distraction and clear a path.'* He looks to Stephan, and the vampire bows his head in acknowledgment. *'Sander, you stay and wait. If there's trouble, you're our backup. Let's go.'*

A snarl tears from his throat, signaling it's time to move. I shift and slink into the shadows with Nesrin on my heels, still in her human form. She is more powerful and protected like this than in her wolf form. My focus is on the upper deck where the bridge is. I hope she's okay.

We make it onto the ship undetected, keeping to the shadows. We have only seen four men patrolling the deck, and they were easy enough to evade. Stephan and Zee will take care of them. They will draw attention to the rear of the ship and clear a path out for us. The sound of tires crunching on gravel meets my ears, and I shift my attention out to the wharf where a shiny black car approaches the boat. I watch as two men get out, helping another from the car. Rage fills my blood at the sight of the third man, the man who killed my family. I close my eyes and take several deep breaths to refocus and calm myself. Letting my anger take over will only put all my friends and Sara in danger. I have to be smart about this.

Nesrin brushes past me. *'Come on, Gabe. Sara first.'*

'Gabe!' Lukas snaps.

I spin around, catching sight of them already halfway up the stairs. I teleport to the top of the stairs and wait for them. Lukas looks around the corner as Nesrin and I hold back. All I want to do is rush forward and get my girl.

'There is one man at this door. I assume the other is on the other side of the bridge, there are always two entrances. l will go around and take care of the other. You two get this one. Get Sara, and get out. I will follow. Make sure we have no surprises on our backs. Be careful, they have guns,' Lukas warns.

Lukas nudges Nesrin, I assume while telling her to be careful and not to be a hero. Then in the blink of an eye, Lukas is gone, leaving nothing behind but an empty space. I face Nesrin, her eyes shining with such intensity that it's difficult to meet her gaze directly.

'Okay, let's go get your girl,' she says with a nod.

'Fuck, yes.'

Slinking around the corner, I melt into the darkness, my paws barely making a sound. A hunter stands up ahead with his back to us.

"I'll distract him. You sneak in," Nesrin whispers urgently, her eyes darting toward the hunter.

I'm just about to argue, to tell her it's too dangerous, but before I can open my mouth, she steps into plain sight. My heart jumps into my throat as the hunter immediately raises his gun, his aim fixed directly on her. Everything feels like it's moving in slow motion—my pulse thundering in my ears, the metallic click of the safety being disengaged. But Nesrin doesn't flinch. With a flick of her wrist, she releases her magic, white tendrils of energy unfurling like living ropes. They snake toward the hunter, moving faster than he can react.

Before he can get a shot off, the tendrils whip around his legs, yanking his feet out from under him with a thud that echoes across the deck. Another tendril shoots out, wrapping around the barrel of the gun and flinging it over the side of the ship, where it vanishes into the dark, churning waters below.

I don't waste time watching. As soon as he's down, I move, slipping through the door with a quick, fluid motion. My heart pounds in my chest as my eyes scan the dimly lit room. And then I see her—Sara—crouched on the floor, her fingers trembling as she works at the handcuffs holding her captive. She's so focused, her brow furrowed in concentration, that she doesn't even notice me approaching.

I sprint across the room, my body shifting mid-bound, my bones cracking and reforming as I morph from fox to human in a single, seamless motion. Sara gasps when she sees me, her wide eyes filled with fear as her hands fly up to shield her face.

"No," I growl, my voice rough and desperate as I crouch in front of her. I grab her wrists gently, pulling her hands away from her face. "It's me. It's okay."

Her eyes meet mine, and for a split second, relief washes over her features. I let out a shaky breath, my heart clenching at the sight of her. "Thank fuck you're okay," I rasp, my voice thick with emotion as I take in her beautiful face.

But then my gaze drops, and I see it—blood. Dark red stains her shirt, seeping through the fabric, and my breath hitches. A sharp, primal fury ignites inside me, blazing hotter than anything I've ever felt. The air around me seems to thicken, my vision blurring at the edges as the world narrows down to one singular, savage thought: *Whoever did this will pay.*

I can't think clearly. Reason and restraint evaporate, replaced by an all-consuming hunger for revenge. My pulse pounds in my ears, and my breathing turns ragged as a red haze fills my mind. All I want—*all I need*—is to tear apart whoever hurt her. To make them bleed like she's bleeding.

"Gabe. Gabe, It's okay. I'm okay. It's just blood," Sara says, trying to reassure me when it should be the other way around.

Every fiber of my being trembles, desperate to unleash its wrath upon them, using nothing but my bare hands.

However, amidst the chaos, I feel a sensation. Warm, gentle hands gently cradle my face, their touch offering comfort. I meet a pair of concerned brown eyes, worry evident in their depths. Before I can fully comprehend the moment, her lips tenderly meet mine, bringing a sense of solace. I tense at the unexpected contact, but then I wrap my arms around her, lifting her off the ground as I stand.

Chapter Thirty-Three

SARA

The relief I feel when I see Gabe is short-lived, cut off by the inhuman sound he makes at the sight of the blood covering my shirt.

"Gabe, Gabe. It's okay. I'm okay. It's just blood."

But he doesn't seem to hear me. I don't think, I just act on instinct, and grab his face, pulling his lips to mine. Gabe stiffens, his body going rigid for a moment, and I think for a moment that he won't respond. But then his mouth moves over mine, and a gasp escapes me as he stands, taking me with him. My legs wrap around his waist. The kiss is urgent and demanding at first, becoming soft and gentle as he calms. His chest emits a low, rumbling sound as he pulls his head away, fixing his intense golden eyes on me.

"I can't believe you left the house," he grumbles.

I smile, pleased to see he's okay, and rest my forehead against his. "I thought they had taken you."

Gabe groans, placing a kiss on my forehead. "Don't ever put yourself in danger for me. Ever. Promise me?"

I bury my head in his neck. "I can't promise that, Gabe. I love you." I hug him tightly, breathing in his scent. My shoulder and arm are screaming in pain, but I push it aside.

"That's the most Taylor Swift thing I've ever heard." Mal sighs. "Now, are you two going to stand there forever making out, or are you going to get me out of these cuffs?"

I gasp, remembering where we are. We have to get out of here. I push at Gabe's arms, and he lowers me to the ground, squeezing my waist before releasing me. As I spin toward Mal, my heart skips a beat when I catch sight of Nesrin walking through the door. The moment our eyes meet, hers ignite, making it hard to believe that what I'm seeing is real. They are completely white, and radiate an ethereal, magical glow. A soft, radiant shimmer envelops her, making her appear as if she belongs to another realm. I am left speechless, completely captivated by her presence. Mal's sharp intake of breath jolts me back to reality.

I drop to my knees next to her. "I can't get the cuffs off her, and I won't leave her here."

"Of course not," Nesrin replies.

Gabe gracefully maneuvers around me, his attention focused on my friend. "What the fuck!" he draws up short at the sight of Mal beaten and bruised. His attention has been fully focused on me since he arrived, completely oblivious to Mal's presence. Nesrin hurries over and kneels down in front of Mal.

"Hey, Mal, I'm Nesrin. We are going to get you guys out of here, okay?"

My friend barely opens her eyes as she nods her head. Seeing her so tired and defeated has guilt slithering through my chest.

I look to the door and the blood seems to drain from my body. My scream echoes through the room as an enormous, menacing black wolf bursts through the door. The wolf skids to a stop and shifts almost instantly, revealing Lukas. Despite sighing in relief, my heart still beats painfully in my chest.

"Nesrin, quick, we have company!" he barks.

I lower my gaze and notice the cuffs glowing and then crumbling into mere dust. Mal remains unfazed by the use of magic, her body slumping as if drained of energy. Gabe reaches for her, his strong arms scooping her up effortlessly.

"Quick. This way," Lukas demands, striding toward the opposite door he came through.

With a strong grip, Nesrin supports me as I rise to my feet. A wicked smile is spread across her face. She's enjoying this. Crazy woman. Wasting no time, we descend the narrow stairs with quick, silent steps, urgency humming through the air around us. The sounds of the battle grow louder with each passing second—the clash of metal, the thud of bodies hitting the deck, and the feral growls of beasts in the fray.

When we finally reach the deck, chaos greets us. At least eight hunters are engaged in a brutal, frenzied fight, their weapons gleaming in the dim light. But they aren't alone. Shadows flicker and dart around them, a blur of movement too fast for me to track. I squint, trying to make sense of the scene, but my focus is drawn to the edge of the fight.

A massive gray wolf emerges from the shadows, its fur matted with blood, its eyes wild and fierce. My breath catches in my throat as I watch the beast stalk toward one of the hunters, who doesn't even see it coming. With a swift, deadly motion, the wolf lunges forward and sinks its teeth into the hunter's leg. A sickening crunch echoes through the air. The man barely has time to scream before the wolf flings him across the deck like a ragdoll. His body slams into the side of the ship with a resounding thud, and he crumples to the floor, motionless.

Nesrin lets out a low, impressed whistle beside me. "Well, that's one way to take care of things."

I'm still reeling, my heart racing from the sheer violence of it all, but there's no time to dwell. The fight isn't over, and we need to move. The air is thick with the scent of blood and magic, a heady mix that sends my pulse racing even faster.

"Let's go," I murmur, pulling my eyes away from the wolf and refocusing on the task at hand.

Nesrin nods, her grin widening as her magic flares to life once more, swirling around her like tendrils of smoke.

The blur of movement slows enough for me to make out a man. *What kind of man can move that fast?*

"Vampire." Nesrin smiles as she watches the supernatural being. I must have made a face, because she elaborates, "You pulled a me and spoke out loud without meaning to."

Then Nesrin and Lukas position themselves in front of Gabe and me, standing side by side. They give each other a look, but I don't know them well enough to decipher it.

Nesrin smiles. "Always, sugar muffin."

I frown with the realization that Lukas has said nothing. When I look at Lukas, I notice he's trying to hide a smile, but failing. Lukas looks back at us, his face serious again.

"Gabe, get them out of here. Take the car and leave if we aren't there in ten minutes."

The feeling of guilt knots my stomach, causing me to instinctively turn my head to the fight. Though the odds appear to be balanced, I am well aware of the ruthless and unscrupulous tactics employed by the hunters.

People are getting hurt because of me. I can't just leave. Two hunters come at us, throwing daggers at Lukas and Nesrin. I cry out in warning, but Nesrin sees it coming and throws her arm up. A wide, shimmering blue shield spreads out in front of the group, the daggers falling uselessly to the ground. Lukas shifts and pounces on one of the men. I look away when I hear a crunch of bones, and gurgled screaming.

"Come on, Sara, we have to go now!" Gabe yells, though I can see in his eyes he's reluctant to leave his pack behind.

We make it all of five steps before skidding to a stop on the wet deck. Coming our way is the man who I thought was my father for so many years. Using a cane for support, he walks with two men on either side of him. The rhythmic tap of his cane on the deck causes my nerves to fray. A rumbling sound from Gabe draws my attention, his body rigid and trembling. I look up at him, and the hatred I see in his eyes takes my breath away. The sound of Mal's whimpering makes me realize that he is unconsciously tightening his hold on her.

"Gabe." I gently place my hand on his arm, feeling the tension radiating from him.

Chapter Thirty-Four

GABE

With my focus solely on the man standing in front of us, everything else blurs into the background. All I can see is the haunting image of my parents lying lifeless on the forest floor. I want to make him pay for the pain he has caused. My grip on reality slips away, and I feel myself on the brink of losing control. Every muscle in my body tenses up, coiled tightly like a spring.

Out of nowhere, Stephan appears right in front of me, blocking my view of the hunters.

"Let me take her." He holds his arms out for Mal.

As if in a daze, I look down at Sara's friend cradled in my arms. She's in pretty bad shape and doesn't need to be part of this fight. I pass her into Stephan's arms, only then realizing how tightly I have been holding her with my anger overpowering me.

"Take care of her," I order.

Stephan raises his eyebrow at me, then glances down at the small hunter in his arms, his eyes betraying a fleeting moment of tenderness before it vanishes entirely. If I didn't know him so well, I wouldn't have noticed the slight widening in his eyes.

"I will keep her safe," he promises.

Then he's gone, the young hunter along with him. I really hope he keeps his word, because Sara will lose it if her friend becomes hurt any more than she already has.

Looking down at Sara, I reach out and clasp her hand in mine, giving it a reassuring squeeze. Her eyes, wide and dilated, reveal her heightened state of alertness.

"Did you just hand Mal over to a vampire?" she asks, incredulous.

"Yes," I whisper, giving her hand one final squeeze before turning to face the man who has tormented my dreams.

Watching us intently, his eyes harden, revealing a mind that is constantly assessing. The two men who stand behind him step closer, their presence adding an extra layer of intimidation. The abrupt sound of gunshots shatters the silent standoff, heightening my sense of urgency. I forgot about the guns. It seems the hunters have acquired new, advanced equipment, stepping away from their usual dagger and fighting skills.

'*Lukas?*' I check through the pack bond.

'*We are fine. Six down, four to go. Make that seven if you include the entourage you're facing. Are you okay?*'

Before I can answer, another car pulls up to the dock, and a group of hunters emerge, running for the ship. '*We are fine, but we have more hunters incoming.*'

Following my words, a haunting howl echoes through the air. The wind brings with it the sound of another howl, followed by a quick bark. Lukas has called Sander to help.

Refocusing on the present, I shift my gaze to Sara, who stands beside me, her posture upright and commanding. Her eyes, normally warm and filled with love, now burn with a fiery intensity. They bore into the man before her, piercing through his facade, unmasking him for the monstrous killer he truly is. Every fiber of her being radiates a potent mixture of hurt and anger, like a storm brewing on the horizon, ready to unleash its fury.

And yet, in contrast to Sara's seething anger, the man she once called her father exudes an eerie calmness. His ice-cold gaze meets hers, devoid of remorse or regret. It is a chilling reminder of the darkness that resides within him, the depths of his ruthlessness that have left a trail of destruction in his wake. His very presence seems to suck the warmth out of the air, leaving behind an unsettling stillness.

Chapter Thirty-Five

SARA

"Sara."

My blood freezes at the sound of that voice, the voice that's haunted my nightmares my whole life.

The man I thought was my father, though he never acted like it, approaches us, his stride off balance. His gaze is fierce and unyielding, leaving me feeling exposed and vulnerable. Cold, calculating eyes briefly flicker to Gabe, his face betraying a hint of annoyance before he looks away and dismisses him completely.

A deep growl rumbles from Gabe, and I startle at the unexpected sound.

"Abe," I reply, trying my best to keep my fear from showing.

Abe's expression stays the same as he stares back at me. I try to drown out the sounds of fighting, but the echoes of fists hitting flesh and angry shouts linger in the air. Last I saw, Nesrin used her magic to make all the guns vanish into the depths of the river, leaving only the sounds of fists colliding in hand-to-hand combat.

"You seem to like causing more trouble than you're worth."

"This is your doing, not mine. Why can't you just leave me alone?"

"You need to pay for your crimes."

"What about *your* crimes?" I throw back, my hands trembling.

Gabe's presence beside me sends a tingling sensation down my arm. It dawns on me that I can sense his magic, a faint but unmistakable presence.

"You need to turn and leave now, or it will not end well for you," Gabe growls.

The muscle in his jaw tightens, causing his face to contort with an unsettling mix of fury and pain. The air around him seems charged, as if an electric current pulses through his body, making the hairs on my arms stand on end. I've never heard him use this voice before. It resonates with a deep, menacing tone, laced with an unfamiliar element. Pain, maybe?

With a blink, Abe shifts his focus toward Gabe. A sinister gleam enters his eyes, making my body lock up from memory. "And who do you think you are to give me such demands?"

Gabe laughs humorlessly, and I move closer to him. I don't know what's happening right now, but I feel like I'm missing an important part of the puzzle.

"You don't remember? I know for a fact I look exactly like my father."

My head jerks back as if I've been slapped. With a sense of dread, I twist my body to face Gabe, silently pleading with him not to articulate the terrifying thoughts that plague my mind right now. Abe studies Gabe intently, his eyes scrutinizing every detail. Sensing the threat, the men at his back inch closer, their expressions growing tense.

"Ah . . . " he nods, pointing his cane at Gabe. "I killed your parents, what? Twenty years ago? I knew they had a child, but I couldn't find it. I figured they used their magic to hide you. Sneaky filthy kitsune."

A rush of anger floods through me as I contemplate the cruel injustice that befell Gabe's family. Worse, at the hands of this man, someone I know. *Is* this *why Gabe ran earlier?*

Then it clicks. The photo Mal sent.

Abe's gaze snaps back to me, his lips curling into a sneer that twists his already hateful features. The venom in his words drips like poison. "Apple doesn't fall far from the tree," he spits. "Just like your whore of a mother."

Before I can process the insult, Gabe takes a step forward, fury radiating off him like a storm about to break. His body trembles, every muscle tensed, ready to strike. My hand shoots out instinctively, gripping his arm in a desperate attempt to hold him back. My fingers dig into his flesh, feeling the raw power surging beneath his skin, the barely-contained rage threatening to unleash something far worse than violence. Waves crash violently against the side of the cargo ship, as if the ocean itself is reacting to Gabe's fury.

"Don't," I whisper, my voice strained with the effort it takes to keep him from tearing Abe apart.

My eyes lock onto Abe's, and for a moment, it feels like the whole world narrows down to this single wicked man standing before us. He has committed countless atrocious acts—hurting people without so much as a flicker of remorse. The pain he's caused, the lives he's destroyed—it all flashes before me in an instant.

The cacophony of the ongoing fight gradually fades away, the snarls and screams now muffled by the enveloping darkness that invades my vision. My skin tingles and feels too tight all of a sudden. All I can focus on is making this horrid man disappear.

A dense mist slithers over the ship, shrouding my surroundings in a veil of obscurity, its ethereal touch curling around my ankles. Turning my head, I study the thick mist that has rendered everyone invisible. It has swallowed us all, its eerie presence permeating the air.

"Gabe?" I whisper.

"It's okay, it's Nesrin," Gabe murmurs in a barely audible voice.

I reach for him, but he is gone.

"Gabe?"

Nothing.

I let out a small yelp, startled by the sensation of something brushing against my legs. It takes a moment for me to realize that it's Gabe in his fox form. As he moves past me, I sink my fingers into his fur and allow him to guide me through the mist. The shifters, with their heightened senses, have the advantage of silently tracking their prey in the mist.

A prickling sensation skates up my spine and my fingers slip from Gabe's fur as I turn sharply. I swear someone is behind me. Out of nowhere, I am forcefully knocked to the side, and a sharp blow lands on the side of my head, leaving me disoriented. The impact of the ground sends a jolt of pain through my skull, intensifying the ache in my injured shoulder. As I gasp for air, I manage to roll onto my back, my vision blurred by tears that I desperately try to blink away. Above me, a thick mist swirls, obscuring my view of everything else. I sit up and instinctively massage my head. I look around, attempting to pinpoint where the impact came from, but I quickly realize that I'm alone. My heart races, and I struggle to catch my breath as panic surges through me.

A thud draws my attention, and I watch in horror as the mist slowly dissipates, unveiling a looming figure standing right beside me.

Frantically, I scramble to my feet.

My eyes strain to focus on the shape inching closer to me. A sudden bark erupts from my left, startling me, just as Abe comes to a stop a few feet in front of me. My eyes widen and the blood drains from my face at the sight of the gun in his hand. My chest tightens with fear as he lifts it, aiming directly at me, causing my heart to race in terror.

I inhale sharply, feeling a shudder in the air as panic overwhelms me. A bolt of lightning breaks the silence, striking the ship and causing us to lose our balance. Acting quickly, I extend my arms wide, desperately searching for something to steady myself. I notice Gabe, in his fox form, leaping toward Abe and clamping his jaws onto his arm. With a forceful motion, Abe tries to shake off Gabe, surprising me with his strength. Despite being injured, Abe doesn't go down.

The sudden blast of the gun makes me scream, and my body reflexively drops to the ground. The mist thins out, and I see two large men moving in our direction. Frantically, I look around for something to use as a weapon. My eyes catch sight of a rope lying on the ground, and without hesitation, I rush over to grab it, swiftly pulling it tight as the men pass by. The impact of their fall creates a tremor beneath my feet, prompting me to lunge forward without pause. I swiftly land on the back of the nearest man, feeling the warmth of his body beneath me. I wrap the rope around his neck, tightening it with precision, ensuring he is securely trapped.

Whipping my head around, my eyes scan the surroundings, desperately searching for a trace of the other man. Damn it, he was just here. I pivot on my heel, my gaze darting in every direction, hoping to catch even the slightest movement. From a distance, I hear a blood curdling scream, and ripples of anticipation move through the air, until it abruptly ends with a loud splash. Someone fell overboard.

The air is pierced by the sound of rapid, echoing footsteps, and my body spins around. Adrenaline coursing through my veins, I brace myself as a body collides with mine. I manage to land and roll straight to my feet, but so does he. *Mike.* With a determined look in his eyes, he wastes no time launching himself toward me, his fist swinging with aggressive force. Despite his relentless assault, I skillfully evade or counter each strike. I can feel the reverberation of every impact deep within my bones, fueling my frantic quest for an opening to hit back. I feel exhausted and drained, the night stretching on endlessly with no hope of a reprieve.

My foot hits something on the ground and my heart lurches in surprise, causing me to falter, just as a hit comes for my face. My body twists in an attempt to evade the attack, but his fist connects with my jaw as I fall to the ground. Landing with a jolt, the force of impact leaves me gasping for air. Spots dance in my vision, and I watch as a dark mass slams into Mike, taking him down. He doesn't even have time to scream before Lukas shifts, clutching his head in both hands, and with a swift motion, snaps his neck.

Lukas stands to his full, imposing height and walks over, holding out a hand for me.

"Are you alright?" he asks gruffly.

I snap my mouth closed, realizing I'm gawking at him. "Yes, but I lost Gabe."

Lukas grunts, his rough hand gripping mine as he helps me to my feet. "I have a feeling he is settling a debt."

"Abe will kill him."

"Not likely. Stay here, stay hidden."

Before I can respond, Lukas swiftly shifts and bounds off, the mist swallowing him up in seconds.

Stay here.

Screw that. I need to get to Gabe.

Making my way through the dense mist, an icy shiver runs over me as the cold, damp air clings to my skin. Up ahead, two figures stand motionless, their bodies tense as they engage in a silent standoff.

Gabe!

I quicken my steps, confusion rolling through me. *What is happening? Why aren't they moving?*

"Gabe," I whisper hoarsely.

As my voice echoes through the air, Gabe's head whips around, his attention fully on me. My breath catches in my throat as I freeze, completely absorbed by the sight of his eyes. They're radiant orbs of pure gold.

"Sara," Gabe growls, not in anger, but in a possessive tone.

Suddenly, as if breaking from a trance, Abe bellows in fury as he lunges at Gabe. Just like a fleeting illusion, Gabe evaporates into a cloud of glistening golden dust, only to materialize again, silently and effortlessly, right behind Abe.

My hands instinctively shoot up to cover my mouth as Gabe tightly grips him in a headlock. Abe's futile attempts to twist and strike Gabe only seem to fuel his anger. I've seen that crazed look in his eye more than a time or two. It's like staring into the depths of madness.

Rain begins pouring from the sky, thinning out the mist and drenching us within seconds. As I breathe in, I sense a faint electric charge in the air, causing a tingling sensation on my skin.

Gabe shifts seamlessly from one moment to the next, his fox lunging for Abe's throat. Abe raises a gun, his finger tightening around the trigger as he takes aim at Gabe. In sheer horror, a piercing scream escapes my lips, and I instinctively raise my hands. Bolts of lightning erupt from my palms, a brilliant flash illuminating the air, striking Abe directly in the chest.

Abe's eyes flare wide with disbelief, his fingers losing their grip on the gun. It falls to the deck with a thud as he collapses beside it. The thick mist that has been swirling around him suddenly dissipates, leaving behind a haunting silence, a sharp contrast to the continuing storm above us.

In a state of shock, I'm momentarily frozen as Gabe transforms back into a human and sprints over to me. My breath leaves me, and my knees start to buckle. As I fall, I feel a gentle cushioning beneath me—something soft and furry. My head droops and I meet a set of amber eyes belonging to the white wolf. She is so beautiful. Lying with my body half draped over her, I feel Nesrin's whine vibrate through her body before she lets out a sudden, sharp bark. Then Gabe's there, pulling me to him.

"Where?" he demands, sounding desperate.

Confusion engulfs me, leaving me disoriented. A wave of weakness and dizziness crashes over me, distorting my vision into a hazy blur.

"I can't see. There's so much blood!" Gabe yells.

Gabe lays me down carefully on the cool, wet deck, his hands frantically ripping at my clothes, desperately searching for any injuries.

"I'm fine, I'm okay," I murmur, but my voice sounds weak and uncertain.

My lips feel swollen and heavy. Speaking becomes a struggle as words stumble and trip over each other on my tongue.

"G . . . a . . . b . . ."

Gabe doesn't respond; his face, striking and gorgeous, pales in the dim light.

"Nesrin." His voice is choked with emotion.

Her voice is like an angel's as she replies, "I'm here. I got it."

Nesrin moves to my side and cups Gabe's face. "Gabe, it's okay. I got it."

What's happening? Why can't I move?

Lukas moves closer, his shadow falling over me. I look up at him standing guard over the three of us. A comforting warmth spreads through my chest, and I try to smile. However, a sudden cough escapes me, followed by the sensation of something wet landing on my face. I turn my head and spit out what's in my mouth. *Blood.*

"That can't be good," I whisper hoarsely.

The sight of a majestic gray wolf silently approaching us draws my attention, its movements exude a captivating blend of grace and elegance.

White light flares to life around me, and I close my eyes from the brightness of it. My body warms painfully, the agony making me scream, but it's drowned out by the thunder rolling overhead. As everything turns hazy, the sound of Gabe's frantic voice and Nesrin's reassuring words reach my ears.

Shouts fill the air, and then Lukas's voice rises above the chaos. In this moment, everything becomes quiet and devoid of noise. I feel something wet touch my cheek, and I roll my head to the side, my eyes barely opening to see the wolf staring down at me.

Huh . . . I know those eyes.

"Zee," I whisper, the sound barely audible.

When the pain eases and my mind grows quiet, I pick up on Gabe's distant voice asking, "Is she alright?"

"Yes, she is going to be fine," Nesrin answers, sounding exhausted.

Guilt snakes its way into my chest, and a wave of remorse washes over me for subjecting everyone to this. I feel the hair being pushed from my face, and I lean my head into the touch.

A soft voice sounds in my head, and it takes me a second to identify it as Nesrin's. *'You're going to be okay, Sara.'*

"Gabe, take Sara home," Lukas orders, his voice sounding so distant. "I'll stay and help with the cleanup."

My outstretched hand quivers, desperately searching for Gabe. The weight of fatigue weakens my muscles, causing them to tremble. Just as my arm threatens to surrender, a firm grip wraps around my hand, providing much-needed strength.

"Don't you ever scare me like that again," Gabe's gravelly voice murmurs in my ear, sending shivers down my spine. I'm gently hoisted into his strong embrace, enveloped by the comforting warmth radiating from his arms.

"Sorry," I croak, resting my head on his shoulder, loving the feel of him carrying me.

As the cool breeze caresses my face, it delicately rustles through my hair, and I revel in the soothing sensation of nestling my head, finding solace and drifting into slumber.

Chapter Thirty-Six

SARA

The car turns onto a gravel road, and I'm jolted awake by the unmistakable crunching sound of the tires. I'm still cradled in Gabe's lap, my head tucked under his chin. I tighten my fingers around the fabric of his shirt, anchoring myself to the warmth of his chest.

"Go back to sleep, baby," he murmurs, kissing the top of my head.

I allow my eyes to slowly drift shut, but I have no intention of falling asleep again. After a few minutes, the car comes to a halt, and Sander quickly jumps out of the driver's seat. He opens the door, allowing Gabe to assist me out of the car.

"I'm fine."

"Someone shot you," Gabe grumbles, keeping an arm around my waist. "In the chest."

Sander's expression softens as he gives me a sympathetic look. "He's right."

Together we make our way toward the house, and a sense of relief washes over me, as if a heavy burden has been lifted. It's hard to describe the mix of emotions I'm feeling now that it's finally over, but it's so intense that it's almost bringing me to tears. *Abe is dead.* My knees give way beneath me, but before I can fall, Gabe's arm tightens around my waist, keeping me upright.

"Easy," he says.

Breathing heavily, I look over to see Nesrin, Lukas, and Zee arrive, their car doors slamming shut, and the sound echoing in the distance.

"That was quick," Gabe greets them.

"I'm going to head home before the boys wake up." Sander's eyes soften as they turn to me. "I'm glad you're okay, Sara."

"Thanks," I reply, giving him a smile.

Nesrin slowly makes her way over, her steps heavy and deliberate. With her shoulders slumped forward, she seems visibly burdened by exhaustion that is entirely because of me. Guilt overwhelms me, and I step away from Gabe, ignoring his protests.

"Are you okay?" I shift nervously on my feet.

Lukas and Zee swiftly reach her, positioning themselves on opposite sides as a protective measure, ready to catch her if she were to fall.

"I'm okay, just tired," Nesrin dismisses our concerns.

A silent conversation seems to move between them all before Lukas steps forward and pulls me into a hug.

"Don't ever run off again. It hardly ever goes the way you want it to. Just ask Nesrin."

"I don't know. Works out fine for me," Nesrin answers with a shrug. "Plus, the makeup sex is mind blowing, so . . . "

I can't help but laugh, feeling my face flush.

Nesrin grins when I look at her, and Lukas shakes his head as he steps back. His hand finds Nesrin's, their fingers entwined as he guides her over to the house. Before joining them, Zee playfully winks at me, giving my nose a tap, adding a touch of mischief to the moment.

Gabe steps in front of me, his hand reaching out and intertwining with mine, urging us to follow. My heart beats wildly in my chest as the air between us becomes charged with anticipation. We slowly ascend the stairs and Gabe leads me down the porch to where the sun is rising over the valley.

We stand in silence on the porch of Lukas's house, the cool morning breeze gently rustling the leaves as we stare out over the valley. The sun rises, painting the sky in shades of pink, a beautiful contrast to the darkness of what has been the longest night of my life. I wrap my arms around my waist, feeling the soft fabric of my shirt beneath my fingertips. I don't know who this shirt belongs to, but it swallows me whole. Still, it provides much-needed relief from my blood-soaked sweater.

"Sara, look at me." Gabe's demand sends a surge of butterflies fluttering in my stomach, and I turn to meet his eyes with a mixture of emotions tumbling through me.

Gabe stands in front of me, his clothes torn and covered in dirt from the fight we just survived. His long, black hair hangs around his shoulders, and there's blood on his chest and face. My blood.

The strength of his attention on me is so overwhelming that it renders me completely oblivious to everything else. I feel my heart pounding, desperate to run into his embrace and never release my grip.

Gabe's hand gently brushes against my cheek as he pushes my hair over my shoulder, his touch lingering, before trailing it down my arm, his fingers interlocking with mine. Gently, he lifts my hand to his lips, planting a tender kiss on the back. With his other hand, he reaches out and firmly grasps my waist, pulling me to him.

"I love you, Sara. I can't picture my life without you or Tyler in it. And I don't want to. I am completely and utterly yours, body and soul." The raw emotions lighting his eyes make mine tear up. "Tonight, I thought I lost you. I can't . . ."

The pressure in my chest intensifies as I fight back the tears. "I love you too," I choke out. "I want forever with you."

"Done," he growls, the noise coming from deep in his chest.

Leaning down, his mouth covers mine in a demanding kiss. I push up on my toes and he releases my hand, cupping my neck. Our lips move in sync, my head dizzy with all that is him.

Scent. Taste. Warmth. Feel.

It's all too much and not enough at the same time.

I gasp as his warm hand slides under my shirt, smoothing across my stomach, creating a tingling sensation.

Like a spark igniting a fire, my veins come alive with a surge of energy. My entire being longs for him, a blazing inferno igniting my soul. Gabe moves to nuzzle my neck, kissing across my collarbone to the swell of my breast, my hands finding their way into his hair. Gabe groans softly, lifting his head to capture my mouth again, his kiss so tender that it creates a moment of stillness, as if time itself has paused. My hands roam his body, tracing every curve and contour, until I finally embrace him, wrapping my arms around his neck and holding him tight. We break the kiss, but remain locked in a hold, our bodies pressed together, feeling the rapid thump of our hearts. As I let out a contented sigh, a sense of peace washes over me. Finally, I've found where I truly belong. The thought that I will never again have to live in fear, constantly running or hiding, fills me with an overwhelming sense of liberation.

"I can't wait to get you home and strip you bare. I'm going to discover every inch of you," Gabe whispers in my ear, making me shiver.

Without warning, a powerful tremor shakes the ground beneath us. The house quivers with force.

"What now?" I whine, holding onto Gabe's arms for support.

Inside, shouts ring out, their intensity matching the thunderous footsteps on the stairs. Gabe and I exchange worried glances before hurrying inside.

"Tyler?" I shout, bursting through the front door.

"Upstairs," Gabe replies, sparing me a fleeting glance before he bursts into a cloud of golden dust.

My brain short circuits for a second as I stare at the empty space where Gabe just stood. Another tremor rattles the house, snapping me into action. Heart pounding in my chest, I race up the stairs, desperate to ensure Tyler's safety. Standing outside a bedroom door at the end of the hall, Zee catches my eye. With that one look, a wave of dread washes over me, and I slow my steps.

Inside the room, I slide to a stop, my mouth agape in astonishment. The room is a disaster zone. The room is in complete disarray, with furniture overturned and items strewn everywhere. Tyler stands at the back of the room, surrounded by a swirling gust of wind that forms a protective dome around him. His wide, brown eyes are filled with a mixture of shock and fear, one arm tightly wrapped around Astraea. The palm of the other hand is facing outward, as if warding off something. I swiftly glance around the room and see Nesrin and Lukas, but if he is familiar with them, why would he feel scared?

Gabe is standing by Lukas's side and looks ready to jump through the dome to get Tyler and Astraea, damn the consequences.

Nesrin's voice cuts through the noise of the roaring wind, "Tyler, it's okay. He won't hurt you, I promise. You are safe here."

She approaches the dome, and Lukas moves to grab her arm, shaking his head. Her eyes meet mine as she instead walks over to me. "You need to talk to him."

I'm still utterly puzzled. *What the hell is going on? Is* Tyler *doing this?*

Sensing my confusion, Nesrin offers me a comforting smile. "He takes after you, it seems."

Before I have a chance to react, a blur of movement catches my eye as a large shadowy figure sprints toward us, skillfully entwining its tail around Nesrin's legs. A head peeks out from behind her, revealing a hidden companion. Startled, I take a step back. My head tilts to the side as I stare intently at the creature hiding behind her.

"What is that?" I ask, even though I know damn well what it is.

The creature's big golden eyes blink up at me, revealing a mixture of curiosity and caution. Mesmerized, I watch as the creature's tail gracefully encircles Nesrin's ankle, its scales morphing into a vibrant display reminiscent of rippling water.

"This is Malachite. He is really friendly, and full of childish charm. He usually sleeps with Astraea, but hadn't met Tyler yet, so they both got a shock," Nesrin replies, running her hand lovingly over the dragon's head as she gazes at him with adoration.

I notice the desperation in her eyes as she glances back to me, silently begging for my help. "He didn't mean to scare Tyler. He won't hurt anyone, I swear."

I believe her. More importantly, I trust her. My eyes sweep across the room, reassured by the trust I have in each person. I move toward Tyler, joining Gabe, who is already crouching, attempting to engage him in conversation, but his attention remains fixated on the dragon.

"Hey, baby, it's okay. You did great, you protected yourself and Astraea. I'm so damn proud of you." My voice breaks as his scared eyes meet mine. "I'm so damn proud."

The wind begins to taper off as he lowers his arm. "Mom?"

I see the dragon out of the corner of my eye, creeping closer. So does Tyler, his arm coming back up. The small dragon goes to where Gabe is crouched and nuzzles under his arm, seeking comfort, and I hear the shrill noise it makes, obviously in distress.

"Tyler, baby, this is Malachite. He is part of Gabe's family. He won't hurt you. See," I assure him, moving over to the two of them.

Gabe stands up and extends his arm toward me, his fingers curling around mine as he pulls me closer. "She's right, Tyler. He won't hurt you."

Malachite is now sitting at our feet, his head tilted back, his intense stare focused solely on me. I slowly reach my hand down and run it over the dragon's snout, and he leans into my touch, nudging my hand with his head, wanting more. I laugh, unable to help myself. This is amazing.

Tyler's eyes are watchful as he concentrates on us, but then he redirects his focus to Nesrin and Lukas as they draw nearer.

Lukas takes a step forward, his face radiating gentleness and understanding. "Tyler, you are part of our family now. I swear you are always safe here. Just ask my little Star there." His deep voice carries through the room. Then he sends Astraea a wink.

Astraea blinks, then looks up at my son with a smile that lights up her entire face. Tyler's eyes widen and he drops his arms, looking down at Astraea in shock and wonder, the wind dying completely.

What just happened?

Chapter Thirty-Seven

GABE

I soak in the feeling of contentment, a warm sensation spreading throughout my body, causing a gentle tingle in my fingertips. The tension that has built up in my muscles during the commotion an hour ago slowly dissipates, leaving behind a sense of ease and relaxation.

Sara and I have claimed one of the sofas in the front room. Her back is firmly against my chest, and I can feel the comforting flow of her breathing as it matches my own. The rhythmic beating of her heart against my chest acts as a soothing melody, calming any lingering worries that plagued my mind just hours ago.

The aroma of freshly brewed coffee wafts through the air, its rich scent mingling with the warmth enveloping us. I stretch out my legs on either side of Sara, mirroring her relaxed posture. The gentle pressure of her body against mine creates a sense of security and closeness, as if we are two puzzle pieces fitting perfectly together.

Following the events upstairs, we all took showers and changed into clean clothing. Since Lukas is the alpha, and the pack house is for everyone, he has an abundant supply of clothes for all. Unable to resist, I lower my head and breathe in the delightful aroma of

Sara's clean hair, a blend of floral shampoo and her own natural scent.

"Did you just sniff me, fox boy?"

I laugh, poking her in the ribs. "Did you just call me fox boy? Cause I can assure you, I'm no boy."

At that exact moment, Zee pops his head into the room and grins. "Can I come in?" He winks at Sara.

"Of course," she replies, moving to sit up.

My arms tense around her, and I hold her tighter to me. Her head tilts back, and our eyes lock, her forehead furrowed in a puzzled expression.

I raise my shoulders in a casual shrug. "I'm comfortable."

Zee smirks and takes a seat across from us, his elbows on his knees as he leans forward. "You're going to have to get used to that," he says to Sara.

I can't see her face, but I can hear the bewilderment in her voice. "What?"

Zee's blue eyes sparkle in delight, flashing me a grin before he looks back to Sara. "You almost died last night, honey. Gabe is not going to let you out of his sight for a long time. He is going to want you right by his side."

She surprises me by leaning heavily into me. "Well, it's all over now. I'm safe, and the hunters that were involved are dead."

"We don't know that," I retort.

"Gabe's right. I think it's best to keep an eye out. Maybe your friend can get in touch with the clan and see what's happening now?"

I feel Sara stiffen, her muscles tensing. "Is she alright with that vampire?"

Zee shrugs his shoulders. "There is no way in hell that Stephan would hurt a hair on her head. Not with Nesrin to answer to."

My mouth naturally curves up at the corners. Nesrin is definitely not someone to be messed with. What's more, she has developed some kind of friendship with that vampire. Nesrin connected herself and the pack to the vampire's only heir. Like a patchwork quilt, our family consists of unique pieces that fit together perfectly. In this moment, admiration fills me with the intricate web of relationships that have been woven within our pack, thanks to our luna. Nesrin, with her unwavering loyalty and her talent for bridging gaps between different beings, is a vital thread that holds us all together.

"Plus, Gabe here can get downright scary as well."

It's my turn to stiffen, my muscles tensing as anticipation fills the air. I haven't had a chance to discuss with Sara what I truly am. She's aware of my ability to shift into a fox, but the intricate world of kitsune and the magic it entails remains uncharted territory. I seldom use my magical powers, only resorting to them when absolutely necessary. In fact, it has been five long years since I last unleashed my magic, that is, until Tony and Abe. It's not a task I enjoy, for it feels like a profound violation of one's privacy to delve into someone's mind.

'*Zee*,' I warn.

Zee's bright blue eyes flare, and his eyebrows shoot up in surprise when he looks at me. '*You haven't told her?*'

'*No.*'

Sitting up, Sara locks eyes with us, her gaze filled with curiosity. "Are you guys doing that creepy thing Nesrin spoke to me about? Mind speaking?"

"Sorry," I confirm, pushing us into sitting positions on the couch.

She turns to face me fully. "Gabe, I trust you. I love you. If you have something to tell me, do it. You can trust me in return."

Zee stands. "That's my cue to leave. See you in the kitchen." Then he strolls out of the room. '*Tell her.*'

I let out a weary sigh, my hand instinctively reaching up to run through my tousled hair. "You know I'm a fox, right?"

Sara nods, her eyes filling with understanding, and I manage to muster a weak smile before I carry on. "Well, I'm what they call a kitsune. Not only can we shift into a fox, but unlike other shifters, we are also magic."

"Like Nesrin? She is a witch and wolf, right?"

"Nesrin is . . . she is complicated. She's what we call a legacy, and yes, she possesses those characteristics, but her essence goes beyond them. My magic is part of the kitsune. We have the magic of trickery. I can . . . " I hesitate.

Sara gently places her hand over mine, offering a reassuring smile.

"My element is water, mainly rivers. I can manipulate water. I can also transport myself short distances."

"Like on the ship when you disappeared into gold dust?"

"I didn't realize you saw that."

"I thought I'd lost my mind," she admits. "Then you did it here, and I knew I wasn't imagining it. But that doesn't seem so bad, right?"

A tight knot begins to form in my stomach as my unease grows stronger. Will she still trust me when I tell her?

"I can manipulate people's minds, create illusions, that type of thing. I have never used it on you, I swear–" But her lips cut me off as they brush across mine.

Leaning back, she cups my face. "Gabe, I trust you. I know you would never use that gift on me. You're a good man."

The weight that has been pressing down on me suddenly disappears, causing me to instinctively draw her into a tight embrace. "Thank fuck."

"So, what's a legacy? I feel like I have a lot to catch up on."

I take a deep breath and chuckle. "Okay, well, a legacy is a mortal descendant of a god or demigod, one who has the powers of the god they have descended from. Nesrin is a descendant of Althaea, the goddess of healing. Althaea's daughter came to Earth and fell in love with a shifter, a wolf. The rest is her story to tell."

Frozen to the spot, Sara's wide, brown eyes capture her shock, while her mouth forms a perfect O of astonishment.

Laughter bursts from my mouth at the expression of shock on her face. "Are you okay?" I reach up and close her mouth.

Sara blinks several times, refocusing on me. "She's a demigod!"

I chuckle. "No, she is a legacy, but most importantly, she is just Nesrin, our luna." I nudge her gently before pulling her into me and kissing her softly.

The air around me seems to shift abruptly, signaling tension within the pack bond. I loosen my grip on Sara and rise to my full height, my attention drawn to the commotion emanating from the kitchen. My body tingles, and without conscious effort, I vanish from the front room and materialize instantly at the kitchen door. The room is alive with the sound of everyone talking at once. I feel Sara's hand gently press against my back as she comes up behind me. And together, we survey the bustling kitchen and its cacophony of voices.

Chapter Thirty-Eight

GABE

"What's happening?" Sara asks.

I shake my head, trying to sort through whose emotions I'm sensing. "I don't know."

Suddenly, Lukas fills the doorway on the other side of the room. "What is happening? Why is my wife freaking out?" he bellows, and the room quiets immediately. The crowd parts, unveiling Nesrin standing in the center of the room. With a dazed look on her face, she clutches something in her hand, and I strain my eyes to see what it is. Next to me, Sara gasps in surprise, her hand quickly covering her mouth as tears well up in her eyes.

I frown at her, thoroughly confused. "What?" I whisper, but she shakes her head, her eyes locked on the scene in front of us.

I look back at Nesrin and watch as Lukas stalks toward her, his full focus on her. He takes her face in his hands and gently lifts it to look at him. "Sweetheart, talk to me," he demands.

Nesrin opens her mouth, but nothing comes out. Worried, I take a step forward and see a tear roll down her cheek and hit Lukas's thumb. What the hell is happening?

Zee catches my eye, and I can see the glimmer of excitement there. I look at Kyra, and she is practically bouncing on her toes, unable to contain her excitement. Sander's wide grin contrasts with the puzzled expressions on the kids' faces.

I'm so fucking confused.

The air becomes heavy with static, making every hair on my arms stand on end. Shadows gather in the doorway where Lukas entered.

Sara's grip on my arm tightens, her nails digging into my skin. "What is that?"

"That is Leila, Nesrin's sister and Zee's mate."

Leila appears in the middle of a portal, gracefully stepping out and taking in the room. Her red hair flows around her as she takes quick steps toward her sister. "What's happening?" she demands.

"I don't know, she won't tell me," Lukas replies, concern edging his voice.

Leila frowns, looking down at Nesrin's hand, and pulls the object from her. Her eyes widen in surprise as she looks back up at Nesrin. "You're pregnant?" she whispers, elation filling her voice as she stares at her sister.

Lukas's head jerks back. "You're pregnant?"

Nesrin nods the best she can, her head still caught in Lukas's grasp. Then, with a grin spreading across his face, Lukas lifts her off her feet and spins her around, her laughter ringing through the air like music. She looks so small in his arms, her dark auburn hair flying around her. My heart swells with a mix of love and excitement at the sight of them together. The thought of them having a baby makes my grin widen, and I can't help but feel a surge of pride for my friends.

Lukas sets Nesrin down, but he doesn't let go. Instead, he smothers her face with playful kisses, and her laughter grows even louder, a joyful sound that seems to chase away the remnants of any lingering daze. As I walk over to them, Lukas finally steps back, though he keeps one arm firmly wrapped around her, his protective nature on full display.

"Congratulations," I say, taking in their joyous expressions. The pack bond pulsates with their overwhelming happiness, impossible to contain such excitement.

Blushing, Nesrin wraps her arms around me tightly, pulling me into a hug. "Thanks, Gabe."

Everyone steps forward then, their eager voices filling the air as they crowd around the couple, their eyes sparkling with excitement. Lukas basically drags Nesrin away after that, and I know we won't see them for the rest of the day. My eyes catch on Tyler's from across the room as he watches Astraea with quiet curiosity, his brow furrowed like he's trying to figure her out. I lean in and plant a soft kiss on Sara's head before heading over to Tyler.

His attention moves to me as I approach.

"Hey, want to take a walk?"

Nodding eagerly, he jumps up and follows me outside to the porch. "What's on your mind?" I turn and lean my back on the railing. Tyler looks back at the door to the house.

"Astraea. She is different, isn't she?"

"We are all different, Tyler, but yes, Astraea is special."

"I heard her inside my head last night. She has never spoken to me before. You said she couldn't speak, that she was mute."

His tone's not accusing, but it carries a sense of hurt, which I hated. "Yes, I said that, but if I had told you she was telepathic, what would you have thought? She communicates in a unique way, making it challenging to understand unless you're familiar with it or open to hearing it. I was waiting for you to be ready."

Tyler's shoulders slump. "I don't understand what's happening."

I sigh, running a hand over my head. "I know you don't, bud."

"What am I?"

I push off the railing and take a seat on the top step, patting the spot next to me. Without hesitation, Tyler plops down beside me, and I bump his shoulder with mine.

"You are your mom's son. You are special, but I think we should all sit down and talk about what's going to happen."

"Are we going to live with you?"

"Do you want to live with me?" I inquire carefully.

With a nod of his head, his expressive brown eyes meet mine. "Yes. I hate our apartment."

I concur. The first chance I get, I'm asking Sara to move in with me. My ears prick, and I turn to the sound of soft footsteps coming toward us before pausing at the door. Sara's listening.

Glancing back down at Tyler, I give him a nudge with my shoulder. "I want to show you something."

I jump up, making my way down the stairs, and look up at Tyler. "Ready?"

"Yes."

A surge of energy moves through me as my magic infuses my body. In the blink of an eye, everything transforms, and I raise my gaze to Tyler and bark.

Tyler's little mouth drops open, a look of pure disbelief crossing his face. "No way," he breathes.

Excitement builds, and I rush up the stairs, loop around him, and nudge his face.

Tyler giggles, and the sound is music to my ears.

"You have four tails!" he exclaims.

I chuff softly, the sound echoing through the air as I fade out of sight, and reappear at the bottom of the stairs. A subtle shimmer accompanies my transformation back into my human form. The steps creak beneath my weight as I ascend, taking my seat next to him. I can feel his excitement and energy as if it were my own.

"That's so cool," he breathes.

"Glad you think so."

"Why do you have four tails?"

"I lost my parents at a very young age. I only recently discovered that when they died, their magic passed on to me, forming a new tail."

"But you have four tails?"

A pang of sadness hits me in the chest, and I look out over the yard before bringing my focus back to Tyler with a small smile. "My grandmother recently passed."

"So, you have no family?"

"None blood related. But I have my pack, they are my family, and so are you and your mom."

"I'm sorry." His words are soft, edged with sadness.

I hear the crunch of gravel and turn my head to see an old beat-up sedan slowly making its way down the driveway. I can see Greta clearly through the windshield.

What is she doing here? How did she know where we were?

The car comes to a stop, and she sits there for a moment, as if contemplating something. Finally, she opens the door and emerges, her eyes meeting ours. Even from this distance, I can make out the tears welling up in her eyes as emotions take hold. I rise to my feet, and Tyler does the same.

"Miss Greta?" His voice betrays his confusion.

Sara pushes out the door and makes her way over to us. "Greta, is everything okay?" Her concern bleeds into her voice.

The tiredness etched on the older woman's face goes far beyond the surface, as if it has seeped into the very core of her being. Gradually, she moves closer to us; her features morphing and shifting with each step. In a swift motion, I shield Tyler by positioning myself in front, and firmly grasp Sara's arm to halt her progress.

"Tyler. In the house now." I don't have to ask twice. He is gone, the door closing behind him with a loud bang. Sara and I watch as Greta changes from an older, white-haired, plump woman to an older version of Sara. With the same brown-tanned skin and dark wavy hair.

Sara's hands fly up to cover her mouth. "Mom?"

The older woman's face is streaked with tears as she nods, her emotions too overwhelming to contain. Sara doesn't ask her anything else, she simply rushes down the stairs and throws herself into her mom's waiting embrace. My chest tightens as I watch them cling to each other, their sobs mingling. I stand here, patiently waiting for them to release each other, before I start making my way over.

"Greta, I have a lot of questions," I admit.

"It's Marnie, not Greta."

"Marnie, then. Did you want to take a seat on the porch?"

She nods her head and wraps her arm around Sara as they ascend the stairs. While I should be glad that Sara has another opportunity with her mother, the questions are making me feel unsettled.

Why has she kept herself hidden all these years?

Why didn't she help her daughter escape the hunters?

Why not tell Sara who she really was earlier?

More and more questions begin trickling in, then another thought occurs to me as I watch them. Nesrin. She must have known about Greta's glamor. She can see through any magic spell.

Sara takes a seat with Marnie on the bench, and I lean against the railing, crossing my arms over my chest. Marnie looks at me and cringes, "I know I have some explaining to do."

"How are you alive?" The hurt in Sara's voice now overshadows the joy she felt a second ago.

"I was never meant to survive what Abe had planned for me. When his plans went wayward and I escaped, he was so angry. To be honest, I'm surprised I got away. That man was a nightmare."

"Why didn't you come for me?"

"I tried so many times. Abe knew I'd come for you. So, he locked you up tight. Never let you leave the compound. Then he married you off, and I didn't see any sign of you for almost a year. I tried to get you out several times, and failed over and over. I was hoping you'd be able to leave, and I could find you then. Abe knew I would keep coming for you, it was another way to control me. I hated that you were there, and all alone. Then when you did manage to escape, I shadowed you, covering your tracks, making sure you didn't get followed. I found you later, and did what I could to protect you. I wanted so badly to tell you who I was. I was worried you'd hate me." Marnie pauses a moment, and takes a deep breath, her eyes going glassy. "I was going to run, you know, when I found out I was pregnant. Your real father and I had a plan, but Abe found out, and we were caught." A heartbreaking sob escapes Marnie's throat, and she hunches over, clutching her own body.

Sara moves closer to her mom, wrapping her arms around her shoulders. "Mom?"

"I loved him so much. He was my soulmate, and Abe killed him in front of me. I will never be able to forget Asher's last moments, the words he spoke. How he loved me when he had no reason to." Marnie's eyes take a far-off look, her voice barely above a whisper.

"What did he say?" Sara whispers, tears clogging her voice.

"'I regret nothing. Because loving you was never an option.'"

Sara wraps her mom in a hug, burying their faces in each other's necks. "It's okay, mom," Sara's voice cracks.

Fuck. I hate this. I hate seeing her in this much anguish. I clench my jaw, looking away. If Abe wasn't already dead, I'd hunt him down and finish him off.

"You know, I didn't believe in love or soulmates until I met Asher," Marnie mutters, pulling back and stroking Sara's hair. "He opened my heart, my mind, and soul. He put fire in my heart, and brought peace to my mind. Our love made you. You are the best part of both of us, and I failed you. I couldn't protect you. Your father, even in death, protected us, protected you."

"I know. Abe mentioned a protection spell."

"Asher put a spell on me before he died, a protection spell that extended to you when you were born."

Anger swells in my chest. "Well, it didn't work." Sara's wide brown eyes snap to mine. "She was starved and beaten constantly." I leave out the sexual assaults, that is hers to tell if she chooses.

Marnie gasps, her breath catching in her throat, as she locks eyes with Sara. "How? No harm could befall us directly."

"He must have found a way around it." Sara blinks, her eyelashes fluttering against her cheeks, and I observe the subtle movement of her throat as she swallows. I want so badly to pull her into my arms.

"When I was five, when you left, it got bad. They branded me . . ." Sara trails off.

Marnie looks forlorn. "What do you mean?"

Sara lifts her shirt and Marnie gasps.

"Why did he keep you around after, and then keep me if everyone knew I wasn't his?" Sara lowers her shirt.

"Control. He wanted to make my life a living hell. And since he couldn't outright kill me, it was the next best thing. Until it wasn't. The night my team was ambushed, they turned on me, I had no choice but to run."

Our attention is drawn to the front door as it opens. With a sheepish look on her face, Nesrin walks out. Marnie stands up and walks toward Nesrin, their smiles widening as they meet each other halfway and share a warm embrace.

And I'm furious.

A tumultuous mix of anger and confusion consumes me as I watch them. How could Nesrin hide this from us?

Sara stands, and I push off the railing, walking over to her. She stretches out her hand, and I tightly grasp it while facing Nesrin and Marnie.

"How do you two know each other?" Sara is clearly confused.

Little does she know, Nesrin is the best at these types of spells. Because she can see magic, her spells and charms are holeproof. Plus, she can see other spells. No glamor would go unnoticed, so even if she didn't cast the spell, she would have seen through it.

"Nesrin was the one who cloaked and glamoured me when I followed you to Portland. I'd heard she was the best, and she helped me not only with the spells, but also in setting myself up," she explains, shifting her weight, and continues, "Nesrin worked her magic on the diner, too. She added a spell so it seemed like it had been there for years, blending perfectly into the neighborhood. No one even questioned it."

Sara stiffens. "Oh, okay. But why didn't you tell me who you were?"

"I was scared," she admits.

Sara scrunches up her face. "Why?"

"I thought you'd hate me, think I'd abandoned you. I didn't know what lies Abe might have spun."

"I thought you were dead."

Marnie's face is instantly drenched in shock. "He told you that?"

Sara remains silent, her head nodding in affirmation. I tug her into my arms, feeling the warmth of her body against mine. My hand gently rests on the curve of her waist, my thumb delicately caressing the contours of her ribs.

"Is that how you knew Gabe was a good guy? Through Nesrin?"

"Yes, Nesrin is someone I trust completely, and she spoke very highly of Gabe," she answers, her attention turning to me.

I'm absolutely fuming at my luna right now. Why didn't she tell me?

"I didn't know at first that she was Sara's mother," Nesrin pipes up, moving over to us. Her face seems pained. *'I hated keeping it from you, Gabe.'*

Suddenly, Lukas shoves out the front door, a thunderous look on his face. The door bangs against the house, causing all of us to jump.

Nesrin spins on him. "What the hell, Lukas? You scared the shit out of us."

Moving into her space, he speaks in a voice deadly calm. "I can feel you and Gabe down the bond, but most of all, you. And I don't like what I'm feeling, sweetheart."

Nesrin deflates. "I hid something from Gabe," she whispers, her voice filled with regret and sadness.

My heart lurches, as if being forcefully pulled downward by an invisible weight.

"Don't be mad at Nesrin. She was keeping my secret, like I asked her to," Marnie pleads, her eyes wide and hands shaking.

"Client confidentiality and all," Nesrin agrees self-consciously, her delicate shoulder rising as she turns to face us again. I know Nesrin, and she would have told me if she thought it was something I needed to know. The tension releases as I let go of Sara, and walk over, pulling Nesrin into a hug.

"Sorry."

Nesrin pulls back and pats my chest. "It's okay. You're acting as a mate would."

"Mate?" Sara and Marnie echo at the same time.

Nesrin smirks at me, then Sara moves into my space, wrapping her arms around my waist, her head resting on my chest. My arms go around her, and she tilts her head back, those big brown eyes filled with affection.

"You're mates?" Marnie wonders softly. Tears fill her eyes as her gaze goes to her daughter.

"Yes," I reply, looking down into Sara's eyes.

"We are truly mates?" she whispers.

My chest warms and my heart races. I lean down and give her a quick kiss on the lips. I want to do so much more with her, but that will have to wait.

"Yes. Sara is my destined. She holds the other end of the red thread."

"Red thread?" Sara asks, her confusion obvious.

"Yes, According to an ancient Japanese legend, when we are born, an invisible red thread is tied to our little finger. The other end of the thread is connected to someone we are destined to meet. The thread may tangle or stretch, but it will never break."

I find Tyler down by the river later that afternoon. My boots crunch on fallen leaves as I approach him. He's found a log along the bank, and is tossing rocks into the water. I take a seat beside him.

"How you doing, Tyler?"

"Fine." He glances in my direction.

This kid is a rock, on the run with his mom from an abusive family. He had her back, stood between us and his mom when he thought she was in trouble. Stood up to a dragon to protect Astraea, and he met his grandma for the first time today, and he's *fine*. I reach over to mess up his hair, and laughing, he pushes my hand away.

"What was that for?" he demands, eyes sparkling.

"I'm so proud of you, Tyler. You are brave and strong. You are going to grow up to be an amazing protector," I say in earnest, making sure he can see how serious I am. "You protected both your mom and Astraea in the last twenty-four hours. Without any hesitation, you stood firm against a threat bigger than you."

A well of tears form in his eyes, slowly trickling down his cheeks. With a burst of affection, Tyler launches himself into my arms, his grip on my neck firm and secure.

"I'm going to ask your mom to marry me," I reveal. "Do I have your permission?"

He doesn't pull away. Instead, he keeps his face buried in my shoulder, his little head gently nodding.

We stay by the river, the gentle breeze rolling over us, carrying with it a sense of tranquility. Tyler's quiet as he stares out into the distance, his eyes reflecting a mix of confusion and curiosity.

I've come to notice the subtle signs of emotional exhaustion etched across his face. His furrowed brows, tired eyes, and the occasional sigh are all indicative of the whirlwind of events that have unfolded in the past month. It has been a rollercoaster of emotions, leaving him in need of time to process and make sense of everything. I have no doubt he will pull through.

With rocks in hand, I stand and flick them across the water, creating ripples that dance and disappear. Tyler jumps up and follows my lead. Together, we throw rocks while I ponder how I'm going to propose to Sara.

Chapter Thirty-Nine

SARA

"What do you mean you're going back?" I stammer as I stare at my mom on the other side of the kitchen table at Gabe's house. It's just the two of us. Gabe and Tyler are down by the river. Tyler is quickly adapting to our new normal. I'm so proud of him. Astraea appears to have left a lasting impression on him since the encounter with the dragon, as he now seems awestruck and fiercely protective of her. Gabe's revelation that she exclusively communicates through telepathy caught me off guard. I don't understand why she would choose to be mute. It's hard for me to comprehend.

"I've thought long and hard about it, and the only way I can keep you safe is if I go back and take over the leadership of the clan. It's time for a change," Mom explains.

"But it doesn't have to be you!" Leaning back in my chair, I bring my nail to my mouth and begin to nervously nibble on it, a habit I can't seem to break. Mom reaches over, her hand warm and comforting as she intertwines her fingers with mine.

"It does."

I stand up and start pacing, my heart pounding in my chest. "I just got you back. You can't leave."

Mom sits there patiently, her eyes never leaving me, observing my every move. She's prepared for my reaction, knowing exactly how I will respond. "I know, sweetie, but I need to do this."

With a sigh of defeat, I feel my shoulders deflate, a weight of disappointment settling upon me. "It has to be you?"

"Yes, I know the inner workings of the clan, and I know many who aren't happy with how things are being run. Your grandfather, who was my father, served as a clan leader for a long time. Shortly after I married Abe, my father passed away, and Abe took over. I had a suspicion that Abe was the one responsible for his death, but it's something I'll never be certain of. This is why Abe could never outright kill me, I was technically the next in line."

"But I just found out you were still alive this morning."

I know I sound selfish, and I'm absolutely whining, but this is my mom. I would have given anything to have her back, and here she is, and now she's leaving again.

"I know, sweetie."

"What can I do?"

"You can stay here with Gabe and be happy. You deserve to be happy."

I'm already shaking my head, getting ready to argue, when she walks up and grabs my hands. "Sweetie, all I want is you to be happy and safe. You are both here with your new family."

"You're my family, too." Emotions render my voice hoarse.

"No matter what happens, I will always be your family. This doesn't mean we won't see each other. It's time I made things right.

I will fix things with the clan, I promise. It's time for a change, and I'm determined to see that change through."

Just as I start to feel a tingling sensation on my skin, shadows start to gather at the doorway, and Leila and Nesrin emerge into the kitchen.

"What are you guys doing here?" I ask, confusion making me slow to react.

Nesrin gives me an awkward smile. Then they both turn their heads to look at my mom, their eyes filled with concern.

"Are you ready, Marnie?" Leila steps forward.

What?

My eyes dart back and forth between my mom and Leila. "You're leaving *now?*" I whisper through my tightening throat.

As our eyes meet, I see the tears welling in hers. "Yes."

Nesrin moves closer to me, her hand reaching out to grab mine. "We need to make our move now before they secure a new leader."

I shake my head furiously, pulling from her grasp.

Mom comes closer, taking my face in her hands. "I'm going to be back, I swear," she promises fervently, her eyes burning into mine.

"What if they kill you?" I choke out the thought, sending a new wave of panic through me.

"No, sweetie, they won't."

She enfolds me in her embrace, and we cling to each other with fierce intensity. When she releases me, planting a tender kiss on my forehead, she crosses over to Leila, who stands stoically by the door. Nesrin clasps my hand once more, her touch radiating warmth and solace as she draws me closer to her side. Leaning my head against her shoulder, I observe as Leila gently grasps my mother's hand, sharing a silent acknowledgment with Nesrin. Then, her gaze meets mine, and in that fleeting instant, I detect a glimmer of empathy in her eyes, yet our time together is so limited, leaving me filled with uncertainty.

Swirling shadows dance around them, creating an eerie atmosphere. Mom glances at me, blowing a kiss in my direction, before turning to Nesrin with a heartfelt plea in her eyes.

"Take care of my girl and grandson."

"I will. I promise," Nesrin chokes out, the emotions in the room gripping her as well.

Mom and Leila melt into the shadows, their figures blending seamlessly with the darkness, until they vanish completely, leaving behind nothing but an empty doorway. I lift my head from Nesrin's shoulder and walk over to the table. As I fall into my chair, I catch sight of Nesrin moving over to the counter and starting the coffee machine.

"Coffee?" she offers, clearing her throat.

"Yes, thank you," I mumble, rubbing my hands over my face.

"It's going to be alright," Nesrin soothes.

I give her a weak smile. "I sure hope so."

The mere idea of her going to the place where I endured years of imprisonment and abuse makes me feel sick to my stomach. That reminds me.

"We have decaf."

"Oh, my goddess. NO!" Nesrin refuses, paling. "I'll have a hot chocolate."

A smile pulls at the corner of my mouth. "Not a fan then?"

"Nope." Nesrin sighs. "The next seven months are going to be torture without caffeine."

Unable to contain my laughter, I realize just how grateful I am that she's here with me.

"I'm literally fueled by coffee and books," she cries.

As the machine hums to life, a sequence of beeps fills the room, alerting that it is ready to brew. I jump up and stroll over, playfully bumping my hip into hers.

"I'll have a hot chocolate, too. I won't subject you to the torment of inhaling the sweet aroma of freshly ground coffee."

Her wide, amber eyes meet mine, and she looks forlorn. "You'd do that for me?"

I try to suppress my smile. "Of course."

Nesrin's eyes fill with tears, and she sniffs. "Damn hormones," she mutters.

Chapter Forty

Sara

My feet splash down into a murky puddle as I jump out of Gabe's car, quickly shutting the door behind me. My gaze lifts to the towering, abandoned church before me, a deep frown forming on my face.

"This is where the vampire lives?" I inquire, skepticism lacing my words.

"Yeah, it's a bit cliché, but Stephan likes to keep people guessing," Gabe responds, his voice tinged with amusement. He reaches out and clasps my hands in his own, the warmth of his touch providing a sense of reassurance. Together, we ascend the weathered stone steps, each one looking as if it might crumble beneath our weight.

As we approach, my eyes wander to the graveyard on the left, a haunting sight of decaying and crumbling tombstones. The silence hangs heavy in the air, broken only by the distant hoot of an owl. The absence of any other nearby buildings or houses is striking, as if this eerie place has been purposely isolated from the world.

A chill seeps into my bones, sending a shiver coursing through me. I squeeze Gabe's hand tighter, seeking comfort in his presence.

In response, he grins down at me, his eyes glinting mischievously, and he gives me a playful wink.

My return smile is weak. "I thought Zee and Leila were meeting us here?"

"They are," Gabe affirms, directing my attention toward the top of the stairs. I follow his gaze and watch as a shadow portal materializes, with Zee and Leila emerging from it.

"Right. Everyone ready?" Zee says cheerfully, rubbing his hands together.

Is he always this easy going? I rarely see him without his dimpled smile or a sparkle in his eye. I like it, don't get me wrong, but serious situations call for serious responses.

"How are you always so happy?"

Leila lets out a snort of laughter, prompting Zee to playfully jab her in the ribs. "It's part of my charm."

I twist my lips to the side and grin. "It does suit you."

Zee stops at the door and pulls it open. Leila and Gabe enter first, then Zee motions for me to go through.

"Shouldn't we knock first?" I whisper harshly. Panic rises in my throat. The last thing I want to do is offend the vampire, especially when my best friend is somewhere in there.

"You didn't wait to be let in," I hiss, a slight note of panic coming through.

"He knows we're here, darlin'." Zee drawls.

Seeing my hesitation, he hooks his arm in mine, basically dragging me inside.

"He won't bite. Actually, he might, but only if that's what you wanted."

Gabe glares over his shoulder at Zee, his almond eyes glowing a soft golden color.

I cautiously enter the building, my pace slowing so much that Zee releases his hold on me. I am completely mesmerized by the overwhelming grandeur surrounding me. The sight of the towering architecture leaves me in awe. The air carries a faint scent of old wood and polished marble, adding to the ambience of the place. Overwhelmed by the stark contrast to the exterior, I can't help but wonder if this is some kind of clever optical illusion.

There are luxury couches and high-top tables scattered about the room, sheer curtains hung from the rafters. The most prominent feature in the room is the expansive bar situated at the back. The wall behind it is entirely covered in glass mirrors, creating a stunning reflection of the bottles neatly arranged on the shelves. Sitting there, my eyes catch on two figures, and I gasp. *Mallory.*

My heart races as I quicken my footsteps, desperate to reach Mallory. Everything else falls away, all that matters in this moment is her. As she stands, I notice she is wearing a long black dress. The material clings to her lithe frame, and the sleeves come to her wrists. I don't think I have ever seen her in a dress before. She looks beautiful. Her short brown hair is straightened into an inverted bob that really suits her. But as my eyes come to her face, I see the stress there. She looks like she hasn't been getting much sleep. The dark circles under her eyes are prominent, and her skin paler than usual. Giving me a weak smile, she moves toward me, and I meet her halfway, wrapping her in a tight hug. We hold onto each other for quite some time before breaking apart, both of us crying softly.

"Are you okay?" I reach up and touch her hair. Mal's usually vibrant blue eyes are dim as she looks back at me and attempts a smile.

"I'm okay. Are you okay? Tyler?"

"We are fine. Great, actually." It comes out as a whisper, tears building up behind my eyes, making my nose sting. "I'm so sorry, Mal."

"Nothing to be sorry about. I knew the dangers. We both did."

My arms tighten around her, refusing to let go.

Murmurs begin to reach my ears, and we gradually pull apart. My hands reach up, cupping her bruised face, and I chew on my bottom lip.

"I'd kill him if he wasn't already dead," I mutter.

Mallory's eyes widen before they drop to the ground. "He's dead?"

I swallow hard, realizing my blunder. "Yeah, he attacked me, and Lukas, the alpha, had to step in."

"Good," she whispers, but her voice sounds broken.

I notice she keeps glancing back at Stephan, so I turn again and smile at the vampire. He's handsome and clean cut, wearing tailored black pants and a black, buttoned up shirt. His equally black hair is short and styled artfully. The black on black really makes his bright ocean blue eyes stand out. I open my mouth to thank him, but he shakes his head.

"You don't need to thank me." Those blue eyes narrow, as if daring me to argue.

"Okay, then, I won't."

It falls quiet and I shuffle nervously on my feet. I've never seen Mal so worn down. She always kept my head above the water, so to speak. If it wasn't for her, I would have given up on life ten years ago.

"Are you ready to come back? Gabe has made you up a room."

Mallory steps back, tucking her short brown hair behind her ear. "I'm staying here."

My body locks up, and I'm lost for words. *What?*

"What do you mean, you're staying here?"

Stephan steps up to Mallory's side and offers her a soft smile. "Mallory would like to stay here with me."

I narrow my eyes at the vampire. "I wasn't asking you," I snap. "Mal, you can't want to stay with a vampire?"

"But I do, and I trust him."

Hurt blossoms in my chest as I stare at my friend. "You don't trust me?"

Mal grabs my hands in hers. "Of course I do. I trust you with my life. I just . . . "

Mal turns her head to glance at Stephan, and I follow her line of sight. In that moment, the air seems to spark with a delicate tenderness, as if a soft melody is playing in the background. A sense of protectiveness radiates from the vampire's gaze as he stares at Mal.

I sigh, my shoulders slumping. "If you change your mind, there's room for you with us."

Mal's eyes come back to mine. "I know. Thank you."

With that, I release her hands and turn to face Stephan, feeling a mixture of nerves and awareness. "I'm Sara." I hold my hand out.

Stephan grins, a dimple showing in his cheek, and he slides his hand into mine. "Pleasure. I'm Stephan, Master of the City."

Behind me, Zee's laughter fills the air, but I pay it no mind.

"If you hurt my friend, I will hunt you down."

Stephan's grin widens, and he nods his head in acknowledgment. "I would expect nothing less from you."

Taken aback, I quickly let go of his hand and retreat a step. Gabe's presence radiates warmth as he stands behind me, his hands gently resting on my waist as he plants a tender kiss on my shoulder.

Mal shuffles nervously on her feet before Stephan's hand slides around her waist, pulling her closer. I watch my friend visibly relax, practically melting into Stephan's side. I'm worried about her. But as I study the two of them, I can't deny the level of comfort between them. She trusts him, and I can see that he cares for her on some level.

'Stephan isn't a bad guy. He will look after her,' Gabe's voice floats through my mind, startling me.

Zee strolls forward with an easy confidence I envy and extends his hand toward Mal. "I'm Zee, and this is my wife, Leila. We all have your back now, so if you need anything, anytime, we'll be there." His voice is warm, sincere.

Mal's gaze shifts from Zee's outstretched hand to his face, hesitation flickering in her eyes. For a moment, she seems unsure, the weight of her past making her wary of trust. Finally, she reaches out and takes his hand in her own.

"Thank you," she murmurs, her voice barely above a whisper.

"You're family," Zee replies.

Mal's cheeks flush with a delicate blush, and I can tell she's as taken aback by their warmth and acceptance as I was when I first met them. It's not easy to be welcomed so openly, especially when you're used to walls and cold shoulders.

"You know Nesrin can heal those injuries for you in the blink of an eye." Zee eyes her injuries.

Mal nods. "Stephan said as much. But I need to get over the pain myself," she replies, a quiet determination lacing her words.

"She won't even take vampire blood to help," Stephan grouses from the side, his tone a mix of exasperation and admiration for her stubbornness.

I raise an eyebrow at him, struggling to stifle a laugh. "Gross," I choke out, the word dripping with mock disgust.

Mal sniffs, trying to hold back a giggle, and our eyes meet, sharing a moment of understanding.

"And with Marnie leading the hunters in Montana, we don't have to worry about retaliation. You're safe," Gabe adds.

"Your mom is alive?" Mal stammers.

"Yes." My heart is pounding. I'm still not used to the idea that she has been under my nose for so long.

"Holy shit."

"Right?"

"I have so many questions."

Laughter escapes my lips, making me feel more at ease. "So did I."

Mal's demeanor shifts, her previously relaxed stance now replaced with a seriousness. "The most important one being why the fuck didn't she come for you?"

As Gabe lets out a single grunt of agreement, the room grows still and silent, the tension thickening in the air.

"I'm choosing to forgive her. She had her reasons, and if she had come for me and we somehow made it out alive, I wouldn't have the joy of raising Tyler, nor the chance to meet Gabe."

Her thoughts are written all over her face. If only my mother had arrived to rescue me, I wouldn't have suffered through the torture, neglect, and sexual abuse. Yet I wouldn't change any of it, not even for a moment, because I wouldn't want to miss out on any of this.

Gabe's protective nature is evident, and I can tell he is deeply troubled by what happened to me. He wishes he could change it for me. That my mother had gotten me out sooner. But I have made my peace with it.

After I fill Mal in on everything that's happened, we say our goodbyes, making our way back to the car. My mind goes to my magic, and Tyler's. It's unpredictable, and we know nothing of the magic world beyond the whispered lies I heard from Kirk and Abe. The big question on my mind is, do we train with the local coven, or do I take Nesrin's offered help?

I look over to Leila, who has been silent this whole time, observing. Her amber eyes glow with magic as we walk down the steps. I feel a little uneasy in her presence, which is unfair, as I only met her today. She and Nesrin look so much alike, but Leila's hair is redder and her skin paler. Noticing my gaze, Leila looks straight at me and smiles softly. '*You have a family now who loves you and will back you no matter what you choose to do.*'

I pause my steps as I try to process the fact her voice was in my head.

"We are heading out. See you at training in the morning." Zee claps Gabe on the back.

"No worries, man," Gabe replies.

I wave awkwardly as they step through a portal and disappear. Leila's words echo in my mind. I've been on my own my whole life, and now I have all these people ready to help me at the drop of a hat.

My nerves are slightly rattled as I climb into the car, and sensing my disquiet, Gabe looks over at me. "You, okay?"

"Can Leila speak to people telepathically?" I blurt.

Frowning as he drives, he casts me a quick glance. "Uhh, maybe? I don't know. She has only ever done that with Zee that I know of, but she can manipulate minds, and get in people's heads, so probably."

"Like you?" My fingers twist in my sweater.

"Similar, I suppose, but we've never really sat down and discussed it. Leila is quite a more silent partner in our family. She barely gets involved, and is tight-lipped on her abilities."

"Oh."

"Why? Did she say something to you?"

"Yes," I confirm, and at his growl, I rush to reassure him. "It wasn't anything bad. I just wasn't expecting it."

"What did she say?"

"Just something about having a family now, and they would back me"

Gabe is silent, and I watch as a gorgeous smile overtakes his face. Turning his head, he looks at me. "She likes you." His attention goes back to the road, and I internally scratch my head.

"Okay." I draw the word out, hoping he'll fill me in.

His deep brown eyes, so expressive, meet mine again. "That's big, baby"

"Okay."

Gabe laughs, the sound rich and genuine, his head shaking in quiet amusement. There's something about the way he laughs that feels infectious, and before I know it, a smile tugs at the corners of my lips. It's beyond my control, the kind of smile that creeps in slowly but stays there, warm and unshakable.

It's been so long since I've felt this light, this free. The weight that's been pressing down on me for what feels like forever has finally lifted, and it's almost surreal. Mal is safe. That knowledge alone has wiped away so much of my fear. Even though she chose to stay, it was her choice—hers. She has control over her life, and that matters more than anything. Tyler is safe, too, and for the first time in what feels like a lifetime, I have my mom back.

Life is finally looking like what I've always dreamed about, but never really believed I'd get. I'm not going to spend my life running anymore, or looking over my shoulder. For the first time in a long time, I can breathe.

I glance over to Gabe, taking in his profile as he drives, the sunlight catching the strong lines of his face. He's undeniably attractive—his dark hair tousled just enough to give him that effortless, rugged look. But it's more than just his looks. There's a quiet confidence about him, an ease that radiates from him, drawing people in. His charm seems to pour out of him without even trying, like he's used to making people smile, making them feel safe.

"What?" he inquires softly. Reaching over, he takes my hand, linking our fingers, bringing them to rest on his thigh.

As I gaze at him, I can feel a warmth spreading in my chest, as if it's expanding. "I'm so lucky to have found you."

With a grin on his face, he gives my hand a reassuring squeeze. "I believe I found you."

"Semantics." I shrug, feeling an overwhelming sense of joy that makes me want to kiss Gabe at this very moment.

"You're gorgeous," he counters, focusing his attention on me, before looking back to the road. My cheeks warm, heating my face, and I lean over the seat to plant a gentle kiss on his cheek.

Chapter Forty-One

GABE

From the balcony, I observe Astraea and Tyler making their way toward the river with Malachite close to Astraea's side. I can sense Tyler's initial nervousness melting away. He's becoming more at ease with Malachite. It must have been a tremendous shock for him to see a dragon.

Nesrin supports both him and Sara in honing their magical abilities, with assistance from Claudia, Marcus's cousin, who possesses similar magical talents. By the water's edge, Nissa and a few other sprites appear, adding an ethereal atmosphere to the scene. It continues to amaze me that Nissa, the queen of the sprites, has been visiting our group ever since Nesrin and Astraea arrived. While it's widely known that Astraea is the reason for Nissa's presence, having her around brings a sense of relief to all of us, as it provides an extra layer of protection with the ongoing interest of the Seelie queen in Astraea. Nesrin went to great lengths to ensure Astraea's safety, with multiple layers of protection surrounding her. In addition, every pack member wears charms to ward off any attempts at mind control, and the entire pack land is heavily warded. If the fae do try to get near Astraea, they are going to have a hard time doing it undetected.

My mind wanders to Sara, and I can feel her presence as she ascends the stairs toward the bedroom. After the tumultuous events of the past two days, Sara and I haven't found the opportunity to discuss what she revealed to us in the apartment. The fact that Abe forced her to marry at such a young age is truly inconceivable. The mere thought of what she endured ignites a fiery rage within me. My fury is so great that I would break every rule I have set for my magic just to inflict the same pain on them that they had inflicted on her. I can't even begin to fathom the fact that he tried to kill her. My fingers curl over the railing, and I hear the wood splinter under my grip. I close my eyes and take a deep breath, loosening my grasp.

I become aware of Sara's presence as she moves through the house and ascends the stairs to the bedroom. I need to calm down. I listen as the bedroom door opens and closes, and I hear her gentle footsteps drawing near. Sara's vibrant energy envelops me like a warm breeze as she steps out onto the balcony. The gentle rustle of her flowing dress mingles with the distant chatter of the forest. A wave of calmness washes over me as her delicate hand makes contact with the fabric of my shirt, a comforting touch that soothes my senses. Gradually, she encircles her arms around my waist, her soft cheek nestling against my back, sending a pang of tenderness through my chest.

"What are you doing up here?" she whispers.

I let go of the railing and carefully grip her wrists, smoothly pulling her around my body. In the sunlight, her beautiful brown skin has a warm glow, and her hair falls in gentle waves around her face. God, she is beautiful. Stepping closer, I feel her hands on my waist as she leans back against the railing. I lightly run my fingers across her forehead and gently trace them down her face, sweeping her hair over her shoulders. I can't stop my fingers trailing over her bare shoulders in lazy circles.

"I love this dress on you," I murmur, dropping my head and kissing her shoulder.

Sara giggles, a shiver running through her at my touch. A rumble works its way up my throat, and I gently bite down on the sweet spot where her neck and shoulder join, her fingers tightening on my shirt, pulling me closer.

"Gabe," her breathless words send a shot of desire through me.

"You're so fucking beautiful, baby." My fists grip her dress, lifting it up her legs.

I pull back, needing to see her face, and finding myself mesmerized by the depth of emotion in her big, brown eyes that shimmer with affection. Our foreheads touch, and a comforting warmth spreads between us.

I sigh, almost regretting my next words. "We need to talk."

Sara stiffens against me, and I drop the material of her dress, wrapping my arms around her waist.

"Those are not the words anyone wants to hear from their partner," she murmurs, an edge of vulnerability to her words.

"I want to talk about what happened, what they did to you."

Sara's body tenses, her muscles tighten like a snake ready to strike. I can practically feel the surge of emotions radiating from her—a mix of apprehension and fear that hangs heavy between us.

She instinctively withdraws, trying to distance herself from me. A soft whimper escapes her throat, the sound barely audible amidst the tension. Her head shakes in a rapid motion, as if trying to shake off the overwhelming emotions, and guilt washes through me.

I reach up and cup the back of her neck, my fingers sliding through the soft waves. "It doesn't have to be now. When you're ready. I want to know everything. You shouldn't carry that burden alone."

"Gabe, I– I'm not sure I can talk about it."

"Baby, they made your life a living hell. They couldn't kill you, so they found ways to make you suffer. Kirk . . . " I grit my teeth, a growl rumbling in my chest. "He almost killed you. He almost killed Tyler."

With each word I speak, my body grows increasingly tense, my muscles tightening like a tautly stretched rubber band. Heat radiates from my skin, causing a prickling sensation that intensifies with each passing second. The room around me blurs, as if a veil of mist has descended upon the world, distorting everything in my vision.

My eyes, normally a calm shade of brown, now shimmer with an otherworldly glow. I know this because I see them reflected back at me in Sara's eyes. The intensity of my anger seems to manifest itself within them, turning them into fiery orbs that burn with ferocious determination. It's as if my very soul has been set ablaze, fueling the torrent of emotions coursing through my veins.

"Gabe, honey," Sara whispers, her words filled with tenderness. My anger at what happened to her seems to drive her fear of the memories away. "I can seek professional counseling to help Tyler and me navigate through our past. But I don't think it's fair to burden you with this."

With a deep breath, I try to regain control over my emotions, willing the haze to dissipate, and the glow in my eyes to fade. Slowly, the world around me sharpens, returning to its familiar form.

"I want you to confide in me. I want to be there for you," I grumble.

Sara's hand smooths over my jaw, and she leans in, brushing her lips over mine. "Gabe, I love you. I love that you want to help me get through this, but I think, at least for now, I need to open up to someone who won't want to set the hunter's compound on fire."

I close my eyes and release a string of curses.

"I can help you find someone," I concede.

Sara smiles and wraps her arms around my neck. "Thank you."

I can't hold back anymore. All of the energy shimmering in my body finally releases, and I lean forward, my arms tightening around her waist as I crush our mouths together.

I trail my lips across the side of her mouth and across her jaw. Now that I've started kissing her, I can't stop. Sara's hands thread into my hair and she sighs. My mouth moves back to hers in a kiss even more filled with need. This kiss is fueled by a deep craving. A kiss that makes my lungs ache and my erection so hard it hurts.

Pressing a kiss to her neck, I gather up her dress and lightly suck on her pulse. I run my fingers along the delicate fabric of her panties, and instantly, her breathing becomes more rapid.

"Gabe . . ."

"I got you, baby."

I scoop her up and carry her into the bedroom, laying her on the bed. My hands run up her silky-smooth legs, feeling the warmth of her skin, before slowly removing her panties and letting them fall to the floor. Before she can react, I spread her knees and drop my mouth to her clit. The breathy moan that escapes her mouth has a satisfied smile pulling at my lips.

I gently push my fingers into her, feeling her warmth encircling them. She cries out, clenching around me, gripping my fingers tightly. She is hot and wet, like a pool of molten honey. I twist my wrist, my fingers sinking deeper, seeking out that exquisitely sensitive flesh. Sara jerks, her hips rolling in response.

"Oh!" she gasps, her back arching off the bed.

I stroke my fingers over it again, curling my fingers and massaging the sweet spot. Her hands dive into my hair, her hips bucking against my mouth.

"Oh," she moans. "Oh, god."

I bite down gently on her clit before soothing it with my tongue. I feel her legs quivering, and I maintain a steady rhythm with my fingers, applying just the right amount of pressure to that sweet spot while simultaneously licking and sucking her clit.

"Gabe . . . Oh . . . " Her body tightens and spasms, a rush of warmth coursing through her as she quivers under my touch. But I'm not finished. No, I continue to work her, drawing out her orgasm.

Raising my head, I sink my teeth into her inner thigh, relishing the sensation of warm skin. She yelps in surprise, and I withdraw my fingers from her body as I rise to my feet, quickly shedding my clothes. I'm unable to stop the smirk from coming over my face. Despite Sara's dazed expression, she reaches out for me as I climb onto the bed, pulling my body close to hers.

My senses are overwhelmed as I enter her, feeling the tightness and heat wrapping around me. Fuck.

"Baby, you feel fucking amazing," I growl slowly, pulling out and driving back in. "Like you were fucking made just for me."

"Gabe!" Sara cries out, her nails digging into my shoulder, her hips rising to meet my thrusts.

I nuzzle her neck and keep talking, knowing how much she likes it. "Made to take my cock," I groan, her walls clenching around me. "Baby, you keep squeezing me like that, and I'm not going to last."

Sara moans, her arms wrapping around my neck. I roll us over, my hands eagerly pushing her dress up and over her head as she sinks down onto me. With a rhythmic motion, I flex my hips, matching her movements as she lifts and lowers herself. Holding her waist firmly, I grind against her, creating a pleasurable friction between us.

White stars burst behind my eyes, and I feel my body tighten. "Baby, I'm not wearing a condom," I grit out.

"I don't care. Do you?" she pants.

My heart jumps in my chest, and I cup her face with both hands, our bodies still moving. "Are you sure?" I ask roughly.

Sara nods, and I fucking lose it. My desire rockets with her silent agreement of having a child with me, should it happen. I flip her onto her back and drive into her. My hand glides down her thigh, and I grip her calf, raising her leg and placing it on my shoulder. My hands move to cup her breasts and roll her nipples between my fingers and thumbs. Her body trembles, causing her to tighten around my cock.

"Fuck," I growl.

Dropping my head, I capture her nipple with my lips and gently tease it with my tongue. Sara's body convulses as she lets out a sharp cry, her hips lifting to grind against my hand. My body stiffens, my release flooding into her warmth as she clenches me tightly, her climax sending waves of pleasure through both of us.

My hands fist her hair as I move inside her, slowly drawing out the pleasure. I nuzzle my face into her neck, her hands skimming over my sides.

"Fuck, baby," I murmur, placing a kiss on her cheek.

"Hmm," she hums in response.

Suddenly, an energy stirs in the distance, and my senses pick up the sound of Tyler and Astraea's footsteps as they race back toward the house, laughter following them.

"Kids are heading back. We'd better get dressed," I tell her quietly.

Sara sighs as I reluctantly withdraw and get up from the bed. I gaze at her, her warm brown skin flushed and radiating a healthy glow. I scoop up her dress and pull it over her head as she stands and tugs it down her body. As she shakes her hair free, strands cascade down her shoulders, swaying with each movement. Swiftly, she swoops in for a brief, stolen kiss, before running out the door.

Chapter Forty-Two

SARA

With a big smile on my face, I bound down the stairs and spot the kids, who have nearly reached the house. *How did Gabe know that?*

Dammit. In my haste, I forgot my underwear. I quickly duck into the bathroom under the stairs and clean myself up.

As the back door slams open, I quietly slip from the bathroom, straightening my dress, and greet the children with a warm smile.

"Have fun down at the river?"

"Yep! Nissa came and brought some of her friends. Did you know she is a queen?!" Tyler exclaims excitedly.

Laughing, I walk over to ruffle his hair. "I didn't know that."

'You're pretty,' a soft melodic voice floats through my head.

My heart leaps, and I glance over at Astraea. Her beautiful blond curls are tied back in a ponytail today, accentuating her small face and making her blue, almost violet eyes appear larger.

'Thank you,' I say in my mind, wanting to test to see if she can hear me.

Astraea's grin widens. *'You're welcome.'*

Gabe enters the kitchen, and Astraea beams, running for him. He scoops her up in his arms and my heart melts. Gosh, he is so good with kids. An image pops into my mind of Gabe holding our little girl, and I realize that I want nothing more in the world. Astraea's gaze briefly lands on me, a smile playing on her lips, before she redirects her attention to Gabe. She must say something to him, because his eyes immediately lock onto mine. I feel a rush of warmth spreading through my body at the intensity in that one look. My cheeks flush, betraying the fluttering in my heart. Shivers run down my spine, and my breath catches in my throat. It's as if time stands still, and the world around us fades into the background.

I can't help but notice the way his eyes soften, filled with a mix of tenderness and longing. The image of him holding our little girl becomes more vivid in my mind, and a wave of affection washes over me, mingling with the anticipation of a future we could share together.

Astraea's smile reflects my own happiness, as if she knows the significance of this moment. Her presence adds a touch of innocence and purity to the scene, reminding me of the joy and love that awaits us. It's as if she's silently urging me to take a leap of faith, to embrace the possibility of building a family with Gabe.

My heart flutters uncontrollably, matching the rhythm of my racing pulse. Every nerve in my body seems to be on high alert. The kitchen suddenly feels charged with electric energy, and I find myself drawn to him, my feet moving instinctively.

As I approach, I can see the reflection of my own emotions mirrored in his eyes. The love, the desire, the unspoken promises—they all dance within his eyes. It's a connection that goes beyond words, transcending the boundaries of time and space.

In that moment, I know Gabe has the power to make my dreams come true. And as our eyes remain locked, I can't help but hope that he sees the same future in me. Gabe reaches for my hand when I'm close enough, and pulls me into him.

"My niece just told me something very interesting," he mutters thoughtfully.

Tyler jumps up on the stool and spins around. "What did she say?"

Gabe tips my chin back and stares down at me. "Baby."

"Yes," I whisper.

"You want a family with me?"

My heart takes off in a sprint. "Yes."

Astraea claps her little hands and leans forward, resting her forehead on mine. Images flash in my mind of me pregnant, Gabe and Tyler fishing down by the river. When Astraea pulls away, breaking the connection, tears instantly flood my eyes, making my nose burn.

Gabe sets Astraea down and then pulls me into a warm embrace, his arms encircling me. "Whatever you want, it's yours, Sara."

Before I can answer, one of the kids opens the door, and Malachite comes barreling through, sending water flying everywhere. I shriek, covering my face, and the kids burst into laughter. Gabe just drops his head, his lips trailing over my bare shoulder, sending goosebumps scattering over my skin.

"I love you," Gabe whispers in my ear.

I wrap my arms tightly around his neck, pulling him closer, our lips meeting in a passionate kiss.

As we kiss, the sound of children's laughter fills the air, blending with the echoes of water splashing on the floor. The room fills with the scent of wetness, mixed with the sweet fragrance of Gabe's cologne. Goosebumps crawl across my skin, a combination of both the cool water and the warmth of Gabe's touch. Despite the chaos, there is an undeniable feeling of love and joy in the air, as if time has momentarily stood still.

Chapter Forty-Three

GABE

The crimson hues of the setting sun paint the sky in a breathtaking display of colors. Sara sits between my legs, and Tyler is down by the river, trying to catch frogs. The river's currents have gained momentum in the past day or two, but the section near my house remains calm due to the protective barrier of rocks.

I wrap my arms around Sara's waist, pulling her close as we watch the sun sink lower on the horizon, casting long shadows over the river. The air is alive with the sound of crickets, and the distant cry of birds echoes through the air, a symphony of nature's beauty.

She rests her head on my chest, and I can't stop myself from leaning down and smelling her hair. She giggles, tilting her head back to look at me. Without uttering a single word, I gently grasp her chin, tilting her face upward, and softly press my lips against hers. My heart swells with love and contentment. In moments like these, I feel as if the whole world fades away, and it's just us.

"Do you feel that?" she whispers, pulling back to meet my gaze.

"What?"

"It's as if the world is holding its breath, waiting for something magical to happen."

I grin, kissing her on the forehead. "Maybe it already has," I muse.

I reach into my pocket, feeling the cool metal band against my fingertips, and carefully retrieve the exquisite gold ring Tyler helped me choose mere hours ago. I hold it in my hand, admiring the princess-cut pink diamond, sparkling in the sunlight, while the delicate diamond accents shimmer with an enchanting allure. My heart races as I bring my hand in front of us, holding up the ring. Sara's hands fly to her mouth as she gasps in surprise. I bend down, softly brushing her ear with my lips.

"Will you marry me, Sara?"

She turns slowly in my arms, as if afraid that it's all just a dream. Kneeling before me, she looks directly into my eyes.

"You're being serious?"

With a grin, I gently grasp her left hand, lifting it up as I slide the gleaming gold band onto her finger. "Of course, I am."

A mischievous glint dances in Sara's eyes as she grins at me, tenderly cradling my face and drawing closer. Our lips brush, igniting a storm inside of me. Running my fingers through her hair, I deepen the kiss, her mouth parting on a gasp. Like a gentle breeze, a current of magic swiftly glides over our skin, my fingers tightening in response, drawing a moan from her.

"Is that a yes?" I murmur, pulling back just enough to look into those warm, inviting eyes.

"Yes," Sara answers with a nod.

"Thank fuck," I reply, giving her a soft kiss. "Tyler will be so happy."

We both look over at Tyler, who has wandered out onto a large rock. With each skip of the stone, he inches farther out onto the slippery rocks that jut into the river.

Sara tenses beneath my hands. I'm about to call out to Tyler when the air is shattered by a deafening screech, and the rhythmic sound of beating wings. Gently, I push Sara backward so I can stand. Just as I do, another desperate screech sounds, making Tyler slip. Time seems to slow down as I watch him plunge into the river, his body spinning and tumbling.

"Tyler!" Sara screams, her voice choked with fear.

Tyler cries for help, but his voice is lost amidst the rush of the water as it sweeps him away with merciless speed. In a heartbeat, I'm at the water's edge. An incantation silently falls from my lips, my hands raised, and the current stops as if frozen in time. My body trembles with the effort to keep the current at bay. I wade deeper into the water, reaching down until my fingers brush against the surface of the water with gentle precision. A ripple spreads outward from my touch, creating a shimmering barrier that encapsulates Tyler, shielding him from harm and guiding him back to the shore. I scoop him up in my arms, and the second he is safe, I let go of the water, the sound roaring in my ears.

I turn, placing Tyler down on the grass, as Sara falls to her knees, checking him over.

The desperate sound of an animal in pain reaches me, and I look up just as Talon comes crashing through the trees. His wings flap in earnest, and he tries to land, but stumbles and falls, rolling several times over the ground. My blood boils with anger as I take in the sight of him. Blood seeps from multiple wounds, and his wing appears to be in a mangled state. What the hell happened to him?

Talon lifts his head, his golden eyes filled with a desperate plea. Without hesitation, I materialize by his side and caress his face, running my hand over his head. The griffin looks starved and in pretty bad shape.

"What happened to you?" I whisper, the words coming out clipped.

He lets out a soft, defeated sound, nuzzling into my chest. The griffin has grown over the last month since I saw him. He's the size of a small horse.

'Lukas, Nesrin!'

'What is it?' Lukas replies instantly.

'It's Talon, he is hurt really bad.'

'Where are you?' Alarm is evident in Nesrin's voice.

'My house.'

'We're on our way,' Lukas assures.

"What is that thing?" Sara's curious tone comes from behind me.

Glancing over my shoulder, I find her and Tyler standing behind me. Tyler appears pale and frightened, wrapped in his mother's arms. The sun is sinking below the horizon now, casting a warm orange glow across the sky, and I notice them shivering in their soaked clothes. My protective instinct flares, causing a low growl to escape from deep within me. "Tyler, get inside and put some dry clothes on before you catch a chill."

"We will, but what is that, Gabe?" Sara asks again.

I let out a sigh as I gently stroke Talon's massive frame, being careful to avoid the deep wound on his side.

"This is Talon, he is a griffin and part of the family, but he went missing about a month ago. We assumed he went off with his parents after they were rescued from a clan of hunters."

"Is he okay?" Tyler's small voice is shaking.

"No, he's not, but Nesrin will be here soon."

Hardly have the words left my mouth when a chilling howl pierces the silence, causing Sara to leap in fright as Talon screeches back in reply. I sense Nesrin, Lukas, and Astraea as they approach.

Lukas bursts through the dense treeline first with Astraea gripping onto him tightly. Her golden curls flow like liquid sunshine in the wind. Despite her petite frame, she appears even smaller against the massive form of his wolf. Nesrin's wolf, as white as freshly fallen snow, follows closely, mere moments behind Lukas. The stark contrast between the midnight black fur of Lukas's wolf and the pristine white of Nesrin's is truly striking.

I hear Sara's sharp intake of breath as she watches the two massive wolves approach.

As soon as Lukas comes to a halt, Astraea swiftly leaps off his back, her small legs swiftly closing the distance between us. Nesrin shifts instantly, skidding on her knees at our side.

"Goddess," she breathes. "What happened to you?"

Nesrin hesitates, her hands hovering over Talon as if she's too fearful to make contact. Astraea, on the other hand, shows no hesitation. Her tiny hands confidently cradle Talon's enormous eagle head, and they lock eyes for a prolonged moment. Finally,

Nesrin gathers her courage and sinks her hands into Talon's fur. Suddenly, a radiant white light bursts forth, enveloping both Nesrin and Talon in comforting warmth.

"So many injuries," Nesrin says, her voice filled with hurt.

"Who would do this?" Lukas inquires.

'Talon was captured by vampires,' Astraea's soft voice answers.

Lukas and I stiffen, but Nesrin's magic flares at the words spoken by her daughter. A surge of power pulses through the air, causing me to involuntarily flinch. Reacting swiftly, I rise to my feet, positioning myself as a shield for Sara and Tyler. Lukas drops down beside Nesrin, wrapping his arms around her as she concentrates on healing Talon. Her eyes close softly, finding solace in the moment. I have no doubt that Lukas is whispering words of comfort and thoughts of retribution in her mind, fueling her determination.

Nesrin takes a good ten minutes to heal Talon during the time I have sent Sara and Tyler up to the house to change. And when she's done, she falls back into Lukas's body, exhaustion lining her face. Talon rises to his full height, looking down at her. She smiles weakly up at him. "All better, Talon."

Talon cocks his head and blinks his enormous golden eyes at her before shifting his gaze down to Astraea, who responds with a nod.

Nesrin's laughter fills the air as Astraea, with her uncanny talent for mind speaking, imparts something to her. Astraea has a unique and remarkable ability to engage in mind-to-mind communication with anyone. Any living being, whether it's an ordinary animal, supernatural being, or mythical creature.

Lukas stands and extends his hand to Nesrin, helping her up. I bend down, swiftly scooping up Astraea, her head resting on my shoulder. Darkness has taken over now, the only form of light now coming from the few magic orbs I keep floating around the area.

Talon steps forward and seems to nuzzle Nesrin's stomach. I furrow my brow, and my eye connects with Lukas.

"Weird." I watch as the griffin protectively moves around Nesrin.

"He can sense that I'm pregnant," Nesrin mutters, her face heating.

Chapter Forty-Four

SARA

The back glass door slides open, and Tyler and I turn to see Gabe walk in carrying a sleeping Astraea. Lukas and Nesrin follow him inside, and my eyes widen when the griffin shakes out his wings before tucking them in close and walking inside. Its curious golden eyes stare at me for a long moment before dropping to Tyler. Instinctively, my fingers tighten on Tyler's shoulders, wanting to draw him behind me. Even though I know Gabe wouldn't allow the creature inside if he thought it would hurt us, I can't quell a mother's instincts to shield her child.

"Hey, Tyler," Nesrin says kindly. "Gabe told us you took a fall in the river. Can I see if you're okay?"

Tyler gives a nod, and Nesrin extends her hand to him. The crackle of magic fills the room, and a soft tingling sensation dances along my skin. Nesrin sways unsteadily on her feet and I step forward to steady her, but Lukas is there in an instant, scooping her into his arms, cradling her against his chest.

"I'm okay, stud muffin," she argues, patting his chest.

"You're not okay," he growls.

Nesrin kisses his neck. "I just got dizzy."

"You're using too much magic."

Nesrin sighs and looks at us. "Tyler is fine, just some bruising which should be gone now."

"Thank you," I reply.

"Of course." She smiles. "Now put me down, please."

Lukas grumbles under his breath, the sound barely audible as he reluctantly releases his grip on Nesrin, and gently places her back on her feet. I press my lips together, feeling the corners of my mouth twitching with the effort to suppress my smile. These two are adorable. Gabe catches my gaze and flashes a warm smile. Tyler steps away from me and makes his way to the bench to settle down, his eyes fixated on the majestic griffin.

Nesrin's gasp reverberates through the kitchen, startling everyone and causing us to tense up.

"What?" Lukas snaps, his eyes scanning for danger, but her eyes are fixated on my left hand. I look down, recalling the events that unfolded just moments before chaos broke loose.

"You're getting married?" Nesrin exclaims excitedly.

"Oh my god, woman, you don't gasp like that unless there is danger." Lukas runs a hand over his ebony hair in exasperation.

Nesrin ignores him and grabs my hand, examining the ring. "Oh, it's beautiful."

"Tyler helped me pick it out." Gabe wraps his arm around my waist, drawing me to his side.

We all turn to find Tyler studying Talon, with a blend of trepidation and awe.

"Well, congratulations to the both of you," Lukas says.

Surprising me, Nesrin pulls me into a hug. "I'm so happy," she whispers, her voice wobbling.

Pulling away, my eyes widen, and I catch Lukas's concern over her shoulder. I sense Nesrin will be very emotional during her pregnancy if my last few encounters with her are anything to go by.

"Me, too," I whisper back.

Nesrin flushes and clears her throat as she steps away. "We need a meeting with Stephan."

Gabe walks over to the counter and tosses his cell phone to Nesrin. She catches it effortlessly and quickly scrolls through it, her eyes lighting up when she finds what she is looking for. With the phone pressed against her ear, she starts to move around the kitchen, unable to sit still. I wander over to Tyler, my fingers running through his hair. The terror I felt when I saw him fall was . . . gosh, I don't even know. I never want to feel that again. I lean down and breathe in the smell of his hair. If anything happened to him, I wouldn't survive it.

"You okay, Mom?" Tyler's voice is soft, carrying a note of concern.

"Yeah, baby. I was just really scared when you fell into the river."

His arms wrap around me, and he rests his head on my chest. "Me, too."

Lifting my head, I see Lukas hold his arms out and take Astraea from Gabe. The giant, intimidating man is smitten with his two girls. It's impossible not to notice how he constantly keeps them within his line of vision.

Nesrin stops pacing. "Stephan, we need to talk." She listens. "No, tonight," Nesrin snaps. "Don't use that tone. I'm not charmed by your antics, remember?"

Nesrin laughs. I know both Gabe and Lukas can hear the whole conversation, and I see Gabe chuckle, but it's Lukas's deep rumbling growl that has my eyebrows raising.

"Fine. Sensations at midnight."

She hangs up and smiles at the room.

"Who's hungry?"

Chapter Forty-Five

GABE

A man only has so much self-control, and mine is teetering on the edge. I watch as Sara steps out of the steam-filled bathroom, her skin still glistening with droplets of water. It's satisfying to see her like this, so relaxed and at home in my space that she doesn't bother closing the bathroom door. Completely unaware of the effect she is having on me, she bends forward, gently drying her hair with a towel. That's it. I can't take it anymore. Pushing myself away from the wall, I move silently and purposefully toward her. Her wide eyes fly to mine as I snatch the towel from her hands, tossing it to the floor.

"Gabe." Her voice is soft and breathy. I love it.

I place my hand on her stomach, feeling the warmth of her skin beneath my palm, and gently guide her backward until her back meets the cold-tiled wall. The sound of her small gasp has my cock becoming painfully hard.

I press my hips against her, keeping her firmly in place, and lean closer to whisper in her ear. "The house is locked up and Tyler is fast asleep."

I lightly nip at her earlobe before teasingly moving my attention to her ample, enticing breasts. My hands skim up her sides and she shivers in response, her hands landing on my waist. Palming her breasts, I take one of her pebbled nipples into my mouth and suck hard. A sexy moan comes from her, and I move to the other breast, running my tongue over the peak. Her fingers tangle in my hair, tugging me closer as she arches her back against my chest. I slip my hand around her body, holding her tightly as I take her mouth in a desperate kiss.

Sara's hands move from my hair, her palms gliding over my chest and stomach, sending a tingling sensation throughout my body as her fingertips dance along the hem of my shirt. Without hesitating, I yank the fabric over my head and let it fall to the floor. Then my mouth finds hers again. My hands wind and twist in her mass of brown locks. A low groan escapes my lips as Sara's hand cups my cock through my jeans, the sensation sending waves of pleasure through my body. With my hand covering hers, I apply pressure, squeezing tightly. My hips thrust against her hand, relishing in the sensation of friction against my skin, a low growl escaping from deep within me. Without warning, I lift her up and toss her over my shoulder. Her squeals fill the air, and I can't resist giving her a gentle smack on the ass.

"Gabe!" she shrieks, in a mix of surprise and amusement.

Tossing her down on the bed, I quickly strip my jeans. The soft glow of the low lights in the room illuminates her wet body. I pause to admire her until she playfully crooks her finger at me.

"Come here, fox boy," she whispers huskily.

I throw my head back, my laughter echoing through the room.

"That will not become a thing," I growl, crawling over the top of her.

"It most definitely will become a thing," she argues, running a finger down my chest.

"Did I mention how much I love you?" I purr, before crushing my mouth against hers.

My arms cage her body. I can't wait any longer. I am consumed by an overwhelming desire to be inside her. By the way Sara presses her body against mine, and the way her legs are wrapped around me, it's obvious that she agrees. I position myself at her entrance and thrust forward, sheathing myself inside her in one swift movement. Sara's eyes flutter at the connection, breathy noises coming from her mouth. Her wet heat and tightness envelop me. I hold still, feeling her quivering around my cock, and mentally count to ten.

"Gabe, move," she begs.

"With pleasure," I grin.

With each push forward, her eyes remain fixed on mine, intensifying the connection between us. I pull out almost all the way and slowly push back in. We both groan, my forehead dropping to hers. My heart pounds like I've done a round in the ring, and we have barely started.

"Hold on, baby," I warn.

Sara's arms grab my shoulders, her long, lean legs wrap tightly around my waist as I pull out again. I thrust back in with force, quickening the rhythm.

This feels right. So right.

Sara belongs to me. She's mine, and I am hers, now and forever. I feel her tightening around me, her body tensing up, and I keep up the pace. I push up on my hands and lean down, drawing her nipple into my mouth. On the next thrust, she comes, her whole body trembling like a live wire.

"Gabe!" she cries out with a few incoherent words following.

The way her voice sounds as she cries out my name like that, sparks a longing in me, urging me to make her scream it over and over again.

I keep moving slowly, riding through the waves of pleasure with her until her body becomes limp. With a gentle roll, I shift our positions, still keeping us connected. Sitting up, the warmth of her legs wrapped tightly around my waist radiates through me. With our chests pressed against each other, our breaths intertwine, creating a shared rhythm. I reach up, brushing her dark brown hair from her face before leaning in and kissing her, slow and deep. Her movements are deliberate, her hips thrusting with a sensuous grace, eliciting a deep groan from within me.

"Hell, baby. You feel so good."

"So do you." She grins, wrapping her arms around my neck and rocking her hips again. With each seamless slide, each guttural moan, each passionate kiss, I inch closer to the edge. Our bodies become slick with sweat, adding to the intensity as we slowly build up again to that sweet bliss.

"Gabe?"

"Yes, Baby."

"Make me yours."

My movement halts in shock. I gently hold her face, looking into her eyes. "What do you mean? I'm already yours. You are mine."

"No, make me your mate."

I frown, confusion rolling through me. "Are you sure? We haven't talked about it."

"I know all about it. Nesrin filled me in."

"Of course she did." My head shakes. "There is no rush. We can wait." The last thing I want is to make her feel pressured.

Love and affection fill her beautiful brown eyes. "I don't want to wait. Mate me."

"You sure?"

Sara rolls her hip, and I bite back a groan. "Yes, Makoto. Please."

"Fuck!" I groan.

There is nothing I want more, and staring into her big brown eyes, hearing my name on her lips, I can't say no. Moving my hands, I grip her ass, pulling her hips tighter against me, hitting new depths.

"Ohh," Sara moans, her head tipping back, making her hair brush over my legs.

Drawing on my magic, I let it run over my skin and hers. I lift her up slightly, my fingers digging into her soft skin, and pull her back down. I can smell the increase in her arousal as I rock my hips in time with her movements.

Panting in unison, our breaths blend together, creating a shared energy. I drag my hand around her body to her clit, circling it with my thumb, and immediately feel her body tense and jerk in my hold.

"Gabe!" she calls out, her back arching.

Once again, I feel the tantalizing flutter of her walls around my cock, sending waves of pleasure coursing through my body.

"Baby," I grit, my jaw clenched with the effort to hold off longer and make this last.

Her walls tighten around me, and I thrust into her with all my strength, relishing in the intense sensation. Reaching up, I tilt her head to the side, my mouth finding the sweet spot where her neck meets her shoulder. I bite firmly, breaking through the skin, and a flood of blood and magic fills my senses. Sara cries out, her body tensing as I channel my magic into the wound. It flows freely from me to her, and I lose control, pushing her backward into the bed and thrusting into her as if my life depended on it. Sara moans, her body trembling violently, her inner walls gripping so firmly around my cock that I see stars.

With a quick motion, I pull back and use my nail to make a precise, small cut on my neck.

"Your turn, baby."

I'm not sure she hears me at first, but then she rolls us, riding my cock as she clamps her mouth over the cut, pushing her own magic into me. My balls tighten with each push and pull of magic. Her pussy spasms as she takes me deeper and deeper inside her. My cock pulses, and I come, hot and hard, my hands gripping her ass, moving her over me, riding out my own orgasm as she collapses on my chest. When I come to a stop, completely spent, I softly trace my fingers up along her spine and then down again. My free hand brushes away the sweaty strands of hair that cling to her face.

Neither of us bother moving, except to tug the sheet up over our tangled bodies, a lazy attempt at warmth as the cool night air drifts through the open window. I feel her breath, her chest rising and falling in sync with mine, her heartbeat a steady rhythm I could listen to forever. The room is dark, the only light a faint glow from the moon outside, casting soft shadows across her face.

I pull her closer, wrapping my arms around her tightly. Her body relaxes against mine, melting into every curve and line, until it's hard to tell where I end and she begins. There's nothing more I could want—just this, just her, right here. A sense of peace settles over me, like a weight lifting from my chest, and I let my eyes close.

Her fingers lightly curl against my chest, her warmth seeping into me. Together, we drift into sleep, our breaths slow and steady, two halves finally whole.

Acknowledgements

I'd like to extend my deepest gratitude to my mum, whose unwavering support has been a guiding light throughout my life. Together, we made it through some of the hardest times, yet you never once gave up or lost hope. Your strength, love, and belief in me laid the foundation for everything I am today. Thank you for always being there, not just as a parent, but as a friend and my first, biggest supporter.

To Hannah and Tess, thank you for the constant encouragement and reminders to keep going, even on the tough days. Your friendship has been a steady source of strength, and your words of support have meant the world.

And, of course, to my incredible husband and kids: thank you for granting me the space and freedom to pour my heart into these pages. I know it often means late nights, missed plans, and scattered conversations that make no sense. But without your love and patience, none of this would be possible. Thank you for letting me follow my dreams so fully—I'm forever grateful.